RESOUNDING
A DEATH I

T0008096

"This is not your usual ex-cop-turned-PI mystery! Malladi captures the Scandinavian sparseness with powerful dialogue and a true sense of place. The reader is gripped from the beginning and led on a complex journey with provoking questions for all of us: how far have we really come, and will we ever get there? An excellent read!"

—Charles Todd, *New York Times* bestselling author of the Inspector Rutledge Mysteries and the Bess Crawford Mysteries

"Part mystery and part international thriller, *A Death in Denmark* is a compelling read. Amulya Malladi weaves together World War II and Nazi sympathizers with current European anti-immigrant politics, as well as the Russian mafia, and introduces Gabriel Præst, a hard-boiled private detective with a cosmopolitan flair who readers will want more of."

Robert Dugoni, *New York Times* bestselling author of the Tracy Crosswhite series and the Charles Jenkins series

"An intricate tapestry of a novel that unflinchingly lays bare the human cost of politically cultivated hate. Gabriel Præst had me firmly in his well-tailored pockets from the very first page. A fast-paced, emotionally rich, and whip-smart read!"

—Sonali Dev, bestselling author of *The Vibrant Years*

"Philip Marlowe meets Nordic noir in *A Death in Denmark*, a jazzy murder mystery that digs up Copenhagen's past Nazi ties in the inescapable context of the country's current refugee policies."

—Iben Albinus, internationally bestselling and award-winning author of *Damaskus*

A DEATH

IN DENMARK

Also by Amulya Malladi

The Nearest Exit May Be Behind You
The Copenhagen Affair
A House for Happy Mothers
The Sound of Language
Song of the Cuckoo Bird
Serving Crazy with Curry
The Mango Season
A Breath of Fresh Air

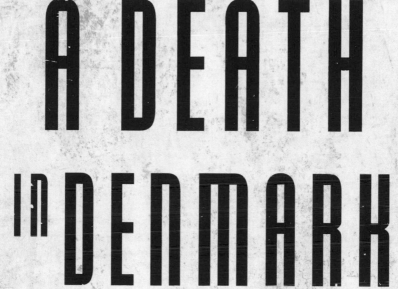

A DEATH IN DENMARK

THE FIRST
GABRIEL PRÆST
NOVEL

AMULYA MALLADI

_wm_

WILLIAM MORROW
An Imprint of HarperCollinsPublishers

A DEATH IN DENMARK. Copyright © 2023 by Amulya Malladi. All rights reserved. Printed in the United States of America. No part of this book may be used or reproduced in any manner whatsoever without written permission except in the case of brief quotations embodied in critical articles and reviews. For information, address HarperCollins Publishers, 195 Broadway, New York, NY 10007.

HarperCollins books may be purchased for educational, business, or sales promotional use. For information, please email the Special Markets Department at SPsales@harpercollins.com.

FIRST EDITION

Designed by Diahann Sturge

Chapter opener grunge grey background © Nataliia K/Shutterstock

Library of Congress Cataloging-in-Publication Data has been applied for.

ISBN 978-0-06-323551-9

23 24 25 26 27 LBC 5 4 3 2 1

For my father, Hanumantha Rao Malladi, who loved a good mystery; and for my friend Radhika Kasichainula, who would have thought Gabriel Præst was as cool as I intended him to be. The world isn't the same without them in it and my heart aches.

Don't you know that a midnight hour comes when everyone has to take off his mask?

—Søren Kierkegaard

When the rich wage war, it's the poor who die.

—Jean-Paul Sartre

LILLE JØDISKE ANNEMARIE
(LITTLE JEWISH ANNEMARIE)

Greater Copenhagen, October 1, 1943

There were twenty of them, huddled together in a truck that Lars Hansen used to transport vegetables from the farm to the market in Copenhagen. Rumbling down the road in the middle of the night, they were en route from Copenhagen to Hansensgård, the Hansen farm in Helsingør.

Annemarie was cradled on her father's lap. Sitting on the metal bed of the vehicle, he leaned against a sack of onions and garlic, the scent of which tickled Annemarie's nose. No one had spoken since they had started to drive. Although Annemarie had only just turned seven, she already understood how important it was to remain silent when she was told. She knew their lives depended upon it. Since the Germans had come to Denmark three years ago, she and her family had been living in fear. She heard her parents talk about it when they thought she was sleeping.

The truck stopped after what seemed like hours. Annemarie

was tired and had dozed off for a while, so her legs were unsteady as she stood and gazed around.

There was a family of four awaiting them, a father and mother and their two children.

Annemarie's father helped her out of the truck, holding her in his arms. She wriggled out of them, not wanting to look like a baby in front of the new people, especially the girl who looked to be her age. She had light brown hair, loose around her shoulders, just like Annemarie. She was wearing a blue dress with white stockings and black shoes, just like Annemarie.

The girl smiled and introduced herself. "I'm Elvira, and this is my brother, Ib."

"I'm Annemarie," she said, her eyes lit with pleasure at finding a new friend.

Around her, the adults shook hands and introduced one another. Everyone looked tired, gray from stress; Helga Hansen, a stout smiling woman, tried to cheer them with her welcome.

"Come on inside where it's warm," she said, putting her arm around one of the women who was holding a baby. "You've had a long ride. The kitchen has a fire going and I have a meatball and dumpling soup simmering on the stove."

Elvira's older brother helped by carrying their bags inside the house, and Lars Hansen spoke to each of the adults and children as they settled into the kitchen.

"You are the same age as my Elvira," he said warmly when he shook hands with Annemarie. "She has some dolls you can play with."

Annemarie looked at her mother, who held a cup of coffee in her hands, and when she nodded, Annemarie almost clapped with glee.

"Let's go." Elvira grabbed Annemarie's hand and led her into her room.

The farmhouse was large and had space for all of them. Everyone slept that first night, scattered around the property. Many slept on beds of hay in the barn, some in the hall of the big house, and two in the large kitchen.

The next day, they'd taken quick baths with cold water in buckets and changed into clothes provided by the Hansens. Annemarie was given a dress that belonged to Elvira. It was white and green, and she loved it. It was now her favorite dress.

That evening they had dinner in the Hansen kitchen, all seated around a big table. It was like a party, Annemarie thought, seeing her parents and their friends happy and smiling for the first time in a long while.

"I wish we could just stay here until the Germans go away," she told Elvira when they went to the barn to see the new baby goat that had been born just two days before.

"Me too," Elvira said. "But you have to go on a boat to Sweden to be safe. There have been others who stayed with us and then left by boat. They always leave in the night so the German soldiers can't find them."

"I'm scared," Annemarie confessed. "What do you think the Germans do to the Jews when they catch them? Put them in prison?"

"I don't know," Elvira said.

"Will they take me away from my *Far* and *Mor*?" she asked.

Elvira gave her a hug then. "Don't worry about anything. You're going to Sweden and there are no Germans there."

They were already best friends—in the way only children could be. They spent that evening together and even slept side by side in the stables on the hay, whispering late into the night about what they'd do when the war was over.

"We can go to the town square and eat ice cream," Elvira said. "Or even go to the cinema. Wouldn't that be fun?"

Annemarie had agreed that it would be *super* fun.

They had barely fallen asleep when they heard loud sounds. Annemarie's mother told Elvira to run to her family in the house.

A German officer was asking everyone to stand in a line in German-accented Danish. Rough hands of soldiers pushed them around, shoving them against one another, squeezing them together.

It was cold and they were all shivering, all twenty of them and their hosts, as they stood in front of the main house.

There were ten soldiers surrounding the farm. Annemarie wondered how just ten men could control so many of them. Because they had guns, she thought. Each one of the soldiers was armed and pointing his weapon at them.

Lars, Helga, Ib, and Elvira had been separated from the Jews. Annemarie and Elvira looked at each other in mutual fear.

"I am Hauptsturmführer Fritz Diekmann," the soldier said. He was a handsome man, tall and lean with bright yellow hair, but his gray-blue eyes were hard. Turning to Lars, he continued in a calm, cold voice, "Is this your farm?"

"Yes," Lars said.

"And you're hiding Jews here," Captain Diekmann said.

"We have guests . . . friends," Lars said.

"*They are Jews,*" the German captain said tightly.

Annemarie knew that the Germans thought Jews were bad people. They made the word *Jøde* sound dirty. Tears filled her eyes, and she tightened her grip on her mother's waist.

"They are . . . ," Lars began, but Captain Diekmann raised his hand to silence him. The Gestapo officer then turned and nodded at two soldiers who strode toward the Hansen family. He stared at the twenty Jews and said, "This is what happens to those who help you. I want you to know that this is your fault."

The two soldiers had handguns with them. They first shot Elvira and Ib in the head. Lars and Helga cried out but before they could rush to their children, the soldiers executed them with cold precision where they stood.

Annemarie couldn't scream. She cried in silent horror. Her new best friend was dead, and it was because of her.

The Jews were thrust into a truck that drove all night. When it stopped, they were herded into a crowd of Jewish captives waiting beside a long train. Annemarie heard whimpers and moans as each of the many cars was loaded with people. Babies were crying while mothers tried to shush them. Young children clutched the hands of their parents, wide-eyed with fear and fatigue.

They had no food or water. Annemarie didn't complain—it wasn't going to make a difference. They were more than fifty people squeezed into a small space; they took turns sitting down because there wasn't enough room.

For Annemarie it was all a blur.

The train started and stopped. Started and stopped. Started and stopped.

When they reached a place where they got out of the train, it was a relief. Annemarie didn't know where they were until a German soldier told the grown-ups. He spoke German and Annemarie couldn't understand him, but she heard whispers among the Danish Jews. They were in Theresienstadt. That name meant nothing to Annemarie.

The German soldiers barked out orders, and Annemarie's mother clung to her tightly. A soldier started to pull Annemarie away and she screamed for her mother.

All the children were taken away, forcefully.

"What's happening?" one boy asked in a language that Annemarie knew wasn't Danish, but she understood enough of the words to know what he was saying.

"They're taking us to bathe," another child said.

"Will I see my mother after that?" someone asked.

"Yes, once we're all clean," someone else replied.

But Annemarie feared she wouldn't see her mother or father again. She feared she wouldn't play in the forest again. She feared she wouldn't hold her doll, open a birthday present, or enjoy an ice cream cone. She feared she was going to die.

CHAPTER 1

Present

I noticed the dark-haired woman as soon as she walked into Mojo on that Friday night in May when it all began.

She was inappropriately dressed for the laid-back blues bar, wearing a severe dark pantsuit, her hair tightly pulled back from her face, black high heels with red soles, which I knew she had a weakness for, and a cool smile. Several eyes, including mine, followed her to the bar, where she ordered a drink from fair-haired Ricky.

She had a striking face. Dark among the blond, blue-eyed Danes. She took her glass of what I guessed was whiskey—she used to be a Johnnie girl—and walked up to the end of the room, right by the smoking booth. She held her drink in one hand, and the other was in her pocket. She leaned against the wall, confidence oozing out of her, as if she were saying, "You *sure* you want to talk to me?" to the men who wondered if they should try their luck with her.

Mojo, the place you went in Copenhagen if you were into the blues, was anything but fancy or chic. It was a hole in the wall. It was also atmospheric, inexpensive, and had been delivering live blues (or jazz or folk music) every day since the mid-eighties. It was not pretentious, and the only thing you had to worry about was arriving early enough not to get stuck at a table behind a pillar, with a partial view of the stage.

There were almost always musicians milling outside the bar with a beer and a cigarette, awaiting their turn onstage. It was a small community of blues musicians and most of us knew one another. I usually played with my band but others, less established, came by on Blues Jam Night on Thursdays, taking turns to play with familiar and new musicians. There were always one or two who were deemed too drunk to perform and kicked off the stage by Thomas, who ran the joint with an iron fist and a friendly smile on his dark face.

We were playing one of the last sets of the night. I was on guitar, while Bobby K finished singing, *I'm gonna shoot you right down.*

It was John Lee Hooker Night.

The woman I couldn't keep my eyes off sipped her golden whiskey slowly as we began to play one of my favorites, "One Bourbon, One Scotch, One Beer."

I watched her watch me as my solo wound down and the clapping began.

"Give it up for my man Gabriel Præst on guitar," Bobby K said, and the crowd applauded. I bowed. "And let's give a hand to John Reinhardt on bass, the elegant Nuru Kimathi on drums, and my drinking partner Valdemar Vong on the sax."

Nuru, a Kenyan who had moved to Denmark after she met and married a Dane, smiled and waved at the crowd, leaned into her microphone, and, in a two-pack-a-day voice, said, "Let's not forget our fearless leader and a man who sings to make angels weep, Bobby K."

After the applause quieted, Bobby K told the crowd that we

would wet our whistles and be right back with "Shake It Baby" and a few other precious gems to close the evening.

I picked up my beer from the bar and walked up to the dark-haired woman.

"Still singing the blues," she mused.

I smiled and leaned in to give her a perfunctory, almost platonic hug and said, "*Hej.*"

She didn't flinch but she didn't lean into my hug either. I would've gone with a handshake, but I perversely wanted to see her response. Now that I had, I had no clue what I was after.

"How are you, Leila?"

She nodded, and something twinkled in her eyes. "When are you done? I need your help."

I raised my eyebrows. Of all the gin joints in all the towns in all the world, she walks into mine after . . . what, nearly a decade?

"My help?" I sipped my beer, simply to have something to do with my hands.

"Yes," she confirmed.

I gave myself a moment to think before I responded, even though I knew I didn't need the time. No matter what was or was not there between us, if she was asking for my help, I'd give it to her.

"Okay," I said. "It's going to be another hour. If it's urgent . . ."

She shook her head.

"Buy me another Johnnie Walker," she held up her nearly empty glass, "and I'll wait."

"You need my help, but *I* have to buy the Johnnie?" I waved to Ricky, the barman, and pointed to Leila's glass. He nodded.

"Yes. After all you *are* making me wait." She was lightening the mood between us, asking me to join in and play.

I smiled as I watched the bartender make a beeline for us, Johnnie in hand. "My man Ricky will take care of you."

As I was leaving, my back turned to her, I heard her softly whisper, "Thank you, Gabriel."

I WALKED MY bicycle, my guitar strapped to my back, beside Leila to Southern Cross Pub on Løngangstræde close to Mojo and Rådhus, the city hall. I knew the pub well, because it was open until 5:00 a.m., and people like me who stayed out late into the morning went there when they didn't want to go home. And the bartender made an old-fashioned that could beat the pants off the designer crap they sold in chic Copenhagen bars, where it cost twice as much.

It was three in the morning and the crowd was winding down. Once I parked my bicycle and locked it, we sat at one of the outdoor tables warmed by an overhead infrared heat lamp. I didn't pick up the blanket that was draped on the chair to cover myself. I was wearing my Burberry trench, because Mojo was a good fifteen-minute ride on my bicycle to my apartment, and even though summer was in the air, the spring chill hadn't quite left the party. I set my guitar case on the chair next to me.

Smokers stood outside, around the door, their alcohol-laden voices carrying through the night.

Leila draped a blanket across her lap.

"You cold?" I asked. "We can go in."

She shook her head. "I'm fine."

A waiter came along, and I ordered an old-fashioned while she ordered another Johnnie Walker, still neat. Her third of the night, I counted, and those were the ones I knew about. One thing about Leila, she could drink most people under the table.

"How can I help you?" I asked once we were settled in, waiting for our drinks.

"You've gotten better," she said and then on a smile added, "at the guitar."

I could've responded with a double entendre about other things I'd gotten better at, but it was too easy and a little unsophisticated, so I said, "Time and practice."

She nodded but didn't say anything. I didn't say anything. I waited for her to tell me how I could help her.

Knowing Leila, coming to me was a last resort. The relationship hadn't ended well. There had been yelling and screaming, and plenty of fighting. She had thrown a few things at me. I had maybe made a few churlish and snide remarks, which had instigated the throwing of things at me. That had been a decade ago. We'd both grown up since then. I didn't enter relationships anymore, so I hadn't had to end any—there was always less drama with relationships that lasted a couple of months than there was for ones that lasted a couple of years and rocked your world.

"If I could have gotten anyone else to do it, trust me . . . ," she trailed off, telling me she was as uncomfortable as I had thought she might be, coming to me for help. It didn't sit well with me. I didn't know why.

The waiter brought our drinks. I took the first sip and sighed in pleasure. I was pumped after playing, as I usually was, and knew that I wouldn't be able to sleep for another hour or so. I was in no rush to get her talking. She'd get there when she got there. In the meantime, I was sitting across from one of the most beautiful women I had ever had the pleasure of seeing naked, with a perfect cocktail in my hand—it was a very good moment.

She toyed with her whiskey glass, took a sip, and then announced, "Yousef Ahmed."

I nodded.

"You know who he is?" she asked.

"Yes, as I don't live under a stone."

"I've taken him on as a client. We intend to appeal."

My eyebrows rose. "Appeal what? The case is over, Leila. The man has been convicted."

She looked me in the eyes, straight, focused, and clear. "I don't think he did it."

"Well, *skat*, they're all innocent, except they're not," I provoked her by calling her darling. The irony of the Danish language is that *skat* also means "tax," very apropos.

She didn't take the bait. "He didn't do it."

"A jury found him guilty. There's nothing left to do except work on an early release," I retorted. "Which I don't see happening."

"I was in London when the trial took place and I couldn't help him then." Her voice was a hoarse whisper. She was affected. "But I intend to help him now."

"How?" I was baffled.

Leila took a deep breath. "I need you to investigate this."

"This? As in the murder of Sanne Melgaard?"

"Yes."

I didn't want to once again say that such an investigation was pointless so I went another route. "Okay. What if I find out he did it?"

She raised her hands, palms up. "Then that's that."

She finished her drink, set the empty glass on the table, and waved at the waiter.

"Why are you doing this?" I asked. "Why even take him on?"

"I know . . . knew his son," Leila explained. "I know the family. It's been devastating for them."

I didn't know what to say, so I shut up. I had never gone wrong shutting up.

Someone called out to an Andreas, who was apparently a son of a bitch, followed by a string of obscenities and drunken laughter.

The waiter came back with a fresh drink and took Leila's empty glass away. He looked at me pointedly and I shook my head. If I drank any more, I wouldn't be able to bicycle home—this was my third and final drink of the evening. Leila, as always, held her liquor better than I did.

"If you knew him, you'd know he couldn't have killed Sanne Melgaard. He's not that man. And I don't give a shit who says what about him. It's like Muslim man plus angry equals murderer," she hissed, and I recognized the fire in her that had drawn me to her.

Leila was a passionate woman. When she believed in something, she went all out. For a short time there, she'd believed in us.

"My law firm will pay you."

"I wasn't planning to do this for free, *if* I was planning to do it."

"And are you planning to do it?" she asked.

"There's a good chance of that happening," I offered, and she smiled, as I wanted her to. Even after a decade, I still wanted to make her happy, I realized, more than a little disturbed by that thought.

"You can talk to your police friends, just make sure they did everything the way it was supposed to be done," she pleaded.

"You know I don't have many police friends." When you ratted out the national chief of police, your former colleagues tended to feel sore about you.

"Meet his daughter," Leila suggested. "She was thirteen when they took him away. She's Sophie's age."

Which made her about eighteen now. Sophie, my daughter, had just turned twenty. Leila certainly had the violins out for this one.

"I can bring her to your office next week. Just meet her and . . . ," Leila faltered.

I raised a hand. "I'll do it. I mean, I'll meet her. I'm saying yes, I'll look into the case."

"Really? Why?"

"Because you asked me to," I said truthfully.

CHAPTER 2

Sophie and I had a father-daughter breakfast every Saturday. It was tradition. We had been doing it since she was four years old when her mother and I separated. I used to have her with me every other week, but even on the Saturdays that I didn't have her, we still had breakfast together, either with Stine, her mother, and Erik, her *bonus* father, or just the two of us.

Stine and I had what one would call an amicable divorce— well, we hadn't been married, so it wasn't exactly a divorce but featured the same elements. I bent over backward to make sure our separation was friendly. Stine had wanted a fight. I didn't give it to her. It helped that she'd already been half in love with Erik when we split up. I never asked her if she was sleeping with him when we were together. It didn't *really* matter beyond my ego. I didn't love her, probably never had. We were both twenty years old when we met. It had been a relationship based on infatuation, in the beginning. She got pregnant a few months after we met and we moved in together, wanting to do the proper family thing. We were kids with a kid. We tried to make it work. We spent four miserable years trying. Then we gave up. One day, we both decided in very few words that it was over. She'd met a man, she told me, one she thought she'd have a future with. I wished her the best. I think she hated that most; that I had let go without a fight, that I hadn't wanted her enough even though she didn't want me. With Erik she'd had the big wedding, the honeymoon in Bali, all of that—everything she'd not had with me. They were good together. They'd not had any children and I secretly liked that, because it meant that Erik and Stine gave Sophie all their love and attention.

It was my turn to pick the breakfast restaurant, so we went to Mirabelle on Guldbergsgade, a street dotted with unique boutique stores and my two favorite restaurants, Bæst and the Michelin-starred Thai restaurant Kiin Kiin. The sourdough bread at Mirabelle was the best one could find in the city.

It didn't used to be like this. When I was growing up, there weren't more sushi bars than hot-dog stands in Copenhagen, which was then a culinary wasteland. But with the famous Noma landing repeatedly on the World's 50 Best Restaurants list, the city had become a gastronomic mecca for food lovers.

We ordered the Mirabelle breakfast with soft-boiled eggs, smoked trout, salmon, and cheese with rye bread. I added Hindsholm sausage to my order while Sophie ordered a green salad. To each his own. And because you couldn't come to Mirabelle and not eat their pastries, we ordered a *pain au chocolat* and a croissant.

It was almost eleven in the morning and the sun was slowly peeking through the clouds, dissipating them so it almost started to feel like a good spring day, for the moment, as the weather report indicated rain in the evening. It was May, and in the fifth month of every year, Danes held their breath and waited for the season to change from winter to fall-like spring to coveted summer because some years, the weather gods skipped summer and went from winter to fall to winter again. And when that happened, Danes comforted themselves by saying, "But we had some good days in May."

I pressed the filter in the French press carafe and poured coffee for Sophie and me. We both liked it black. The place wasn't exactly packed, but patrons sat both indoors and outdoors—more outdoors than indoors, as Danes would and did take the opportunity to enjoy even a sliver of sunshine when granted.

"What's new?" Sophie asked after she finished half her coffee, and I refilled her cup.

"I'm closing *that* case for Erik's firm," I said. Erik was an attorney and I worked for his firm on retainer as an investigator and used their premises for my office.

"The rape case?" Sophie wrinkled her nose.

I nodded.

"And . . ."

"We got nothing." I sighed.

"*So*, there's no justice?"

I shrugged. "I could ask Bør to beat him up but that's about it."

"Bør is still beating people up?" Sophie asked.

I shrugged again. "I don't know. But he's the only man I know who's ever killed someone."

"He has a media company and a podcast." Sophie beamed. "I don't think he's a *gangster* anymore."

Bør and I grew up together in Brøndbyvester, a tough neighborhood. My father was a policeman and his was a mechanic. I became a policeman like my father. Bør became an honest-to-god biker. He went to prison for five years while I was a cop. He'd come out reformed and now helped former gang members get rehabilitated, which prompted his very popular podcast about life and forgiveness. We were still friends.

"He cleaned up nice," I said.

"I feel really bad for the girl. She gets raped and he gets . . . away." Sophie seethed.

"I feel like I failed her and . . . well, all the other women he's probably going to rape in the future."

"So that's it? It's over?" she demanded.

I didn't know what to say, so I did what I did well—I shrugged.

"You're going to do something about this, aren't you?" Her mouth was set mutinously, like when she was a child and was scolding me for disappointing her about something.

I smiled gently. "I may. I'm thinking about it. And speaking of *failing*, I just took another no-win case."

"Tell me about it," Sophie said, and I did.

"Oh my, Leila is back." She clapped gleefully. "I always liked her."

"You don't even know her," I protested.

"You lived with her . . ."

"For three months . . . She was gone for a good part of that time. You met her like twice."

"And liked her. *Mor* met her once and hated her," Sophie said.

Stine wouldn't admit it and took umbrage if anyone pointed it out, but she'd disliked Leila on sight because she was with me *and* she wasn't Danish. She'd accepted my Turkish friend Eymen, mostly because he'd married into a wealthy Copenhagen family, which redeemed him. Leila, with her Iranian heritage, was difficult for Stine to accept. Leila, with her magical hold on me, even harder. Erik, on the other hand, was the most inclusive man I knew, so inclusive that he accepted everyone with open arms, including me, his wife's ex.

"How do you feel, now that the love of your life is back?" Sophie was enjoying herself immensely at my expense. I didn't like talking to her about the women I dated in general, and Leila in particular.

I ignored the "love of my life" part of her comment. "She's not back, not like that. She wants me to investigate this case. That's all."

"And you're right, you're going to fail at this. Everyone knows Yousef Ahmed killed Sanne Melgaard." She tore off a piece of the croissant.

"I know." I heaped smoked trout onto a slice of rye bread, and then cut a small piece. I held it up to her on my fork and Sophie bent down to take a bite. She'd eaten half the eggs and all the salmon and left the smoked trout for me.

She ate faster than I did, and she had steadily eaten while I had told her about my new case, so she was already on dessert with the croissant while I was still only on my second slice of rye bread.

By the time I finished my *pain au chocolat* and all the coffee, Sophie was checking her phone and responding to text messages. I knew it was time for her to get to the next appointment on her calendar.

"You're coming tomorrow, right?" Sophie was moving out of Stine's home. Leaving the nest to share an apartment with a friend while she studied psychology at the University of Copenhagen.

"Yes."

"And Eymen is coming along to help."

"Umm . . . yes . . . of course," I said.

She looked at me suspiciously and I caved. "Okay, I forgot. I'll tell him now."

"What if he's busy?" Sophie remonstrated.

I grinned. "He won't be."

"How do you know?"

"Because I'll ask him not to be. And he's the one bringing the truck to move your stuff."

"It's a good thing he's such a nice guy," she said, shaking her head, and then leaned down to kiss me on my cheek.

As soon as Sophie left, I texted Eymen to let him know he was helping me move Sophie the next day. He responded with a thumbs-up emoji.

Eymen and I had been friends since university, and we were still each other's two-in-the-morning phone call. As in the call you get in the middle of the night when your friend tells you, "I have a dead car at the Polish border, can you come and pick me up?" and you get up and get in your car to drive the ten-odd hours to Poland.

Eymen was now the chief financial officer for a Danish pharmaceutical company, which was an achievement for a second-generation Dane from Turkey. He lived in Frederiksberg with his wife and the mother of his two children, Clara Silberg, who managed her family's foundation because hers was one of those old-money Danish ones that had their own compound in Klampenborg with a view of Nivå Bay.

I ordered a second filter coffee, put on my DITA sunglasses, and sat in the sun, contemplating Leila and her request, which was ridiculous, almost like saying *maybe* Chapman didn't kill Lennon and could someone *please* investigate.

I watched as a couple was seated at a table next to me. Probably in the first month of their relationship, I thought. It was all still fresh and new. They were in their twenties and very much in love because neither of them was looking at their phone. They held hands. They were immersed in each other. It was refreshing.

Since I was already in Nørrebro, I texted Nicole Bonnet, a friend and journalist at *Politiken* who lived close to Mirabelle. She texted back saying she was at home, she didn't have her son with her, and sure, she'd let me buy her a beer at Mirabelle.

Nico was tall, beautiful, and blond. She wore tight jeans, red Chucks, and a T-shirt that said JOURNALISTS GET LAID (OFF). She was half French and half Danish, and we had a healthy relationship based on casual (but superior) sex and the exchange of information. But first and foremost, we were friends. Good ones. The kind you could rely on.

We hugged. She kissed me on my cheek and sat down. She took her Ray-Ban sunglasses off and closed her eyes in pleasure. "Sunshine. Come to mama."

The weather in Copenhagen was an important character in the drama of everyone's life. When it was good, which was not often, it was great; when it was bad, which was most of the time, it was depressing Nordic noir background.

She put her sunglasses back on when the waiter came and ordered a beer on draft while I stuck to coffee.

"Tell me about Yousef Ahmed," I asked once she had drunk a quarter of the beer and we'd stopped talking about the weather, family, and common friends.

She crinkled her nose. "Why?"

"You wrote about that case," I reminded her.

"A few of us worked on that story and it was a long time ago," she said suspiciously. "What's going on?"

"Nothing."

"Is someone asking you to investigate this? Please tell me that's not so."

"Tell me what you know. I know what you wrote, but I'd like the journalist's subjective assessment."

"And your next stop is Tommy?" she mused.

Tommy Frisk was a *chefpolitiinspektør*, chief police inspector, in Copenhagen and used to be my boss when I was a police officer in the Financial Fraud Division many years ago. He had been the one who had fired me from the force. He'd had no choice, as I'd been investigating Karina Jensen, the chief of National Police, for corruption, and had maybe not always stayed within the bounds of Danish law as I did so. Until then my career had been on the up and up, but after that . . . as Maverick would say, *it crashed and burned.*

Ultimately, Karina Jensen was convicted of corruption because she had given nearly six million kroner of the Danish people's money to friends and family members by alleging they were contractors. Tommy offered me my job back once Karina was found guilty, but I'd fallen in *like* with the private investigator life by then. It was not bound by the hierarchy of the police and I didn't have to wear the unflattering uniform.

I neither denied nor admitted to Nico that I'd be seeing Tommy next.

"It's all public information," she noted. "It was, what . . . five years ago? Yousef Ahmed found out that his son had been tortured and murdered by ISIS for being a translator for the Danish military."

We had all found out because ISIS had released a video of the torture and execution, and even though the video had been removed from many sites, it hadn't prevented most of the world from seeing Raheem Ahmed die. His only crime had been to help the Danish military, the military of the country whose government denied him asylum.

Raheem came to Denmark at the end of the war, when troops returned and it became unsafe for Iraqi citizens like him, branded collaborators, to stay in their own country. He was housed at Sandholm, a former military barracks and the largest reception center for asylum seekers, while he waited for his request for family reunification to be processed. Raheem had thought it was just a formality. After all, his father, mother, and sister were permanent Danish residents, having been granted asylum five years ago. But after four months of waiting, his request was denied, and he was forcibly put on a plane and sent to Baghdad.

He was brutally murdered three days later.

"A day after the video was released, there was a protest at city hall against Sanne Melgaard," she continued.

Sanne Melgaard, an open and proud "Denmark for Danes" politician with a strong anti-immigrant agenda, had then been the attorney general of Denmark and claimed she'd followed the government policy in not offering Raheem asylum and sending him back to Iraq.

After his death, in television interviews, Sanne Melgaard said she was sorry about what had happened to Raheem but took no responsibility for it. Instead, she blamed Raheem and his family for how they'd lived their lives in Iraq, which she claimed led to this tragedy. Anyone else would've backed down, considering how awful the torture-murder video was, but Sanne pressed on, undeterred.

"On the day of the memorial service for Raheem, Sanne did an interview with *Politiken* and said Muslim men want to rape white women and weren't we all lucky that Raheem Ahmed would not be one of those men. She retracted it right away, saying she was taken out of context, but the damage was done," Nico said and sighed. "That was just too much for the father. The day after, he killed her."

"She was one *classy* lady, was our Sanne," I remarked.

"No kidding," Nico quipped in disgust. "They didn't even get Raheem's body. ISIS burned it. That video kept me up several nights. It was heartbreaking. You know Kim Stroustrup?"

I nodded. Yes, I knew of the editor in chief of the top Danish newspaper, *Berlingske*.

"He's a friend, and right after Raheem's murder he wrote this open letter to Sanne. It was chilling. During World War Two we turned away Jewish refugees . . . we were on the wrong side of history then and . . . history is repeating itself now."

"I thought we saved Jews by sending them to Sweden," I said, confused.

"Well, we saved Danish Jews, but we apparently turned away non-Danish Jews, so they ended up in concentration camps," Nico told me. "But we won the war."

"And the victor writes history."

"Sure does."

"How do they say Yousef Ahmed killed her?" I asked.

"By *they* . . . you mean the police?" Nico asked, and I nodded. "I repeat, this is all public knowledge, Præst."

"Just walk me through what you remember." I had spent a good part of the morning reading about the case, but Nico saw things through a reporter's lens and gave me a different perspective.

Nico narrowed her eyes. "You're up to something."

But since she knew I'd tell her when I was good and ready, she continued, "She was at her summerhouse in Gilleleje. Yousef went there to talk to her. God knows how that conversation went. Probably not well because he killed her . . . slit her throat as ISIS did his son's and stabbed her about fifteen times, just to be sure. The photographs were awful. A terrible way to go, even for Sanne."

"How did he get to and from Gilleleje?" I asked.

"According to *them*, the police, he took the train. There isn't CCTV footage, but they canvassed and found some people who saw him. Yousef also admitted that he took the train to get there and back."

"And no one noticed he was covered from head to toe in blood?" I asked.

"He wasn't," Nico said. "It was Sankt Hans Aften and it was raining as it always does, which is a bummer for the bonfires. So, there weren't that many people on the train, because they were at the beach, trying to light damp wood. The police theory is that he wore a coat over the bloody clothes or that he had a change of clothes. They weren't sure and didn't care because his bloody clothes and the knife from Sanne's kitchen were found in a trash can close to his kiosk in Søborg."

Sankt Hans was celebrated on the shortest night of the year, midsummer, in the end of June, with large bonfires on beaches.

"And we know for sure it was Yousef that people saw?" I asked.

"This is not one of those oh-someone-else-did-it-Agatha-Christie mysteries," Nico said. "He was there. She was dead. There was blood on his clothes."

"Did he confess?"

"Of course not," Nico said, bemused. "He maintains his innocence, just like everyone else in prison."

"Is he that stupid that he didn't get rid of the evidence along the way? That he disposed of it close to his own place?"

Nico shrugged. "Crime of passion. People do things when they're angry. And remember, criminals are not the smartest people, that's why they're criminals."

"But he didn't confess."

"No," Nico confirmed. "Just because he did it out of righteous anger doesn't mean he wants to go to jail."

She held up her empty beer glass and pointed to the waiter, who brought her a refill. I asked for another fresh carafe of coffee.

"I was hoping you had something new for me, not old and done." Nico raised her freshly filled glass. "At least I get free beer out of this."

I smiled. "Free beer and *something else*."

"I can't," Nico protested. "I *really* wish I could. But *something else* will have to wait. It's my father's sixtieth. I have to leave in a bit for Lolland and deal with the whole family birthday party nonsense."

I had hoped that the afternoon beer would turn into a late lunch and *more*. Nico was always game, just as I was. It was the easiest relationship in my life. She expected nothing from me except when we were together, and I did the same. If we didn't know each other as well as we did, we'd have become a couple—but we did, and she wasn't any more interested in being involved with me in *that way* than I was with her.

"In that case, how about something on the Hassing case?"

"It's the twenty-first century and we're still not able to convict men who rape women."

I nodded. "It's not fair, but *skat*, you know most things in life are not."

"You've been loud about it," Nico observed. "Heard you said to the young rapist he deserved to be castrated or something outside the courthouse."

"He was being smug." I sighed. "I should've been more professional."

Nico snorted. "The stoic Gabriel Præst with not a single hair out of place went wild."

I stroked my bald head and winked.

Outside the courthouse I had not been the Gabriel Præst I had become; I'd reverted to the Gabriel Præst I used to be. The angry police constable. I wasn't proud of losing my temper in front of the media, but I didn't regret it either. It was what it was.

"What do you have?" Nico asked.

"A lead."

"What kind of lead?" she asked, excited.

"Christina Hassing wasn't the only girl he raped, there are others, and I can give you a list of names that we couldn't use in court because none of them would testify. But you could investigate," I suggested.

"And why are you giving it to me?" she probed.

"I'm giving it to you, a good journalist, because that little asshole isn't going to prison and I think he deserves to be punished."

"Public humiliation?" she wondered.

"You don't always get what you want . . ."

"But if you try sometimes . . ." she sang.

"Exactly," I said.

She stepped away for a moment, and I finished my coffee. While I waited for the check, I found the open letter from the editor in chief of *Berlingske* to Sanne after Raheem's murder and began to read.

Ren Religion (Pure Religion)

From the desk of Kim Stroustrup, editor in chief of Berlingske, to Sanne Melgaard, attorney general of Denmark

Dear Sanne Melgaard,

Brandla Wassermann thought her luck had changed in October 1942 when a young Dane helped her and her three children, Ursula (7 years), Jacky Siegfried (5 years) and Denny (2 years), and brought them from Berlin to Copenhagen. Brandla had believed that their lives would now be spared.

But the Danish government was not as kind as that Danish man. Brandla and her three children were expelled from the country a few months after she had been allowed to live in Copenhagen and marched back to the German border, from which point they were sent straight to Auschwitz. The children were murdered immediately. Their mother, Brandla, was executed by an injection of phenol into the heart in Auschwitz on 15 December 1942. Researchers found a list of her belongings, compiled by Berlin authorities from her apartment in Keipelstraße 41, which were secured to compensate for the rent she didn't pay when she was in Copenhagen.

Why is it that Brandla was not granted any of the sympathy enjoyed by 7,300 Danish Jews who were secretly transported to safety in Sweden? The answer is quite simple. Anti-Semitism didn't stop at the German border but infiltrated into Denmark. Danes saved Danish Jews because they were Danes first and their religion was secondary. But in the case of Brandla and other Jews, their religion came first.

Brandla was permitted to enter the country pending review, but in the report written by a Dane and Nazi sympathizer at the Department of Immigration of the Danish State Police, it said, "She is a pure Jew, also of religion."

Then there is the story of Schulim and Ruth Fanni Niedrig, a young Jewish couple who was expelled by the Danes in 1940. Ruth was bitten to death by dogs in Auschwitz in 1943; Schulim lived through Auschwitz and was one of the few who survived the Danish expulsion of Jews from 1940 to 1943.

Is what we did then any different from what we're

doing today? Is what happened to these Jews different from what happened to Raheem Ahmed?

Is Denmark going to stand on the wrong side of history again?

After I finished reading it, I sighed deeply. If we were honest about our past, did it mean history was repeating itself . . . that we'd look back at the Muslim refugees that we refused to protect today with the same guilt as we did the non-Danish Jewish ones we abandoned before and during the Second World War? It was an uncomfortable feeling.

CHAPTER 3

How much did that suit cost you?" Tommy asked.

Tommy was a tall man, even by Danish standards. He had a full head of blond hair. He was in shape, unlike some people his age who tended to nurse a beer gut. Tommy combined his Nordic god looks with a deep voice made to play audiobook characters who've lived a hard life. He wore a pair of jeans with a black shirt and blazer, and cowboy boots. Give him a cowboy hat and a straw to gnaw on, and he could give Clint a run for his money.

"I think that's considered a rude question in polite society," I warned.

"Then we should be okay because we aren't in polite society. Italian?" he speculated.

"Savile Row actually."

"You dress like a metrosexual from southern Sweden," Tommy observed. I sat up and dramatically moved my arms to broaden my chest and he nodded. "Yeah, yeah, you're in shape. What else are you going to do but go to the gym when you don't have a real job."

"I don't go to the gym. Too much spandex. And I have a *real* job. How do you think I paid for my suit?" I asked.

Tommy grinned and waved his hand at the waiter. We had met at Café Victor in the center of the city and were sitting outside because the weather had promise, even if mostly unrealized at this point.

Under its green awning, Café Victor had sturdy infrared heat lamps, allowing customers to eat alfresco nearly year-round if they were so inclined or, like Tommy, had a pack-a-day Marlboro Red habit.

Tommy looked at his watch when the waiter came and ordered a Laphroaig 10, neat.

"It's past five, I can drink the good stuff," Tommy insisted. "Especially since you're paying."

"Isn't that bribery?"

"Hell, no. It's charity. I'm a poor public servant."

I ordered a coffee, black. I had dinner plans at Bistro Boheme on Esplanaden with a friend later in the evening and didn't want to ruin my appetite.

"You're not drinking?"

"Dinner plans," I explained.

The waiter brought his whiskey and my coffee, and I let Tommy take a swallow of scotch before I asked him about Yousef Ahmed.

"Oh, Præst." He sighed. "Why are you poking your nose into that?"

I shrugged. It was my go-to move.

"Who's your client?"

I shrugged again.

Tommy thought about it for a moment and said grimly, "Leila Abadi Knudsen."

I drank some of my coffee.

"She's his lawyer now, isn't she?" Tommy didn't sound happy. "Your dinner plans?"

I shook my head. "Who led the case? Do you think I can see the murder book?"

Tommy chuckled. "Sure, and Scarlett Johansson is going to give me a blow job."

"Don't be a pervert, Scarlett is young enough to be your daughter. You can tell me about the case. It's all old news anyway."

Tommy drained his glass and signaled to the waiter to bring him another. His mood went from sunny to not so bright.

"This is a two-drink conversation," he elaborated. "Henrik Morck was lead detective on the case. He was heading the murder section at Rejseholdet then."

The National Police Travel Team had gained fame due to a popular television show in the early aughts.

"Henrik's a good guy." I remembered the man from my days on the force. "Where's he now? Promoted?"

"He moved *down* to the Financial Fraud Division, your old department, and not as its leader," Tommy said. "He had his pick, but he wanted that. He took some time off after the case. I don't think his heart has been in it since then."

"Case was too much?" I wondered.

Tommy stretched his long legs under the table, and I aligned mine away to avoid getting my brown Alessandro Galet shoes with an asymmetrical Scritto pattern nicked by his not-so-clean cowboy boots.

"Look, Yousef Ahmed did it," Tommy stressed. "You need to remember that no matter how hard Leila is grabbing your dick."

"I'm just looking into the case one more time to reassure my client," I said lightly and added, "And she's not grabbing my dick. Not even if I ask nicely."

"She isn't falling for your handmade suit nonsense?"

"No," I stated emphatically. "I think Leila wants me for my other qualities. You know, as a private investigator."

"We did a thorough job, so reassure your fucking client," Tommy declared and then sighed. "Stop staring at me like that."

"Like what?"

"Like a dog with a bone. Look, I'll introduce you to Morck, that's all I can do. Sound good?"

I nodded.

"Who's your dinner date?" Tommy asked.

"A friend."

Tommy looked at me keenly. Sometimes it didn't help to have friends who knew you as well and for as long as Tommy had known me.

"Is it that blond reporter from *Politiken*?" He knew Nico and I were friends, and we had recently bumped into Tommy and a friend at Le Jardin restaurant next door. Copenhagen was a small city, almost a village.

"No, it's not Nico," I denied. "It is, if you must know, an *old* friend."

"An old friend *with* benefits?"

"I don't sleep with every woman I have dinner with," I retorted. "She's a friend who lives in Helsinki and when she comes to Copenhagen for work, and we can square away our calendars, we have dinner."

Tommy nodded gravely. "How does Leila feel about your Helsinki connection?"

"How are your plans of moving to the city coming along?" I asked, changing the topic. Sometimes with Tommy, I had to be as subtle as a chainsaw on fire.

"They're not," Tommy scoffed. "Nadia wants to make sure we have room for the kids and grandkids. So, we're staying in a big house, just the two of us, waiting for my kids to get knocked up. They are not planning to reproduce anytime soon, so we have a huge house for the fucking dogs."

"How's Nadia?" I asked of his wife, a dog lover with a penchant for German shepherds.

Tommy smiled. He was one of my few friends who had stayed married. Tommy never cheated on his wife, and always smiled when he spoke of her. I had known Nadia almost as long as I'd known Tommy, and I thought the world of her. She was an intelligent woman who had navigated a career as an ER doctor, a mostly male profession, with diplomacy, humor, and a core of steel. The daughter of Palestinian Christians, she'd met Tommy when he'd ended up in the ER after a druggie split his lip with his fist.

"She's now the head of ER at Rigshospitalet," he said with considerable pride. He talked about his two daughters after that. One was in the United States at the University of Notre Dame on a soccer scholarship. His older daughter was in Brussels, working at the EU Parliament, in their media and Public Relations Department.

Tommy regaled me with stories about his daughters and their boyfriends until it was time to leave.

"Don't waste your time on this," he advised as we left the restaurant. "Yousef Ahmed is guilty and there's absolutely no doubt about it."

CHAPTER 4

I don't think Yousef Ahmed did it," Henrik Morck told me when I met him the next day at Byens Bodega, near the police headquarters on Niels Brocks Gade. Henrik was built like a bull and was all muscle. He was clean-shaven like me, but unlike me had bloodshot eyes framing gray-blue irises.

I called him in the morning at around nine to ask him if we could meet to talk about the Yousef Ahmed case. He asked me to go fuck myself. He called back fifteen minutes later and said he'd heard from Tommy.

"The boss said you dress like a banker."

"Yes, I'll be the one in the suit," I told him.

"I'll be the one at the bar," he replied.

He was already at the bodega by the time I got there, and not on his first beer, I suspected. He was drinking a tall draft of an indeterminate pilsner. It was eleven in the morning and the place smelled of stale beer and cigarettes, and something else that I suspected was a disinfectant valiantly sanitizing the place.

A local pub, Byens Bodega was where hardcore locals went and lost tourists ended up. This wasn't a place that showed up on Tripadvisor or any of the "where to go when in Copenhagen" blogs. A large room with a bar in the back, it was simple and not overly clean but oddly welcoming. If you wanted a beer and to smoke indoors, this was the right place.

I refused Henrik's invitation to have a beer on his tab and asked the bored blond waitress who was wearing a white T-shirt that read EAT SHIT and a pair of distressed jeans to get me some black coffee. The waitress was in her mid-twenties; she didn't look like the type that was going to university and doing this part-time to pay the bills. She looked like a lifer. This was it. She was going to stand behind a bar, her eyes glazed over for the rest of her life.

She served me coffee in a white cup and left the French press on the counter.

"Why did you arrest him if he didn't do it?" I asked Henrik.

He looked at me. "Do you always wear a suit?"

I nodded. "When I'm working."

"Why?"

"Uniform."

"Tommy said you get into a lot of trouble."

"Trouble is the common denominator of the living. It is the great equalizer."

"And that you quote fucking Kierkegaard."

"I also have a penchant for Sartre."

"Whatever," Henrik quipped.

"Tommy said you moved to fraud after the Sanne Melgaard case."

Henrik snorted. "I moved to the bodega, *baby*." He said the word *baby* in English. I hated how Danes mixed Danish with English swear words and endearments.

"I heard that too," I responded. "I thought you'd be celebrating. You caught Sanne Melgaard's killer."

He asked the waitress for a refill. He called her Mette. She didn't smile at him as she brought him another tall pint of beer. I felt better. Her not smiling at me wasn't personal.

"'Once you hear the details of victory, it's hard to distinguish it from a defeat.'"

I raised an eyebrow in appreciation. "Sartre."

"And you thought I was just a dumb fuck."

I didn't answer.

"Yousef went to her summerhouse. He says he knocked, no one answered, so he left a letter for her and came back home," Henrik said blandly. "I believe him."

"What did the letter say?"

"Never found a letter."

"But you believe him?"

"Yes."

"But then there's all the evidence," I suggested, pouring myself a second cup of coffee. Surprisingly, the coffee wasn't bad.

Henrik grunted. "The knife that he used to slit her throat with. Blood on his clothes."

"Seems like he lost his head and killed her."

Henrik shook his head. "Too obvious. In the police business you know that criminals are stupid, that's why they're criminals. But Yousef isn't stupid. The man is smart. Has some big degree in economics from Iraq. No one cares in fucking Denmark because he's from Iraq, so he does what Iraqis do—he opens a grocery store and puts his economics degree to use selling fruit, veg, and fifty different kinds of Turkish delight."

"Still doesn't explain why you think he didn't do it," I countered.

"What happened with Karina Jensen," he demanded, suddenly going off topic.

I didn't like discussing the former chief of the National Police, who was out of prison after her three years there and was getting paid handsomely to write a book about her experience, probably still pissed at me for starting the investigation that got her ousted. But Henrik wasn't asking because he was interested in the old case, he wanted a quid pro quo. You show me yours and I'll show you mine.

"I have a *cand.merc.*, a master's in economics from the Copenhagen Business School, so they put me on the Corruption and Bribery Task Force in the Financial Fraud Division. We were looking into the case of a member of parliament using money from a nonprofit company he was on the board of to pay for a pair of Gucci loafers and for his mistress's apartment in Paris," I explained.

"I can't manage one wife and these assholes have mistresses."

"I met the wife, so I can understand the mistress," I said. "Anyway, I started there and then I kept pulling on that thread. As good old Deep Throat advised, I followed the money and ended up finding out what Karina was doing."

"And then what happened?"

"She managed to get the investigation blocked and they sent me to look at some summerhouse fraud scheme in Randers."

"But they did investigate, and she did go to prison. How did that happen?" Henrik asked. Drunk he might be, but he knew how to interrogate an uncooperative witness.

"Because a young journalist at *Politiken* started to ask a lot of questions, wrote some stories, and then they *had* to investigate, and they found proof that put Karina in jail."

"Why did they fire you?" he probed.

I sighed. "Because I gave confidential case files to the journalist at *Politiken*."

"How did they find out that you leaked confidential files?"

"When the story broke in the papers, Tommy asked me if I was the leak, because I was friends with a journalist at *Politiken*, and I told him that I was. He fired me on the spot," I told him. It had taken nearly two years after the *Politiken* story for the investigation to be completed and then another year before the court case reached its verdict. It had worked out for me. I got a PI license and set up shop.

"Why did you tell him?"

"He's a friend. I couldn't lie to him."

"Would he have found out if you hadn't told him?" he wanted to know.

I shrugged. "I don't know. Probably not. My friend didn't break that story, someone else in her newsroom did. I was the source of a source . . . I was pretty safe, I think."

"You knew he'd fire you for that," Henrik drawled.

I nodded.

"You told him the truth anyway."

I nodded again.

"He didn't do it," Henrik said. And he didn't have to tell me who the *he* was.

"Why?"

"There are enough holes in the timeline and the story to drive three trucks through. I mean, witnesses said he was wearing a dark coat and the detectives determined that's why no one saw the blood on his clothes. The coat makes sense. It was Sankt Hans and it was fucking cold because it always rains on that damn day, just to poke us in the eye on the one evening when we can legally have a bonfire. He slit her throat . . . that blood splatter is major. And he stabbed her fifteen times too. I think you'd need more than a coat to hide that kind of carnage."

"Maybe he brought a change of clothes," I suggested. "Changed and then went home all cleaned up. Took the bloody clothes with him, thinking no one would be the wiser."

"There was evidence that someone washed up in the kitchen sink with industry-strength cleaners, in case you were wondering why we didn't CSI the place, because we did and found fuck all. So, let's say he cleaned himself up and changed his clothes. *But* why would he have a change of clothes with him? You carry a change of clothes wherever you go?" he challenged.

"If I was planning to kill someone I would," I replied.

Henrik shook his head. "Let's say he had the foresight to bring a change of clothes because he was planning on killing her. He brought the spare clothes but forgot a murder weapon and used *her* butcher knife?" I saw fire flash in his eyes. "And then he takes it home with him? What kind of an idiot brings the bloody murder weapon home and then tosses it into a trash can close to his place of business and his home?"

"Adrenaline can do crazy things to us humans," I offered, though I could see the holes in the story.

"Those are not the only problems. I got a dozen more," he growled.

"Why didn't you tell anyone?" I pondered. "About your . . . ah . . . concerns?"

"I'm telling you," Henrik said.

I raised my eyebrows.

He smirked. "No one wanted to listen. The entire Danish population wanted the Muslim refugee from Iraq to be the killer. It was like *The X Factor* and he was the first and only contestant. I didn't have a choice. I'm now responsible for Yousef Ahmed spending his life in jail, right after he saw his son tortured and murdered for helping Danish soldiers who interfered in a war that was none of our business to start with. I'm a fucking hero."

"Why not go to the media?" I suggested.

"With what? Conspiracy theories? Look, I'm a regular cop. I solve crimes, go home, eat my food, talk to my kids if they're home, fuck my wife, and on weekends I do some gardening if the weather is nice," he said flatly.

"Why are you telling me?"

"You're the only one who's ever asked if the man is guilty." Henrik raised his glass in celebration. "Congratulations, you won the lottery."

"What did I win?"

"The murder book with my notes." He pulled out a USB stick from his pocket and gave it to me. "If you get caught with this, I don't know how you got it. Okay?"

I put the USB stick into my suit jacket's inside pocket.

I rose from the barstool and we shook hands. "How long are you planning to keep this up?"

"Day drinking?" he asked.

I nodded.

"As long as I need to," he said.

CHAPTER 5

Stine glared at me when I arrived at the apartment she shared with her husband. She wasn't happy, as I knew she wouldn't be. Sophie was moving out and she wasn't ready for it.

"Do you know how dangerous Nørrebro is?" she said to me. "Do you know there was a gang shooting on the street right where her apartment is?"

"It's those fucking immigrants," Eymen said as he walked in and kissed Stine on both cheeks. He was as tall as me, around six two, but he had a full head of dark hair with some salt thrown in, a beard that was a result of laziness rather than fashion, and a face that said, *I'm a good guy, you can trust me* if you overlooked the fact he was Turkish.

"I can't believe you're both okay with Sophie moving out to . . . why can't she live in Østerbro or even Vesterbro? Why Nørrebro?" she demanded.

"Because that's what she can afford, and it's a lot more fun than bourgeois Østerbro." Sophie rolled a large suitcase into the foyer.

Eymen grabbed the suitcase from her. He had brought his truck, the 4x4 that he used when he went camping in Norway with his father-in-law and sometimes me.

"Where's Erik?" I asked.

"At work." Sophie sighed. "He said he'd come over to the apartment to help unload, but you were both on your own here."

"Like that's my fault?" Stine screeched; her voice had that shrill quality I recognized from years of hearing it. I sympathized with Erik.

"*Mor*," Sophie crooned and took her mother's hands in hers, "I'll come back for dinner tomorrow night. But if you keep on like this, I won't come for dinner on Sundays."

"That's what she's promised me. Dinners on Sunday." Stine sniffled. "What's the big rush to move? You could wait until you finish . . ."

"University?" Sophie snorted. "You're crazy. None of my friends have had this problem with their mothers. They moved out when they were eighteen and it was *just* fine."

"Because those mothers are selfish women who don't love their children," Stine declared.

Eymen and I went into Sophie's room and started to carry boxes and furniture down four flights of stairs to his truck, which was illegally parked on Rothesgade, where Stine and Erik had a *herskabslejlighed*, a master's apartment in Østerbro. Stine had lived here since Sophie was four years old and it was the only real home Sophie remembered. She had been too young the years we'd lived together in our little apartment in Vesterbro.

"Why is Stine freaking out?" Eymen wondered as we carried Sophie's bed frame to his truck.

"The shooting," I explained, mentioning an incident, which was the result of an ongoing gang war. "It rattled her because one of her colleagues had been on the street when it happened. Since then, Nørrebro is a hellhole."

"So, Erik and Stine are okay?" Eymen asked as we heaved Sophie's bed frame onto the truck.

"Yes." I grunted. "He leaves when she's in this mood. Comes over and helps me with the house. We drink some beer, tell some lies, and then he goes back when she's calmed down."

"How long does that take?"

"Longest was three days."

"You're the weirdest divorced couple I know." Eymen and I took the stairs two at a time to go back upstairs.

"We were never married," I reminded him.

"You know what I mean. Erik and you are friends," Eymen noted. "I don't think I could be friends with Clara's new husband."

"That's because you love her," I told him.

It was nearly six in the evening when Erik, Eymen, and I finished moving Sophie into her apartment, where we left her to unpack. We went to Manfreds on Jægersborggade, close to Sophie's new place, for a beer and something to eat.

Manfreds was one of those "small dishes, two or three per person" kind of places, so we ordered the entire menu and a bottle of the Carignan-Grenache blend, thinking it would go well with the pork and sauerkraut, the tartare of beef, the cod roe, and the other small plates on the menu.

We didn't talk until we'd finished a beer and half a glass of the wine and the first small plate, which was blanched potatoes with cod roe. The basics first.

"Sophie tells me you took on a new case," Erik inquired.

"Yes, I did."

"And it's a favor for Leila," Erik added.

Eymen raised his eyebrows. "The one who got away." He whistled.

"It gets better." Erik chuckled. "He's looking into Yousef Ahmed."

"Looking into what about Yousef Ahmed?" Eymen wanted to know.

"His innocence," Erik said, and they both let out a laugh.

The waiter brought a Swedish lentil soup and salad to the table. We steadily dug into the food and bottle of wine.

After dinner, Erik walked to his apartment and Eymen offered to drop me off on his way home.

"You should be careful poking into this Yousef Ahmed business," Eymen cautioned me.

"Because he's enemy number one?"

"Because he's a Muslim man who murdered a white politician," he responded.

"Maybe because he is Muslim, he might have been framed," I told him. "I am under no illusions, and neither are you, that most of Europe would accuse the outsider to maintain our sense of superiority. With a case like this, I might have a chance to make a difference and free a potentially wronged man."

"You think this one case will put an end to racism in Denmark?"

"No. But I think if we don't go after every such case of blatant racism, then there is little chance of ever living in a Denmark where you are treated as an equal."

"Between you and me, I am the superior one," Eymen joked and then added, looking at me after he stopped at a red light, "Are you doing this for Leila?"

"No."

"You sure?"

"Yes. But let me put it this way. I'd take on a case less worthy because Leila asked me to," I answered.

"You are one self-aware son of a bitch," Eymen derided.

He drove across the lakes, turned right onto Øster Søgade, and then left onto the narrow Eckersbergsgade. He parked by my town house, in front of which was a picnic table and a small children's playhouse. A red truck lay abandoned outside the playhouse and there were fading kids' chalk drawings on the road.

"I don't think an ex should be all this trouble," Eymen insisted.

After talking to Henrik, I knew that this wasn't *just* about doing Leila a favor. I had had every intention of doing the basic investigation and telling her that Yousef Ahmed was as guilty as everyone thought he was. But within a day of digging, I had found a detective drowning his guilt in several glasses of pilsner and evidence that looked convenient. I couldn't turn away from it anymore.

"Maybe Leila isn't worth it?" Eymen suggested.

I shrugged again.

Eymen shook his head. "Do your shoulders just reflex into a shrug or are you communicating something?"

I shrugged yet again.

Eymen sighed.

I patted him on his shoulder. "Thanks for the ride."

I watched Eymen drive away and opened the small white gate to enter the stamp-size lawn in front of my town house.

I inherited the house from my grandmother a decade ago, to the chagrin of others in the family. But I had been her favorite. I hadn't been surprised. I loved the *Kartoffelrækkehus* (potato row town house) that had been built in the 1800s. The town houses were three floors and people had remodeled their homes in different ways. I loved the street I lived on; there were often kids playing by the playhouse and adults having tea, coffee, or a glass of wine on the benches in the center of the street. We knew one another and twice a year had a potluck block party.

At the end of the street on Øster Farimagsgade was my favorite bakery, Emmerys, where I enjoyed a morning coffee along with a cinnamon roll on lazy Sunday mornings. The street was dotted with cafés, bars, and shops—I could get a cup of coffee, do my grocery shopping, and even buy a bottle of good wine all within a five-minute walk.

I loved my home, even though it was a work in progress.

My *Farmor*, my father's mother, had had her living room on the ground floor along with a kitchen and a washroom; I had left it that way because I could step into the tiny paved backyard for my morning coffee and cigarette and my evening scotch and cigarette. I allowed myself two cigarettes a day—three if the day required it but there had to be truly extenuating circumstances. Last time was when my mother passed away. My father and I had drunk a bottle of scotch and smoked a few packs of cigarettes that night, keeping vigil, saying goodbye to her.

I had converted the third floor into my office, opening into the master bedroom with a walk-in closet and an attached master bathroom that was not quite complete. The bathroom had an antique cast-iron eighteenth-century French bateau clawfoot tub with a hand-burnished natural iron exterior. The bathtub had cost me as much as some people paid for an entire bathroom upgrade, so the room now had only the bathtub, standing on a partially tiled floor. I had found enough of the perfect black and white antique Spanish ceramic tiles to cover half the bathroom. I was on a mission to find enough of the same tiles for the rest of the bathroom, where a functioning modern toilet stood on a cement floor. It was one thing to buy an antique bathtub, quite another to get an antique toilet. I fervently hoped that when I did find the tiles, I'd also have the funds to purchase them. Sixteenth-century Spanish tiles were not inexpensive.

The second floor was Sophie's, with a bedroom, a study, and

a bathroom with a shower and a toilet, and it was completely done. The original wooden floor was polished but maintained its rawness—and the room was painted in some cream color she liked. She and I had a fight when she insisted on painting the original beams in that same cream color and I wanted to keep them raw as they were meant to be. I had won on the beams; she had won on the flowered curtains. No one was happy.

My bedroom was *almost* done. I still hadn't decided (even after a decade) what color I wanted the walls. I had one wall painted a deep blue, which worked for me; but the rest was a mishmash of sample colors I had tried out to find the right bluish white to make it all work. The bed was king size, the frame was from Portugal (not an antique but a replica), and the mattress was comfortable. My mother had taught me never to compromise on a mattress. It was good advice.

For those who had a *Kartoffelrækkehus*, it was a labor of love. For me, it was a mission to build a home that fit me like a glove, a home where there were no compromises, where I loved everything except Sophie's hideous curtains. It had been only ten years since I started working on the house; there was plenty of time to reach the point where I didn't have to spend every weekend fixing a little of this and a little of that.

For Stine, my house underscored why we hadn't worked out. She was an engineer by profession and worked for an IT company. She craved stability. For her, it was all about the destination, and I thrived on the journey. But if I could've been honest, which I'd never be with her, that was not the reason we didn't work out; neither was it because we became parents at a young age. It was simpler than that. I'd never loved her, not the way I or she wanted to love, and she'd never loved me the way I wanted to be loved.

But if I wouldn't compromise on my home, what were the chances of me compromising on a partner.

CHAPTER 6

Aisha Ahmed was a darker version of Sophie. They were the same height and build, and they wore the same kind of light pink shiny lip gloss, the same style of eye makeup (it was called "cat eye," Sophie had told me).

Leila brought Aisha to my office on Adelgade. I subleased my office from Dall og Digman Advokater, the law firm at which Erik, last name Digman, was a named partner. They had the entire floor of the building on top of the French restaurant Pastis and an Aldi supermarket. I worked as an investigator for them and several other law firms in and around Copenhagen. Corporate theft, embezzlement, industrial espionage, corporate corruption, insurance fraud, and cheating spouses made up most of my business.

My office had a view of the stores across Gothersgade, and I had a hand-waving relationship with the owner of the antiques store Le Boheme Interieur. We'd never met, but we often acknowledged each other with a cheerful smile and a wave. Next to the antiques store was my favorite coffee shop and sometimes office, Café Boheme, which was owned and run by the delightful Marlene Engstrup, who served superior Peruvian coffee and some of the best *pain au chocolat* in Copenhagen.

When Leila and Aisha came into my office, I was drinking coffee in a Café Boheme porcelain cup. All that was left of the *pain au chocolat* was the paper bag it had been wrapped in.

The young woman was intimidated and sat stiffly. She wore a pair of jeans, black ballet flats, and a white peasant blouse. She did not cover her hair like many Muslim women did and wore it in a ponytail, and she looked like any Danish woman her age. She had brought along a Fjällräven backpack that she put on the floor, leaning against the leg of my oak desk, which was made from a tree my father had helped cut with my grandfather when he was a young man. The client chairs were made of the same wood, with handles on the sides. I had had them reupholstered with burnished brown leather, the same color as the office chair I sat on. The chairs were comfortable. I did not believe in sacrificing comfort and utility for good looks.

We started with small talk. Leila told me that Aisha had just finished *gymnasium* (high school) and would be going to Copenhagen Business School to study finance. This summer, Aisha was going to intern at Ernst & Young in Amager, where she hoped to find employment after she finished her *cand.merc.*, a master's degree in finance, in five years, like I had.

Leila wore a black dress, short and fitted in all the right places, with four-inch black heels. She had a jacket to go with the dress, which she had removed and hung on the arm of her chair. The day was going to go down in the year's history as one of the *good days in May*, and my office was warming nicely. I had removed my suit jacket as well and hung it in the wooden closet that I had in my office for exactly this purpose.

The closet also contained spare dress shoes and sneakers, as well as jeans and another suit and several ironed dress shirts. It was handy when I came into the office in the morning, still sweaty from my run. I would take a shower in the law firm's bathrooms and then dress for the day. I ran every day, regardless of the weather; and when I could, I would run to the office straight from the lakes. I didn't cheat when it came to my morning run because I loved food, and this was the only form of exercise I could stand to do. I had tried going to the gym and doing some of that CrossFit crap, but all the spandex and tight asses made my eyes bleed.

I was wearing a charcoal-gray Saint Laurent suit with a white Brunello Cucinelli dress shirt and a blue, gray, red, and silver Christian Dior tie. If it were winter, I'd have worn a matching vest. In fact, the tie was going to come off before long. My office, like many others in Copenhagen, did not have air-conditioning.

After they'd refused my offer of coffee, which I could get from the law firm kitchen, where they massacred the environment with Nespresso cups, I decided to broach the subject of their visit. I had another appointment in an hour with Nico, whom I was taking to lunch at Pastis downstairs.

"He didn't do it," Aisha said in a small voice.

I nodded.

"You don't believe me," she accused.

I raised my hands, palms up. "I pass no judgment. I'm all open ears and mind."

She swallowed. Leila put her hand on Aisha's in support.

"My father is a good Muslim. Violence is against our religion, no matter what *you* all say," Aisha said sincerely.

I wanted to tell her not to generalize, but I was a middle-aged white man living in one of the whitest countries in the world—what the fuck did I know about what it meant to be Muslim. So, I shut up and went back to nodding and drinking my coffee.

"He came home that day and there was no blood on him. I told the police this, but they didn't believe me . . ." Aisha trailed off.

"Tell me what happened," I urged. "From the day when you found out about your brother."

Her eyes went from angry to sad in an instant, and then they became wet from unshed tears, and I wanted to put an arm around her and tell her everything was going to be all right. According to Stine, I had never learned to deal with Sophie's tears. "You're such a sap that she has you twisted around her little finger. If she asked you for a pony and cried about it, you'd go and get her a fucking pony." This was true.

"The video . . . of my brother . . ." She paused to suck in some air.

Leila squeezed her hand.

I waited.

"We found out about it from a reporter from *B.T.* He came to the shop and asked Abba about it. He showed him the video and Abba fell. He fainted. The reporter called out for help and I heard them. Our apartment is upstairs, so I came running down and then Ammi did. Abba sat up but he wasn't well. When my mother asked him what happened, he just . . . he started to throw up and then clutched his chest. We thought he was having a heart attack. The reporter was nice. He called an ambulance for Abba, and he came with us to the hospital. He never put any of that in the paper—that Abba fainted, that he wouldn't let Ammi or me see the video. When we asked him, the journalist, he didn't show it to us, saying that he couldn't do that to us."

She stopped speaking and licked her lips.

"I'll bring you some water," I said and left the office.

I walked down the corridor to the kitchen and pulled out a bottle of water from the fridge and three glasses from the cabinet. Despite the Nespresso cups, which assaulted my green senses, Dall og Digman's thoughtful office manager made sure several glass bottles of water were in the fridge for use and reuse. There were no paper cups either; we all used glassware.

I put the tray with the bottle of water and glasses on the table. I added a bowl of raspberry-and-chocolate-covered almonds from Summerbird, the chocolatier that the law firm bought from in bulk for meetings.

Aisha drank the water; I ate one of the almonds. They were rolled in chocolate and then in powdered raspberries, so the sweet and bitter of the chocolate blended to enhance the tartness of the raspberries and vice versa.

"What happened after that?" Leila gently prodded Aisha.

"Abba was fine, just dehydrated, they said, and shocked. We went home and that night Ammi and I watched the video." Aisha began to cry.

I pushed forward a box of facial tissues made from recycled paper. She took one and wiped her tears. She crumpled the tissue in her hand and balled it into a fist on her lap.

"The next day it was on the news and then everyone was talking about it. Abba spoke to TV 2 News. We were in mourning and everyone from the neighborhood came by the apartment." Aisha's eyes sobered as she remembered. "Ammi and I couldn't stop crying. I still remember everything about that video. Everything. Raheem was . . . He helped the Danes and then they wouldn't let him stay here. They sent him home from the asylum center. They said he could not get asylum, but he could apply for family reunification from Iraq."

She shook her head.

I knew what had happened after that. Sanne Melgaard went on TV 2 News and said that Raheem wasn't Denmark's problem, that she didn't see why everyone was so up in arms about someone who had been killed in Iraq. Weren't people killed by ISIS every day? Were we upset every day? Her lack of compassion had been accepted as "racists will be racists" by the leaders of the ruling party with which Sanne's party was associated. Some had said that maybe Sanne had been misunderstood. But no one had openly reprimanded Sanne, except a few media outlets that published opinion pieces on compassion.

"Then the protests happened." Aisha shuddered. "That was crazy. We stayed home that day, locked inside. The next day everything was quiet, and we could finally mourn Raheem during his memorial service. Abba didn't want any other father to go through something like this, so he decided to talk to Sanne Melgaard. He called her office and they told him she wasn't there. But then someone called from her office a day after the memorial service and told us that she was in her summerhouse in Gilleleje if he wanted to go see her. So . . ."

I raised my hand. "Someone in Sanne Melgaard's, the attorney general's office, told your father where she was?"

Aisha nodded. "Yes."

"Someone called your father and told him?" I wanted to be sure.

"Yes," Aisha said. "He took the train and went there. He said he knocked on the door and no one opened it. So, he left the letter and came home."

"You are sure there was a letter?"

"Yes," Aisha confirmed. "I know because I helped him write it."

"What did the letter say?"

Aisha took a deep breath. "That he forgave her. That he felt no hate toward her. That he would pray for her to learn compassion so she could help people instead of hurting them. He wasn't angry." She turned to Leila. "To stab her fifteen times would mean he was angry, very angry, wouldn't it? He's not capable of that kind of rage."

"There is no mention of a phone call." I knew not only because of what Henrik Morck had told me but also because I had gone through Henrik's notes and the murder book the night before. It was common knowledge that Sanne Melgaard had a summer-house in Gilleleje and everyone who followed her on Instagram knew she was there the morning of her death because she'd posted a picture of blooming daisies in her garden.

"Did your father use Instagram?" I asked.

"What? No. Even I don't use it. I think it's a waste of time."

"So, you didn't follow Sanne Melgaard on Instagram?"

Aisha scoffed. "No. Like I said, I don't have a profile . . . on any social media. It's stupid."

Probably, I thought, but a gold mine of information for a PI.

"Where did your father leave this letter?" I asked.

"He slid the letter under the door."

"No one found the letter," I mused, and when I saw Aisha shrug, I made a gesture for her to continue.

"He came home after that," Aisha continued. "Then in the morning, the police came and took him away. They searched the house, and . . . well, you know they found the knife and bloody clothes in a trash can close to the kiosk. He wasn't wearing bloody clothes when he came home . . . He wasn't."

"But they were *his* clothes, and the blood was Sanne Melgaard's," I reminded her.

"Yes," she snapped, "but I don't know how that happened. Someone . . . made it up."

"That's a pretty elaborate scheme to set your father up. Who knew he was going to see Sanne Melgaard at the summerhouse that day?"

"Ammi and me, and some of our friends," Aisha said thoughtfully. "It wasn't something he announced to the world. But it wasn't like he was hiding it."

I nodded. Several people had known what Yousef was planning to do; several people and the person who had called to make sure Yousef Ahmed knew where Sanne Melgaard was that day. The call that the police didn't believe was real.

"The trial was short . . . ugly but short. They found him guilty. He'll stay in prison until he dies." Tears streamed down her cheeks. "None of this makes sense. He had no reason to kill her."

"Anger and grief can make people do things that we never think them capable of."

"You think he did it." Aisha accused me. Her tone was hostile. I knew that tone well from Sophie.

"I don't know," I admitted. "When I know, I'll tell you."

Aisha looked at me for a long moment and then asked, "And you won't judge?"

"No," I promised.

"My father is a good man," she concluded and stood up.

I joined her and thought of what the American historian Henry Adams once said, *It is always good men who do the most harm in the world.*

I held out my hand to shake hers. She did so with a firm hand. I liked her.

CHAPTER 7

I watched Leila and Aisha walk on Gothersgade toward Kongens Nytorv from my window. When I couldn't see them anymore, I called Henrik Morck.

"What?" he barked.

"Yousef's daughter says that someone from Sanne Melgaard's office called to let him know that she was going to be in Gilleleje in the summerhouse," I told him.

"Whatever."

"Was there a phone record?"

"He said the call came to the landline in the kiosk," Henrik said. "You know how many people call a kiosk?"

"So, you checked."

"There were calls but no one called him from her office," Henrik asserted.

"But what if someone did?"

"*One more beer, Mette*," I heard Henrik say.

"Henrik?"

"Let me tell you this in police speak. We couldn't determine with any certainty that someone had called Yousef Ahmed to tell him where Sanne Melgaard was. We stick to our theory that he found out from her Insta account or from *Jyllands-Posten* or any news outlets that had her feed on their sites."

"His daughter said he didn't use Instagram," I said. "I mean, most old people don't."

"My mother-in-law is seventy and has an Instagram account. @DitFarmorsKøkken. She has fifty thousand followers. She posts pictures of stuff she cooks. The Crown Princess Mary follows her," Henrik said dryly.

"Did his smart phone or computer—"

"No smart phone. Yes, to the computer," Henrik confirmed, cutting me off. "He had been on news sites that day. He knew where she was."

"Right."

"Have you found out anything new or are you just wasting your time going over things I already went over?" he asked.

"You did such a bang-up job that I thought following you was the way to go."

"As you know, I'm a *very* busy man, don't waste my time with these useless fucking questions." Henrik hung up.

I texted Leila: **Can you set up a meeting for me with Yousef Ahmed?**

She responded immediately: **Yes. I will send details once I arrange it.**

I put my phone aside and stared out the window until I saw Nico bicycle up Gothersgade to Pastis. It was indeed a good day in May when women started to wear short skirts and dresses while bicycling. Nico was wearing a flowing yellow sundress that cheered me.

I met Nico as she locked her bicycle. She leaned into me and touched her lips to mine.

"I'm famished and I've been dreaming of *steak frites* all day," she announced as we walked into the restaurant. I was a regular, so I took my usual table, which was half inside and half outside the restaurant when the café windows were left open to welcome the start of spring.

She ordered a bottle of Perrier that came in a green bottle made of plastic, which would end up in the ocean in a whale's gut, while I asked for *postevand*, tap water.

"All right, what have you got?" I asked after the waiter took our orders of beef tartare for me and *steak frites* for her. Since it was the middle of the day, we decided to order a glass each of red wine instead of a bottle. We agreed that the 2016 Guigal Châteauneuf-du-Pape would go well with our food, and the waiter concurred.

"Well, Hassing wasn't the first person to have made a complaint against Mr. Goody Two-Shoes." She beamed. "Apparently, this isn't Frederik Vinther's first rodeo . . . rape accusation."

"I told you that."

"But I found the sealed legal documents," Nico said triumphantly.

"How did you do that?"

"Because I'm a fabulous journalist"—she preened and when I raised an eyebrow, she laughed—"and because I know people who know people who can give me access to sealed legal documents."

"Why are they sealed?"

"Because that's how the wealthy function. I interviewed some of these young girls. Most of them were bought off and made to sign an NDA; didn't even get as far as the police. A couple went to the police but there was hardly any evidence. Hassing was the only one who came this far." Nico raised her glass with a smile. "*Skål.*"

"What happens now?"

Nico's smile broadened and lit up her face. "Your evidence may not be good enough in a court of law, but it was just fine for my editor, with corroboration from the victims, of course. We're still waiting on some fact-checking to come through, but maybe this weekend you could spend twenty kroner on a *Politiken* Sunday edition to learn more about the sins of Frederik Vinther."

I raised my glass. "*Santé*," I toasted. "This was fast, even for you."

"It's easier when you don't have to do all the research," she said. "I can't believe that this creep has been getting away with this for so long."

"Many creeps like him."

"Too many," Nico agreed.

Our food arrived and we talked about her son, whom she co-parented with her ex-boyfriend. He was thirteen going on thirty, she complained.

"And the ex is being his usual asshole self," she told me. "I don't know how you and Stine managed to raise Sophie without killing each other."

"It took some work." I had learned early on that the key to dealing with Stine was not to go to every fight she invited me to.

"I met someone. Blind date that a girlfriend set up," Nico informed me while she nibbled on macaroons, and I was drinking coffee.

"Serious?"

"We met last night and"—Nico smiled—"it has promise."

"Good for you." I felt a slight pull in my chest.

The world was moving on, while I was spending my time looking for antique Spanish tiles rather than a partner on the many dating apps that I did not have on my phone. I was too old-fashioned to meet a woman by swiping left or right. After a certain age, you wanted bedmates you enjoyed both in and out of bed. This was what it meant to be an adult, more satisfying and infinitely more complicated.

"How about you?"

"Still an uncompromising romantic."

"Præst, there are just not enough men like you left in the world."

"I know," I said. "Is this your way of saying that we won't be catching a nooner after this lunch?"

Nico laughed. "Yes, I believe it is."

"I'm heartbroken," I said dramatically.

"Oh please," she protested.

She knew and I knew she knew that I was fond of Nico and she of me. We liked to have sex because it was *very* good sex. We liked each other's company. We weren't in love. We were never going to be.

"If not a nooner, can you help me get in touch with someone?" I requested.

"Who?"

"Sanne Melgaard's husband."

CHAPTER 8

Palle Melgaard was a professor of art history at the University of Copenhagen and met me at Paludan Bog & Café on Fiolstræde at the edge of Strøget, the walking street. The café was popular with university students and professors. A political science student I was seeing some years ago introduced me to the place. The relationship had lasted only a few weeks, but my visits to Paludan continued. There was something comforting about an old-fashioned bookstore that served coffee and had weathered leather sofas to enjoy a book while drinking that coffee.

I had googled Palle Melgaard and seen pictures of him with his wife, so I knew what he looked like. I watched him from the window as he made his way in. He was a tall man with white hair. There was a beaten-down quality about him. His shoulders drooped. He had bags under his eyes and held a limp cigarette in his hand, his head bent against the rain. It had been steadily drizzling all day and the wind had a bite to it. He wore a pair of dark pants with a half-heartedly ironed light blue dress shirt. He was huddled inside a striped blazer with elbow patches.

He threw his cigarette on the road. I waved at him when he

came in. He looked at me quizzically for a moment and then nod-ded as if to himself and walked toward me.

It was around two in the afternoon and the café wasn't overly crowded. There was enough room to have a conversation with-out being overheard. Nico had arranged the meeting and had ex-plained to Palle what I was doing, so I was surprised that he had agreed to meet with me.

He carried a leather messenger bag, which he put on the empty chair next to him when he sat down across from me at the small square wooden table. I asked what he'd like to drink, and he said a latte. I got him what he wanted and myself a cortado, which I knew they made well. I also ordered two slices of *jordbærkage*, strawberry cake topped with fresh cream. He had not asked for cake, but I wanted to be polite, and this was a bribe I could afford.

"Thank you for meeting me," I said once we were settled with our coffees and cakes between us.

He took a sip of his latte and then, as if approving it, nodded. "The only Præst I know is Karl Præst, the football player."

I had heard that before. Karl Aage Præst had been a Danish football player who won a bronze medal in the 1948 Olympics. He had played for Juventus.

"No relation," I told him.

"I said yes to meeting with you because I wanted to tell you to go fuck yourself." Palle picked up a fork and disassembled the strawberry cake with a jab.

He spoke calmly. He wasn't upset. He was drinking coffee and eating cake. He was relaxed. He might have been talking to me about soccer.

"I was hired by the family," I informed him.

"Do you think *that man* is not guilty?" he asked, dabbing the corners of his mouth with a paper napkin as some of the whipped cream smeared his upper lip, which he entirely missed. He continued to eat his strawberry cake as if he had not a worry in the world. Either he was truly within himself or a complete sociopath.

"I'm not paid to think. I'm paid to look at evidence objectively."

"You were fired as a policeman," he said smugly.

A sociopath, I thought, someone who enjoys the humiliation of others.

"Yes."

"Why?" he wanted to know.

"That was a long time ago. History."

His eyes narrowed. "History is my stock-in-trade. I heard you investigated Karina Jensen."

"That was a long time ago," I repeated and then after a short pause added, "You found *her.*"

"Yes," he said, his eyes not changing, not showing a hint of sadness or loss.

"It's been some years."

"There was a strong scent of blood." Palle sniffed as if testing his sense of smell.

I nodded. *Definitely* a sociopath.

"He slit her throat." Palle ate a bite of the cake. "And stabbed her fifteen times," he added with his mouth full.

"Yes." I had seen the pictures in the materials Henrik had given me. It should evoke some emotion in a husband; it had disgusted me, and I didn't even like the woman.

"And you think *that man* is not guilty?" he asked calmly.

"I don't know."

Palle snorted. "This fucking Muslim trash comes into our country, uses our resources, kills our people. And you people want to give them a free pass."

I didn't think asking him who he meant by "you people" was

going to elicit a response that would help my investigation, so I refrained from indulging in sarcasm, which would be only marginally satisfying. Hitting him would be vastly more satisfying. I refrained from that as well. It was clear Palle didn't turn racist because he thought Yousef killed Sanne, he believed Yousef killed Sanne because he was a racist prior to his wife's murder.

"Can you tell me what happened on *that* day?" I tried again to get him back on track.

"Why?"

"It's a place to start."

Palle finished his coffee and cleaned his plate of cake crumbs and whipped cream. He stood up and looked down his nose at me. "No, it's not a place to start anything. It's where it all ended."

He then left without another word or even a backward glance.

I texted Nico: **He drank coffee, ate jordbærkage, which I paid for, and then left. Told me fuck all.**

Nico texted back: **You're welcome.**

SANNE MELGAARD'S SISTER, Ulla Bernsen, whom I met a day later, was more forthcoming than Palle.

She lived in Værløse, in the outskirts of Copenhagen, in a large villa that had been split into two apartments with a shared garden. Her husband had passed away three years ago, and she now lived alone. She was sixty-three years old, two years younger than Sanne. Her white hair was cut short in a bob, and she wore a pair of jeans with black Ugg boots and a sweater. She resembled her sister, but she had more polish, more grace—a softness that no one would ever have accused Sanne Melgaard of having.

Ulla used to be a social worker for Gentofte Kommune and had specialized in spousal abuse before she took early retirement a few months ago, she told me. We sat at her dining table. She served me a cup of black coffee and a chocolate roulade cake with a small cloud of whipped cream.

"Sanne and I had our differences," she acknowledged. "Especially on the immigrant issue. I'm *Venstre* Party all the way. I've always voted blue."

"How did Sanne feel about that?"

Ulla laughed. "Christmas dinners were loud. My husband, Brian, and I are the opposite of Palle and Sanne. Our children accepted their aunt and uncle for who they were. They didn't like them always, but their love never wavered. You know, Sanne never had kids so our kids were theirs too. My daughter and son would tell us not to discuss politics for the sake of peace, but my husband was an elected member of the city council; how could we not discuss politics?"

I liked her frankness and her baking. I cleared my plate of chocolate cake and didn't turn her down when she offered me a second slice.

"I spoke to Palle," I told her.

"What did he say?"

"He told me to go . . ." I paused and she finished for me. "Fuck yourself."

"Yes," I confirmed with humor.

"Palle is and has always been an emotionless turd. He and Sanne suited each other. Two people with hearts shriveled like raisins."

"Well, tell me how you *really* feel." I was now enjoying myself.

She picked up her cup of coffee and drank some. "She was my sister," she said softly, and her eyes filled with tears. "And I miss her. No one should die the way she did, but I am sure many think she deserved it because in a world where we talk about diversity and inclusion, Sanne defended homogeneity and exclusion. I keep thinking about how scared she must've been. There must be such horror in dying a violent death."

"What do you know about the murder? Where were you when it happened?"

"We were here." Ulla waved a hand around her house. "Palle called us, it was around eight in the evening. He was screaming. We couldn't understand what happened at first, but I knew they were in the summerhouse because she'd posted it on Instagram. He told us Sanne was dead. Brian and I immediately got in the car and drove. When we got to the summerhouse the police were there. Palle had taken the train from the city, and she'd been driven the night before by her assistant. He told us that the house was dark when he arrived and that was unusual. The door was locked, and that's when he knew something was wrong. He had had to look for his key to open the door. They never locked the door, no one there does."

She took a deep breath as if preparing to tell me about what Palle saw when he turned on the light.

"She was on the floor in the living room, right there on their white rug. I never liked that rug. White, you know, shows every speck of dirt." Ulla sighed. "Blood . . . it was everywhere. Palle was covered in blood too because he'd checked on her, tried to revive her. It was ugly, the way she had been killed. How could a human being do that? Isn't our humanity supposed to stop us from doing something like that?"

"There is nothing with which every man is so afraid as getting to know how enormously much he is capable of doing and becoming," I quoted Kierkegaard. "The beast lives within the man."

She put her coffee cup down, and her shoulders dropped as if weighed down by what she had told me. "And then they said that this man, Yousef Ahmed, did it. Why do you think that's not true?"

"I don't know if it's true or not," I told her. "My job is to either confirm or not, based on evidence."

"Isn't there already enough evidence to confirm? They convicted him, didn't they?" she asked.

"I'm being asked to take a second look."

"Which means that you might confirm that he did kill her," she mused.

"That's entirely possible."

Ulla nodded. "Sanne was getting death threats before this happened. I mean, she was always receiving death threats, because she was the attorney general. Her anti-Muslim agenda didn't help. Every time they changed the rules of immigration to make it harder, the death threats came from immigrant groups. When she did something even mildly to support the immigrants, the white supremacists sent death threats. PET would investigate, but this . . . this . . ." She paused, and I waited.

One thing I had learned since I became a policeman was that everything was relevant; the pieces of a puzzle that looked as if in discord with the others sometimes were exactly the pieces you needed to see the final picture.

She took a deep breath and said, "She didn't tell anyone about it. Just me. We had gone to Odense as we did every year for our father's and mother's birthdays. They are two days apart. We take . . . we used to . . . now I do . . . take the train, visit Seden Church, where they're buried. We used to stay the night at Hotel Munkebo Kro. Eat dinner there and then the next day we'd come back home. It was a ritual for us. We never missed it. I still go. There is comfort in tradition."

I looked wistfully at the remnants of the second (and last) slice of chocolate cake on my plate, drank my coffee, and waited.

She stood up then. "Can we go sit outside? I don't smoke inside the house."

I nodded. I poured some more coffee in my cup and we went outside. She offered me a cigarette. Her hands were shaking slightly. I turned down the offer, even though I was tempted. When it came to cigarettes, I was always tempted. But if I didn't stick to my two-cigarettes-a-day rule, I'd be chain smoking.

"She was writing a book," Ulla told me.

"A book? A memoir? Fiction? What?"

Ulla lifted her shoulders, let them drop, and sighed. "A book about World War Two, about the Nazi occupation in Denmark. She was collecting articles and stories, talking to people, finding documents." Ulla smiled softly and added, "She wanted to tell the *real story*, she told me. Many Danes were heroes, she said, but many were villains who had gotten away with murder and more. She went to Berlin several times to look through some Nazi archives and she talked to a lot of people there. Her German was very good, you know."

"I've been talking to a lot of people about your sister, and no one has mentioned this book." I emptied my cup of coffee.

"She told me that no one knew and that she was only telling me because it was a secret and . . . she made it sound like she would expose some *very important* people with her book," Ulla explained. "I didn't take her seriously. She exaggerated like that sometimes. Everything was a *big deal all the time*. I mean, everyone knows everything about the occupation, there are no secrets left. I didn't think anything of it. She was angry . . . you know, because she felt that the Elias Juhl government and her own party were kicking her out, forcing her to retire."

"Why didn't you tell the police or anyone else about it?" I asked.

Ulla shrugged. "I don't know. I didn't say anything because . . . well, I just didn't. It never came up."

"How much had she written?" I asked.

"She said she was done, just waiting for some last documents from Germany. She was worried, she told me that night when we had dinner at Munkebo Kro. This was a few weeks before she died. She said that she had been told to stop working on the book . . . by someone *important*." Ulla took a long drag from her cigarette and then laughed as if remembering something. "She said *der er ugler i mosen*."

It was an old quirky Danish idiom, "there are owls in the bog," which meant that there was something suspicious afoot. Originally, the saying was "there are wolves in the bog," but when wolves left Denmark, the *wolves* changed to *owls*.

"It seemed so farfetched," Ulla continued. "She was behaving like she knew a secret and there are no secrets left about that time . . . so . . . I thought she was just blabbing, making herself feel important."

"Did she tell you *who* was threatening her and why?"

Ulla took another deep puff of her cigarette, making me want to draw the nicotine in like the addict I was. "No."

"Who else would know? Someone must have helped her research the book?" I prompted.

"My first guess was Palle," Ulla replied. "He's a history professor. But when I asked him about it, he said he didn't know."

"Was she working on it on her computer?"

"Where else? But . . . I don't know," Ulla said uncertainly. "She went through a stack of printed pages on the train when we were coming back to Copenhagen. She told me that was the book. I didn't pay attention. I was reading a Sara Blædel novel, much more interesting than World War Two conspiracies."

"Did she tell you *how* she received the death threat?" I asked. PET, the Danish Security and Intelligence Service, would have documented every threat received by Sanne Melgaard, as they did for all politicians and the royal family.

Ulla crushed her cigarette. "No."

"What was she going to do about the threat?"

"Nothing." Ulla smiled. "She was going to see the book through, she told me. 'Let them bring it on. I'll show them what Sanne Melgaard is made of.' She was tough like that. She didn't scare easily."

"Why did you tell me when you didn't tell the police?"

"I don't know. Honestly, I had forgotten about the whole thing and didn't think of it"—she paused and then smiled—"well, until you showed up."

"Thank you for talking to me and for the coffee and the cake."

"It's my pleasure." She beamed. "You're a good young man. And it's nice to have company."

"If you think of anything, please call me." I gave her my business card.

CHAPTER 9

Ulla had been kind enough to set me up for a meeting with Aleksander Ipsen, Sanne Melgaard's personal assistant at the time of her death. Aleksander now worked for the prime minister's media advisor, honestly called a spin doctor in Danish politics, Mikkel Thorsen.

"I'm not sure why I'm here," Aleksander said as soon as we sat down at one of the benches outside Coffee Collective at Torvehallerne, an urban covered marketplace where everything—produce, food, alcohol—was more expensive than it needed to be.

I liked Torvehallerne and spent a good amount of my office time in the summer outside Coffee Collective during the day before moving a few meters down to Vino Fino in the evenings. It was a convenient meeting place, as it was right next to the Nørreport train and metro station, and they had good Wi-Fi so I could work at 125MB/s with excellent beverages.

"Ulla said you'd be a good person for me to talk to about Sanne Melgaard," I explained.

He nodded.

He was nervous.

I knew he was in his early thirties from his Facebook and

LinkedIn profiles, but he looked much younger. He was a slender man, wearing a slim-fitting Danish-designed dark blue suit with pants that were slightly above the ankles and shoes without socks. He had on a white V-neck T-shirt under his jacket, committing a fashion faux pas that was difficult to forgive, even if I could accept the shoes-without-socks situation, which I couldn't.

Aleksander kept touching his gel-soaked blond hair, pulled away from his face artistically, as if to test that his pouf was where he had left it when he'd dressed this morning. Now, I had no problem with a man who paid attention to how he looked, but that was predicated on the result being palatable. I hoped Aleksander's assistant skills were better than his sartorial ones.

Since it was yet another good day in May, I had chosen to wear an off-white Tom Ford linen suit with a pale blue Eton dress shirt. You never wore a suit jacket with a fucking T-shirt. I completed my uniform for the day with a pair of blue suede derby shoes *with* socks. I never used hair gel, *even* when I had hair, because it was uncouth. A good and regular haircut beat gel or oil or whatever else misinformed young men drenched their hair in. However, this had not been a problem for me for the past five years, when I had made a genetic inevitability of baldness a voluntary choice and started to sport a shaved head. This had the bonus of my acquiring a variety of hats and caps that made me feel more like Philip Marlowe than a cheesy PI taking pictures of a woman's husband fucking her best friend.

I adjusted my blue Giorgio Armani straw hat, which I had picked up at a vintage store in Rome, so I could look into Aleksander's eyes. "It's just a casual conversation over a cup of coffee." I smiled the smile I had used on nubile young women when I was a young man—the smile that said, *I'm not a serial killer* and *I'll make sure you have a good time you won't regret.*

Aleksander sat stiffly. "I didn't tell Mikkel about this meeting."

"Mikkel Thorsen? The PM's spin doctor? Why would you?"

"He is my boss." Aleksander looked around as he spoke, like he was worried that Mikkel Thorsen could catch him talking to me.

"I'm sure your boss has better things to do than follow you around," I said. "And why would he care if you talk with me? The PM and Sanne were not even in the same party."

"They were friends." Aleksander licked his dry lips. "Old friends. Did you know that?"

"I may have heard that somewhere."

"Anyway, what do you want to know?" Aleksander focused on me, his tone getting sharper. "I have a meeting in thirty minutes."

"When was the last time you talked to Sanne?" I wanted to ask him about the book she was working on but decided to soften him up a bit first.

"That morning . . . the morning . . . of the day she died . . ." He sighed. "I drove her to the summerhouse and then took the car back for Palle. She was in a good mood. She was going to spend the day gardening and working on some articles she was writing."

"You went back to the city and then gave the car to her husband." I wanted him to confirm that because Ulla had said that Palle had taken the train. *Why did he do that when we had the car with him?*

"Yeah." Aleksander was nonchalant. "Look, I know what people thought of her, but she was a good boss. She was a great politician. I learned a lot from her."

I was proud that I didn't sabotage the meeting by asking him if he was also a racist bigot like Sanne Melgaard.

"She was very knowledgeable. She knew politics and," he continued, "she knew Danish history better than anyone I know."

Ah, that I believe in the PI handbook is called an entry point, I thought cheerfully.

"Someone told me she was working on a history book," I said casually.

Aleksander looked confused. "History book? I don't think so. It wasn't her style. She didn't even want to write a memoir. She thought it was vulgar." He smiled as if remembering something fondly. "She got into a fight with the PM. He wasn't the PM then; he was just an MP. His father had written his memoir and Sanne told the PM that the reason Gert had to write it himself was because no one liked him enough to write it for him. The PM was really angry about that."

Gert Juhl had been the prime minister of Denmark in the eighties and now his son, Elias Juhl, was the prime minister. The Juhls were political royalty.

"Ulla mentioned that Sanne got a lot of death threats." Since the history book was a dead end, I moved on to my next question.

"Oh, those were the wildest. And not all from immigrants, mind you, many were from Danes, *real* Danes." He was animated now, excited. "We looked through them to see if Yousef Ahmed had ever sent one."

"Had he?"

Aleksander shook his head.

"He said someone called him from Sanne's office to tell him she was at the summerhouse," I said.

Aleksander snorted and took a sip of his coffee. "Yeah, that's what we do, we call *randos* and tell them where the attorney general is."

"He says he left a letter for Sanne the day he came to the summerhouse, do you know anything about that?" I asked.

"No," he replied snootily. "Look, you can investigate all you want, but that won't change the facts. I hope that *perker* rots in prison."

"I think the right word is *udlænding*, foreigner," I said mildly.

"Oh please. It's like what Pernille Vermund said, let's call things what they are. If you're a *perker*, you're a *perker*; if you're a Dane, you're a Dane," Aleksander said.

And what did it mean to be a Dane? I wanted to ask him, but I suspected he was another person who believed that being Danish meant being white. He wanted to *make Denmark white again*, I thought, heartily tired of the poorly dressed man.

I stood up. "Thank you for your time," I said and left.

I didn't shake hands with him. I also didn't punch him in the face.

"How's it going?" Leila asked me when I answered my phone.

"I'm doing fine. How are you?" I said loudly into my AirPods, over the sound of traffic.

I was bicycling to my office from my meeting with Aleksander.

I heard her sigh. "Where are you?"

"On my way to my office. I have a meeting with a lawyer at Dall og Digman."

"Have you made any progress?" she asked.

"No." I ignored the bicyclist who gave me a finger for passing him aggressively.

"Nothing?"

"Nothing to talk about."

"Damn it, Gabriel." Her voice rose. "Can you give me a straight answer?"

I cycled into the parking lot in front of Pastis. I parked my bicycle and locked it. I took my Tumi messenger bag, which I had secured in the front of the bicycle, and hung it crossbody on my right shoulder. I was silent the entire time.

"Gabriel?" Her tone had a tinge of impatience with a sprinkling of tired acceptance.

"I talked to a few people, and I know fuck all." I went into the building and took the stairs two at a time to the third floor, where my office was.

"Who did you talk to?" she demanded.

"Leila, when I have something, I'll tell you." I entered my office.

I pulled my laptop out of my messenger bag and put it on the table before hanging my bag in the closet. I took my jacket off as well. Linen or not, it was fucking warm. It looked like climate change was finally benefitting Copenhagen this year. Last year, it had rained all year round, including the summer. Plane ticket prices to guaranteed warmer climates had gone through the roof. This year, staycations would be popular if the weather continued to be this pleasant.

"Can we meet for a drink tomorrow evening?" she asked.

"I'm playing at Niels Lan Doky." I didn't want to see her, I thought, even as I felt a tingle in my heart at the idea of seeing her again.

In addition to Mojo, I also played at Niels Lan Doky International Jazz Collective with a jazz band. *Gabriel Præst was not all blues!* I also had jazz in my soul.

"I just need fifteen minutes." She wasn't exactly pleading but there was a tremor in her voice, and I caved. "I start at nine, how about a drink around eight at not your USUAL wine bar?"

"Where is that?"

"It's a wine bar, it's called *not your USUAL wine bar*," I explained dryly. "It's on Lavendelstræde."

"I'll find it," Leila said, and then paused for a long moment before saying, "Why are you so angry with me?"

"I'm not angry with you." My tight voice belied the statement.

"You sound angry. I . . . are you still angry about . . ."

About your cheating on me. Yeah, I think I still might be.

"Leila, I have a meeting." I hung up on her.

While I met with Casper Dall of Dall og Digman about one of his insurance cases he needed my services for, I thought about how Leila made me feel. Eymen hadn't been wrong when he said she was the one who got away. Of all the women I had ever had a relationship with, ever had sex with, Leila was the only one I had imagined living with for the rest of my life. We had dated for two years and lived together for a short three months. Still, she had been the one, the love of my life, not that it did me any good, because I couldn't have her. Wouldn't have her—because the acrid taste of betrayal was still ripe in my mouth.

Goddamn Leila, she had slept with an ex-boyfriend while we were living together, after I'd finally made a commitment to a woman since Stine. It happened while she had been on a business trip to London, where she'd gone to university. She'd come home and told me.

It was a mistake. *Can you forgive me? I love you and I want us to work.*

I said I forgave her and then proceeded to make our lives miserable with some textbook passive-aggressive behavior. We fought all the time, and even though I never brought up the fucking she'd done with someone else while we were living together, it had been the subtext.

Then my grandmother died, and I moved out of our apartment and into the town house, finalizing what we had been on the brink of since she'd told me about her ex.

I had seen her since then, here and there; after all, Copenhagen was a village and you bumped into people you didn't want to see all the time. It had taken a few years but eventually I had been able to smile at her and say hello, instead of looking away.

But it looked like I was back in that place of anger. I had never *really* let it go. I was surprised at that realization.

CHAPTER 10

You never dealt with it. What did you think was going to happen? *Voilà*, you'd be over it?" Ilse Poulsen said to me when we met the day after in her home office.

I had booked an emergency session with Ilse, a therapist whom I had been seeing for the past three years so I could become a better version of myself. Her office was in Østerbro, in an apartment above another one of my favorite Copenhagen French eateries, Restaurant Le Saint Jacques.

I met Ilse when she had come to me because she thought she was being stalked. It had been one of her clients, who was now a resident at the Brønderslev Psychiatric Hospital in Nordjylland, where he would be for a very long time as per the instructions of a judge.

We had gotten to know each other, and since we'd managed not to have sex, probably because she was not attracted to me, she had agreed to accept me as a client.

"I did deal with it," I protested.

"How? By fucking every woman that moves?"

"I was young. I'm more circumspect now."

"Yes, you are, but you still haven't dealt with Leila," Ilse persisted. "You loved her. You felt betrayed. And then you felt guilty for treating her like an asshole when she was trying to save the relationship."

"She slept with another man." I felt the old anger surge. "She *fucked* this guy and not just once and then said *Oops*, no, she had a two-week-long affair with him while she was in London, ignoring my phone calls. Come on, Ilse."

"I'm not talking about how she treated you. I'm saying that you have not allowed yourself to deal with it. She hurt you."

I took a deep breath and then sighed.

"She hurt me," I admitted. "And it hurt like a motherfucker."

"And it still hurts?"

"Yes. Seeing her hurts."

Ilse nodded.

"I didn't want to lose her. I wanted to make it work, but I couldn't. I was angry all the time, and every time I looked at her, all I could see was that she didn't love me, because if she did, she wouldn't have been able to have sex with another man." The words rushed out as if they'd been waiting to be spoken all these years. I had never talked about it with anyone. Not even Eymen. I told him we were done and when he'd asked why I had simply said she'd met someone else. After that I slept with many women, so I'd assumed that I must have gotten over her.

"We never had sex after she told me. She tried . . . but I couldn't." I remembered vividly how much I had hurt and how much I had hurt her.

"And now? How did you feel when she came to ask you for help?"

I raised my eyebrows and then gave out a short laugh. "Triumphant."

"That she broke first and came to you?"

"Pathetic, right?"

"A little." Ilse smiled. "But not unusual."

"Do you think she's been waiting for an opportunity to come to me and ask for help? Or is it really a last resort?"

Ilse shrugged. "You can't control how she feels or thinks, you can only control your reaction to it. My question is, how does it make you feel that you're helping her?"

I rubbed my face with both my hands and then looked up at Ilse. "Like, I maybe have a chance with her again. Even though I don't ever want to be with her again. It's . . . confusing."

Ilse nodded. "What does it mean to you to have a chance with her? Does it mean that you'll have sex with her? Or that you'll have a relationship with her?"

I let the façade fall away and said the most honest thing I could. "I was happiest with her. I feel like I have forgotten how to be *really* happy. Maybe being with her will make me happy again."

"You already know she can't make you happy, Gabriel," Ilse reminded me. "You know that only you can make yourself happy."

"Yeah, I know. And that's why this is such a clusterfuck," I said.

REGARDLESS OF WHAT Ilse said, seeing Leila waiting for me at the wine bar made me happy. She was wearing a pantsuit, a blue one with white stripes. She had on matching heels. Her hair hung loosely around her shoulders, and she was massaging her scalp. A black elastic hair tie was wrapped around her right wrist, as if she had just taken it off to let her hair down. Her white shirt was unbuttoned lower than I had seen it in the past few days, and I wondered for a half moment if she was trying to flirt with me.

That thought changed when she tied her hair back severely, away from her face, as soon as she saw me come up to her, and then buttoned her jacket's top button to hide the flesh that had peeked from above her shirt.

"*Hej*," I said and sat down.

She was drinking an orange Riesling. The weather was right for it.

I had discovered not your USUAL wine bar with Eymen, whose friend had invested in the establishment, which focused on unusual wines from Moldova, Georgia, Hungary, Armenia, and even Denmark. It also catered to wine snobs like me by offering wine from the old countries.

I took my fedora off and put it on the bar next to my guitar case before I ordered one of my new favorites, a Cabernet Fetească Neagră, the Black Maiden from Moldova.

"Still a wine aficionado," Leila said when we clinked our glasses together.

"This is the Black Maiden, lots of dark cherry, plum, and chocolate, and it hasn't seen oak, so, no vanilla or butter."

"Thank you for seeing me." She smiled. She didn't have any lipstick on, which meant she hadn't bothered to refresh her makeup to see me, while I had spent more time than I normally did on what to wear. I had decided on a black silk dress shirt with black pants, a dark gray fedora, a dark gray John Varvatos velvet blazer, and black Oxford shoes. Ideal for a night of jazz *or* seeing your ex.

"My pleasure." I lifted my glass. I was less angry now that I had talked to Ilse and figured out that I was angry, and somehow knowing that made me less hostile.

"You look good," she said. "Even without the hair."

I took a sip of wine. "You look good as well. The hair is different." She used to have a short bob, and she used to look like a 1920s sex goddess.

She frowned for a moment, as if trying to remember what her

hair had looked like when we were together, and then nodded. "I let it grow. I tie it up now. It's easier to manage."

I wasn't angry with her, I thought exultantly. And I wasn't in love with her. I felt good for reaching that realization. I felt it was a win.

"You look good. Happy." I could be generous now that I was confident about my feelings toward Leila.

"I am. I made partner at my law firm," she said and then hesitantly added, "I . . . I'm seeing someone. We . . . we're getting married."

I hadn't noticed the sparkling diamond on her ring finger . . . no, I would have noticed. She had taken it off, I realized. What had she thought? That I'd fly off the handle because she was *engaged* to someone? I didn't give a shit.

"Congratulations."

"How about you?"

"Still renovating the town house," I noted. "Still Sophie's dad. Still a PI. And still single."

"*Still renovating the town house*. You've had it for . . . what? A decade," she said with warm amusement.

"It's a labor of love."

"And you're still on the edge with your sartorial splendor . . ." She paused and then sat up a little. "Tell me who you've been talking to about the case."

I told her about my conversations with Tommy, Henrik, Palle, Ulla, and Aleksander. I told her everything except about the book Sanne was supposed to have been working on. It appeared that Sanne had been keeping it a secret, and I wasn't ready to talk about it until I knew more.

Around eight thirty, I told her I had to leave and get ready for my set at Niels Lan Doky.

I put on my hat and was about to leave when I turned around. "I *was* angry, but not with you. With myself. I didn't present well in the end. I'm sorry for that."

"I cheated on you."

I nodded. "Yes, you did. And I behaved like an asshole. Both statements are true."

"I'm sorry for cheating on you." She took a deep breath. "I don't want to make you angrier, but I'm now living with *him*. He moved to Copenhagen from London and . . ."

"Like I said, I'm not angry anymore and I'm glad you're happy. I'll call you as soon as I know more."

As I walked out, I had the desire to smoke a cigarette or punch my fist through a wall.

Fuck it. I was still angry.

That night the guy on drums said that I was playing like I wanted to beat the shit out of someone, more anger than joy, more aggression than elegance. I agreed with him. I wanted to beat the shit out of someone.

CHAPTER 11

see you're drowning your sorrows," Eymen noted as we sat on his balcony with a view of the Frederiksberg Gardens.

"I'm not sorrowful," I grumbled. "I'm drinking because this is a lovely 2001 Barolo, which was a good year for wine in Piedmont and Barolo."

"I got it on discount from a friend. Bought a case." Eymen looked at the bottle closely and added, "And the vintage is 2000 not 2001."

I sighed. "Two thousand was not a good year for Barolo—too much alcohol, too sweet. But after the third glass of wine, who cares how the fucking thing tastes."

Clara, Eymen's wife, came to the balcony then. Petite and fair next to her tall and dark husband, she was wearing a black gown, and her diamonds were as big and bright as her blue eyes. Her blond hair was tied up in a loose chignon. She'd gone to the opening of *Tosca* at the Royal Danish Opera House, as her family was a patron.

"I hear that Leila is back. The one who got away." Clara sat down on the arm of my chair. She leaned down and kissed my bald head. "I don't think I've seen you like this since you got dumped by . . ."

"For the last time, I did not get dumped. I dumped Merete." A relationship in our university days that had shown promise until it hadn't.

"He's drinking better wine now," Eymen pointed out.

Clara looked at the bottle of Barolo and frowned. "This was not a good year for Barolo."

"You're both such wine snobs," Eymen said. "This is pretty *fucking* good wine for fifty kroner a bottle."

"What confuses me, Gabriel, is that you were not like this when you broke up with Leila." Clara's lips stretched into an all-knowing smile. "You moved into your grandmother's town house and slept around without fear of STDs."

"There are ways to avoid STDs."

"But now, she's back and she's *fucking* with that Gabriel Præst calmness. I'm loving this." Clara was amused, maybe even a little gleeful.

"With friends like you . . ." I poured some more wine into my empty glass.

"I'm enjoying this as well." Eymen winked at me. "It's good to see you like this."

"Like what?" I asked.

"A mortal with feelings," Clara explained.

"Like in the old days," Eymen agreed.

Clara rose then. "I'm going to go change and when I come back, I'd like to talk to you, Gabriel, about this Yousef Ahmed thing you've gotten yourself into."

"You just had to go tell her," I complained. "I think it's time to move to coffee."

I poured the rest of the wine in the bottle into my glass and drank it, bottoms up. When Eymen raised his eyebrows, I said, "No point wasting fifty-kroner-a-bottle wine."

"Sacrilege," Eymen agreed.

Clara and Eymen had started dating in university, where we'd all met. Clara was a Silberg, an old Danish name, old money, old white privilege, and it had been a scandal when Clara married Eymen, a Turkish Muslim. Even though Eymen was now accepted, he carefully chose the Silberg family events he attended. Clara never pressured him, just as he never pressured her to go to his family gatherings, either in Istanbul or in Denmark.

Of all the couples I knew, Clara and Eymen were the most balanced, and a big part of that was that they had no desire to control each other and had lives that didn't always intersect.

Clara came back wearing Daisy Duck pajamas. We sat around the small dining table in the large kitchen and Clara asked Eymen to pour her some of her favorite port. I thanked Eymen for the espresso he slid in front of me.

"I met Mikkel Thorsen today," she announced.

I raised my eyebrows. The prime minister's spin doctor and Alcksander's boss.

"He knows you and Eymen are friends," she added with a smile and took a sip of her port. She reached out to a drawer behind her and pulled out a box of Summerbird chocolates and put it in front of us.

"He knows me?" I was astonished. "I'm a nobody . . . well, I did meet his assistant. Maybe he mentioned me."

"But then how would he know that you and I are friends?" Eymen wondered.

"I'm assuming that he has looked into our Mr. Præst," Clara suggested. "Intriguing, isn't it."

"Confusing," I said.

"What did he say?" Eymen asked as he picked out a chocolate filled with nougat from the box.

"Just that he knew about Gabriel helping Leila and that it was such a waste of everyone's time, and couldn't I let you . . . Eymen, know that, so that you could let your friend Gabriel know that." She was smiling brightly. "I think this is terribly exciting. I mean, Elias Juhl's spin doctor wants to stop you from investigating something. I want to know why he gives a shit. Don't you?"

Eymen shook his head. "The strangest things excite you, my dear. I think we should be worried. Mikkel Thorsen is a powerful snake. I wouldn't want to be on his wrong side."

"Mikkel is a dabbler, a wannabe." Clara's tone was haughty.

"You can say that, but Gabriel's last name isn't Silberg." Eymen took his wife's hand in his and then turned to me. "Præst, you should think about stepping away from this case. Yousef Ahmed is guilty and all you'll end up doing is rattle everyone's chain and in turn they may rattle your entire world."

"I don't have the same problems you do in defending a Muslim. I have white privilege." I looked him in the eye when I spoke.

Eymen dropped Clara's hand and rose from the table. He put his hands in his jeans pockets as if preventing them banging on a hard surface in frustration.

"You think that I don't defend Muslims because I am one?" he demanded.

Eymen was a calm guy. Usually, not much got under his skin. But Clara and I could always push his buttons and sometimes, like this time, we did so.

"I think that you're careful." I didn't want a fight. I was about a bottle of wine down and the espresso wasn't bringing down my alcohol level enough that I could have this discussion.

"Because I have to be," Eymen bit out.

"That's what I said."

When we were in college, three white guys had started to beat up Eymen when he'd been leaving a bar at five in the morning. I had been behind him by about five minutes and had dispersed the assaulters by simply yelling at them and running toward them. Two guys had held his arms while the third had repeatedly punched him in his stomach. The beating had been accompanied by racist slurs. Even though the bruises faded, I knew that was when Eymen had accepted that he had to be careful. He might hang out with me, but he wasn't white and in Denmark, he wasn't safe from random racial violence. It could happen anywhere and anytime. It could be violent, as it was that day outside Heidi's Bier Bar, or it could be subtle, in a meeting room.

"I'm not a coward," Eymen said, his eyes storming. "I want you to be careful, because you could get hurt."

I drank my espresso. I had nothing intelligent to say to that.

Clara put a hand on my shoulder. "You do what you need to do. And tell me how I can help. I'm going to a gallery opening next Wednesday and I know that Mikkel will be there. Any message you want me to deliver?"

Eymen shook his head. "Don't encourage him, Clara."

"If you don't like what he's doing, you don't have to be involved," his wife told him. "But you don't get to tell him what he should do. That's not in our remit as friends."

Eymen sighed. He flung his hands up in the air and sat down. "I give up."

I didn't want to rile up Eymen but . . . I'd riled him up before and knew how to bring his temper down, so it wasn't a huge concern. "Could you ask Mikkel, as if in passing and nothing to do with this case, if Sanne Melgaard was working on a book?"

"What kind of book?" Clara asked. "Like an autobiography?"

"No. It was about Denmark during the Nazi occupation," I told her. "I think someone didn't want her to write the book."

Eymen raised his eyebrows. "Why would anyone care? Sanne was . . . well, as notorious as she was, she was on the last legs of her political career."

"A swan song," Clara murmured thoughtfully as she sipped her port.

She heard a small cry from their seven-year-old daughter and put her glass down. "Keep me posted, Gabriel." She gave me a kiss on the cheek and went to check on Nysa.

"Are you sure about what you're doing here?" Eymen drank some of the port from his wife's glass.

"No. I have no fucking idea what I'm doing."

"Well, that's comforting, now that you've gotten my wife involved."

CHAPTER 12

I was sitting at a table at Pastis, drinking the perfect kir royale because the bartender knew just how much crème de cassis to add to a good Nicolas Feuillatte Champagne, when Politiassistent Freja Jakobsen came and sat across from me.

"You couldn't have that drink for lunch if you were still on the job." She picked up my glass and took a sip.

"Would you like me to order you one?" I asked.

"Against the rules." She sighed.

I closed my laptop and set it aside. "You were in the neighborhood?" I asked sarcastically. Freja was a *Politiassistent* in Gentofte Kommune, so she had obviously come out of her way to find me.

A waiter came to check on us and she pointed to my drink and the waiter nodded.

"It's on you," she told me.

"Of course." I smiled. "What are you doing here besides breaking the rules of drinking on the job?"

Freja and I had gone to the academy together. But that was a long time ago, and since then we saw each other with mutual friends at social gatherings and most recently at work during the

Christina Hassing rape case, which was handled by her police station.

"Can't a friend drop in to see you?"

"So, do you want to talk about FCK, or do you want to get to the point?" Freja was a diehard Football Club København fan.

"*Fine*. Where were you last night?"

"Wow." I raised my eyebrows in mock horror. "I have to buy you a drink and tell you about my evening. You sure this isn't a date?"

She grinned and thanked the waiter when he placed a frosty glass of the Champagne cocktail in front of her. "Can you also bring some of those toasted almonds and olives?" she asked the waiter.

"Am I paying for those too?"

"Someone beat the crap out of Frederik Vinther last night." Her voice was steady.

"Maybe I should be buying *that* guy a drink." It warmed my heart to hear the little rapist had gotten some of what was due to him.

Freja took a sip of her drink and closed her eyes, as if she had been dying for a drink all day.

"I know you leaked the story about him raping that other girl to *Politiken*." Nico's story had published the past weekend.

I smiled at her. "Women. Plural. You know I don't kiss and tell, Freja."

"Where were you last night?" she asked again. "Between seven and eight in the evening."

"Is foreplay already over?" I knew she was doing her job, but I knew she wouldn't mind the banter—hell, I think she expected it.

I had been vocal about how much I disliked the twerp who'd raped not only Christina Hassing but also numerous other women and had gotten away with it because his daddy had money. But Freja knew me and knew that beating him up would not be my style.

The waiter placed two small white bowls in front of us, along with cloth napkins. One bowl had large olives and the other toasted almonds. When we assured the waiter his services were not required any longer, he left.

"Come on, Præst." Freja picked up a large olive and bit into it.

"I don't have to tell you anything." I knew I was being perverse.

"I *can* bring you in," she warned.

"Do you know that I work for a law firm now?" I pointed up to the ceiling. "Dall og Digman would love to know why you think you can come and ask me questions. I'm a humble private investigator doing my job."

"You have never been humble. We also asked Hassing's lawyer, your ex-wife's new husband, where he was," she said. "So, yes, we're asking everyone involved. He was beaten with a baseball bat by a masked man . . . men, he isn't clear on that."

"The plot thickens. But Stine is not an ex-wife. We were never married. And what did Erik tell you?"

"To go fuck myself. I told him I didn't do that sort of thing." Freja batted her eyelids.

"You know me, I'm all about the rules, and if the lawyer told you to go fuck yourself, I'll have to follow suit." I took three almonds and tossed them into my mouth.

"*Av for Satan*," Freja swore. "You threatened the boy outside the courthouse. You said in front of God, media, and everyone else that you'd beat the shit out of him."

"I was a little annoyed then. I've calmed down since."

"And then you leaked the story to that blonde you're fucking from *Politiken*," she continued.

"Her name is Nicole Bonnet and she's a damn good journalist," I said softly and added in the same tone, "And don't talk about her like that."

Freja raised a hand in apology. "I'm sorry, that was uncalled for." I could see she was genuinely remorseful.

I emptied my glass of kir royale. "I had dinner at Eymen's house. Didn't leave until two in the morning and was too drunk to beat anyone up."

Freja relaxed. "My *chef* is certain it was you. I told him it couldn't be. So, if I check with Eymen . . ."

"Or Clara," I offered.

"Right. Clara Silberg. That should shut my boss up."

"What happened to the Vinther scion?" I wanted to know how much damage had been done.

"You know I can't discuss an ongoing investigation." Freja's smile was saccharine sweet.

"You know you guys fucked up on the Hassing case."

"Rape cases are not easy, you know that." She raised her hand before I could respond. "Doesn't make it right, just makes it what it is. Anyway, the boy was going to Jolene Bar for a night of debauchery when he was pulled into an alley off Flæsketorvet by a masked man . . . men . . . who beat the crap out of him. A broken jaw, two broken ribs, a concussion, and a twisted ankle from when he tried to run and tripped on a trash can. He's at Rigshospitalet and Herr Vinther is pointing his finger at you."

"Broken jaw?"

Freja grinned. "Yeah. Wired shut. He gave his statement by typing it."

"Good." I was *very* pleased.

"Who do you think beat him?" Freja asked.

"Fuck if I know."

"Any guesses?"

I shook my head.

"Come on, Præst. I know you didn't do it, but I don't put it above you to encourage someone else to do it."

I shook my head again. "It's not my style. If it were me, I wouldn't wear a mask. I'd want him to know it was me beating the living daylights out of him."

CHAPTER 13

I was painting my living room a lighter shade of pale blue when Eymen called to let me know that some policeman from Gentofte Politistation had called to ask him about my whereabouts the previous evening.

"Since you didn't say anything to me, I assumed you wanted me to tell the truth."

"Yes."

"Good. Clara was worried that maybe you wanted us to say something else," he said.

"And Clara wouldn't mind lying to the police?" I asked, knowing the answer.

"Of course not." Eymen hung up.

I went back to the wall, happy with the choice I had finally made. It had taken me two years to decide the color for the living room walls. Even I, who could live in absolute chaos, was starting to feel that a decade had been long enough. I now needed my living room and kitchen to be finished, done—neat and tidy. I would then start tackling my bedroom and bathroom.

Nico knocked on my door when I finished painting the walls of the living room and was making my way to soak my sweaty body in my vintage bathtub. She had a large paper bag with the logo of Madbaren Marmorkirken, a hole in the wall that served some of the best Italian pizza in Copenhagen, and a bottle of wine.

"I'm done with my maybe who could become serious." She lifted a box of pizza in one hand and the bottle of wine in the other. "I come with food and a bottle of Chianti."

"That is the correct password. You may enter."

I decided to forgo the bath and took a quick shower while Nico set plates on my granite kitchen counter. She knew her way around my house. By the time I came downstairs, the counter was set with plates, thick white cloth napkins, and some tea lamps for ambience, and Bill Evans's *Interplay* was playing on my retrofitted Victrola Jackson turntable.

She held out a glass of wine and I accepted it.

"If I didn't know any better, I would say you're trying to seduce me." I sat down next to her.

"I know that the fastest way to a man's . . ." She touched her glass of wine to mine.

The bottle of Chianti was almost gone, along with the pizza, when I told Nico about Freja's visit. "Who do you think did it?"

She looked at me with innocent eyes. "I have no idea."

"Are you sure? You look like you know something." I emptied the bottle of Chianti by filling her glass halfway. I rose to find another bottle in my wine refrigerator. I settled on a Beaujolais Villages—no point drinking the good stuff this late in the game, when our taste buds were becoming less discerning with each passing glass.

"The little prick left me a threatening voice mail and sent me some offensive emails after the story came out," Nico explained. "It happens. People see my byline and sometimes they say nice things and sometimes they don't."

"Right." I leaned against the counter, my legs crossed at the ankles, and watched her.

"I told Pierre, and *you know how he is*."

Pierre Bonnet, Nico's uncle, used to be a football star, playing for AC Milan, where he racked up more yellow cards and goals than anyone else on his team. They called him La Furia in the Italian media, because he had a temper both on and off the field. He was retired now, in his mid-fifties, and was active as a soccer coach with an organization that worked with underprivileged immigrant youth.

"Why did you tell La Furia about Frederik Vinther?"

Nico made an exaggerated gesture with her hands. "He is my uncle; we talk *all* the time."

I closed my eyes to resist the urge to yell at her. "Please tell me it wasn't Pierre."

She scoffed. "Pierre is fifty-six years old and a teddy bear."

"Can it be connected to you?"

"Can what be connected to me?" She smiled mischievously.

"Nico . . . Vinther isn't going to let it go. He's going to make sure the police look into it."

Nico shrugged. "Did I tell you that Pierre and some of his friends left this morning for the U.S.? They're going to buy Harleys and then ride from Milwaukee all the way to California. The old man and his friends are going to have a three-month-long adventure."

I put my glass of wine down and walked up to her. I framed her face with my hands and kissed her on her mouth. "For a journalist . . . you're . . ."

"Very sexy." She caught my lower lip with her teeth. "Can we take the wine upstairs? I like the occasional kitchen-floor sex, but I went to the gym today after several weeks and my muscles are sore."

I picked up the bottle of wine. "Let me see if I can help unknot some of those tight muscles."

I LEFT NICO sleeping and went for my morning run around the lakes. When I came back, the sun was shining brightly and there were two women in my kitchen, drinking coffee. They were laughing as they talked and for a moment, I wasn't sure I was in the right house.

Leila, with her dark hair, was wearing a severe dark pantsuit, while Nico was light and blond, dressed only in one of my shirts with the sleeves rolled up. There was no doubt what Nico and I had spent the night doing.

"Good morning," I said as I walked up from behind them.

Leila smiled uncertainly.

"I'm going to take a shower and get to work." Nico drained her coffee cup. "Præst, do you still have some of my clothes from last time?"

I smiled. Nico wanted to help. Make sure that Leila thought we were a couple. But the fact was that, on more than one occasion, she had left some of her clothes in my house. "In my closet in a dry cleaner's garment bag."

"You had my T-shirts dry-cleaned?" she asked, incredulous.

I shrugged. "Lena takes care of the clothes."

I was perfectly capable of taking care of my laundry and house-work, but I didn't like doing it. A few years ago, I'd hired Lena to come in once a week and take care of the cleaning, changing of sheets, laundry, and everything else in between for me. Lena had been with Stine and Erik for nearly ten years and had adopted me as well.

"I'm sorry. I didn't mean to intrude." Leila looked as uncomfortable as Nico had probably meant her to feel.

I started the Jura coffee machine. Once I had a cup of coffee in hand, I stepped out into the backyard. "Do you mind if we talk outside?"

"Oh . . . your morning cigarette." She remembered. "You still smoke."

It sounded like an accusation. "A cigarette in the morning and a cigarette in the evening. Actually, last evening I didn't even have a cigarette."

"Maybe because you were having Nico instead." Her voice was crisp; and as if realizing that, she added smoothly, "None of my business who you fuck."

"Don't talk about her like that," I said lightly, but the warning was obvious. I lit my cigarette and sat on the table, where I had an ashtray, my sneakers resting on the bench.

Leila took a breath, closed her eyes. When she opened them again, she said, "I'm sorry. That was unfair."

"Apology accepted." I took a puff. "What can I do for you?"

"Someone beat up Yousef Ahmed in prison last night."

"Seems to be going around." I looked at my cigarette as I spoke, feeling weary. First Vinther and now Yousef.

"What?"

"Nothing. Go on."

"They think it was one of those neo-Nazi types," she explained. "He's at Rigshospitalet. He's in the ICU. He has a ruptured spleen."

"How severe are his injuries?"

She shrugged. "They think they've managed to control all the internal bleeding. The man who beat him told Yousef he should stop trying to get out. He said, 'Ask that Muslim lawyer bitch of yours to back off or next time you and she are both dead.'"

"That's specific." I thought of what Eymen had said about being careful.

"Yes."

"Do you think they meant you when they said 'Muslim lawyer bitch'?"

"Well, I'm one of the few Muslim lawyers in Copenhagen . . . and a total bitch." Leila laughed.

I smiled. "Okay. Thanks for letting me know."

"That's it? *Thanks for letting me know*?" She was annoyed.

"What do you want me to do?" I asked.

She looked at me sharply. "I just wanted you to know."

"Okay. Now I know."

I was rude. My back was up. She just showed up without warning and she'd seen Nico here. She had those vulnerable big brown eyes that were tempting the hell out of me while my lover from the previous night was taking a shower in my bathroom.

"I've asked for special protection for Yousef and the police are on board."

"He's in the hospital, so that will be easy to do," I said. "Do I still get to meet him?"

"In the hospital." Her voice was a little wobbly. "I met him, and he looked . . . he looked so small. Beaten, literally and emotionally."

I nodded, taking a last drag from my cigarette.

"I don't want him to die, Gabriel. I feel that this is my fault and . . ." Tears sprang in her eyes and ran down her face.

If I had an Achilles' heel it was seeing a strong woman cry. I stubbed out my cigarette and walked up to her. I put my arms around her, and she leaned in.

Nico came down then and mouthed, "All okay?" from behind Leila.

I shook my head.

She nodded and mouthed, "Call me."

Leila moved away a few moments later, her crying under control. "Thank you."

"I'm doing everything I can to move this as quickly as possible," I soothed. "And I'll keep at it."

"What if they come after you?"

"Or you."

"Right," she said. "I am, after all, the Muslim lawyer bitch who they want dead."

"I'm going to be careful. And I want you to be careful."

After she left, I called Tommy.

"I don't know if you know this, but there are criminals in prison, this is the kind of stuff they do," Tommy said.

"They threatened him, Tommy," I told him. "They specifically talked about Leila and threatened her. How would some random criminal even know who Leila is?"

I heard Tommy's long sigh. "You want me to look into it?"

"Yes."

"Are you making someone nervous or is she?" he asked.

"Probably me. I'm asking questions."

"If you are making someone nervous, then maybe Henrik Morck is not an asshole with buyer's remorse." Tommy sounded as tired as I felt.

"Maybe."

"Who have you talked to so far?"

I told him.

"This Aleksander fellow, he works for the PM's spin doctor now?"

"Yes."

"And the PM's spin doctor asked you to back off via Clara Silberg?" Tommy asked.

"Yes."

"He might be saying that because it could cause bad publicity," Tommy suggested.

"Yes, it might be."

"He's a fucking spin doctor, publicity is his business," Tommy said.

"That's what I was thinking."

"Still, why does he give a damn about you?" Tommy wasn't asking me, he was ruminating.

"Good question."

"I can't officially reopen the murder case, that will cause an epic shitstorm. I *can* officially investigate who went after Yousef Ahmed and why. And I'll make sure Leila has protection." He paused and then added, "You be careful. Understood?"

"Yes, *chef.*"

"Fuck you, Præst."

"No, *chef.*"

Tommy hung up, laughing.

CHAPTER 14

Clara wore a burgundy Gucci dress that made her look slutty and sophisticated all at once. I didn't know anyone who could pull that off but her. I had been instructed to dress formally by Clara, so I had worn a dark blue Christian Dior suit with a burgundy shirt to match her dress. I had forgone a tie and instead finished the look with a Loro Piana Laurence blue velvet fedora.

Clara met me outside Galleri Feldt. She looked me up and down and nodded with appreciation. "It's a good thing you are not white-white Danish."

"I am white-white Danish, with the undeserved privilege to go with it."

"You know what I mean." She ran a finger along the base on my hat. "Whoever in your family dallied with some Latin blood should be applauded, because without that olive skin, the burgundy would make you look like Dracula."

I bowed.

"And it's a good thing you're fit, because any man who dresses like you would most definitely be considered . . . feminine and you'd never get laid."

I offered her my arm and she took it, leaning a little into me.

"Now, don't leave me and run away with some attractive woman like you normally do."

I patted her hand that rested on my forearm. "I have the most attractive woman in this place on my arm, I couldn't do better."

"You're such a charming flatterer."

After what had happened to Yousef Ahmed, Eymen and Clara both agreed with me that I should join her for the gallery opening, where we were going to meet Mikkel Thorsen. It was overt but if this was truly a lead, a face-to-face meeting would either get the ball rolling or tell me that it was a dead end, and I should look elsewhere.

Galleri Feldt specialized in modern Scandinavian design and was unveiling the artwork of the designer Hans Jørgensen Wegner. I was fond of his work and had invested in a vintage Flag Halyard chair for my living room. I admired how the chair brought together leather, stainless steel, and Icelandic sheepskin to give it its iconic look. It was enormously comfortable, and I had spent many winter evenings listening to music and reading a book in its luxury.

"Clara, I'm so glad you could make it." Norma Silberg, one of Clara's many aunts and a close friend of the Feldt family, gave her air kisses. Norma was in her seventies and smelled heavily of Chanel, both in perfume, jewelry, and attire. She looked at me with a little disdain and added, "Eymen couldn't make it."

Clara smiled broadly. "Instead he loaned me his best friend, who enjoys art as much as I do. Tante Norma, this is Gabriel Præst."

Norma haughtily responded to my hello with, "Take off your hat, young man, and show some manners."

"He has no hair, Tante." Clara snuggled up to me. "And both Eymen and I like him with his hat on."

Norma snorted in disgust and walked away.

"I think you gave her a distinct Eymen, you, and me ménage à trois vibe," I said.

"She deserved it for being such a snob." Clara then smiled for real when she saw her father.

Victor Silberg was a tall man with blue eyes and a full head of gray hair. He ran an investment firm and had more money than God, and because of that did whatever the fuck he felt like. He liked Eymen, and even though the rest of the Silberg clan, including Clara's mother, had gone into apoplectic shock when she introduced them to a twenty-year-old Eymen and told them he was her boyfriend, Victor had welcomed him with open arms. They both shared a love of camping and hiking and went away on long weekends to Norway and Iceland. I was always welcome, and I joined them whenever I could. Victor didn't like wine, but then, no one was perfect. However, the man knew his scotch and how to catch, clean, and cook trout on an open fire with nothing more than a fishing line, a Swiss knife, and a box of matches.

"I hear that you're in trouble with the law." Victor and I walked up to the bar to get a drink as Clara mingled.

"You'll have to be more specific."

"Frau Astrid Vinther is here today," Victor warned. "The minute she sees you . . ."

"They have a son in the hospital and she's at a gallery opening?"

"Nothing comes in the way of social climbing," Victor said. "Did you beat the boy up?"

"No."

"If you had I'd congratulate you." At the bar, Victor ordered a Macallan 18 neat for each of us. Since it was a very fine scotch, I was happy to forgo Champagne in its favor.

"And I hear that you're working with Leila Abadi Knudsen." He raised his glass.

I touched mine to his. "You are very well informed."

Victor smiled. "Always. Especially when it comes to my boys, and I take care of what is mine." Clara was an only child and Victor had called Eymen and me his boys since we were in university and had become friends with Clara.

"Just leave me a little something in your will. It would help me finish the house."

Victor snorted. "That house of yours will never be finished because you don't want it to be finished. Perfectionists keep looking backward to fix things."

I nodded. "The most painful state of being is remembering the future, particularly the one you'll never have."

"Who said that?"

"Kierkegaard."

"And are we talking about the future you'll never have? And is this about your house or Leila?" Victor smoothly moved to lead me out of the way of Frau Vinther's glare. "She's not going to attack you as long as you're with me."

"The all-powerful Victor Silberg." We walked to the other side of the room, where we saw a flash of burgundy.

"Though you're probably safer with Clara," Victor said with pride. "She can be vicious."

As he left me in the company of Clara, who was talking to Mikkel Thorsen, I realized that father and daughter had orchestrated my movements to ensure this exact result. Stay away from the rapist's mother and meet with the prime minister's spin doctor.

"Now, be nice," Victor whispered in my ear. "He is *truly* all-powerful."

Mikkel Thorsen looked like he had walked out of *GQ* magazine's blond edition or a casting call for a handsome German SS officer for a World War Two movie. His hair was cut stylishly, and even though it wasn't a crew cut, no one would say it was long. The man understood the value of a good haircut. He wore a suit that fit him well, and the dark gray enhanced his cold blue-gray eyes.

"Loro Piana?" He pointed at my fedora with his Champagne. I nodded appreciatively. Most men didn't know a fedora from a baseball cap.

"I'm going to find Signe and tell her how much I loved her book." Clara gave me a kiss on my cheek before she walked away.

We watched her leave. Mikkel took a deep breath. "She's a very special woman."

"Yes."

As if by tacit understanding, we walked out to the garden, where there was an unrestricted view of the blue Øresund, the sound that separated Denmark from Sweden. One of the busiest waterways in the world, the northern part of Øresund saw traffic from nearly seventy ferry departures every day. But where we stood, the waters were not inundated with industrial ferries but expensive yachts and motorboats—which were probably docked in the pricy Tuborg Havn marina. The sun was still sprinkling light on the water as it sank, but as May stretched into June and then July, the sun would stay up longer and longer.

"I hear you talked to Aleksander Ipsen." Mikkel set his drink on a high round table.

"Yes." I took a sip of my superior scotch and decided to enjoy both the liquor and the good view until Mikkel got to wherever he wanted to go. Politician types always took the long road.

Mikkel nodded. "I quit smoking two years ago, but right now, I'd kill for a cigarette."

"I don't have any cigarettes on me."

"I know," Mikkel said, just with a touch of smugness. "You smoke a cigarette in the morning and one in the evening. One right after your run and one right before you go to bed."

I wanted to say, *Now why would the PM's spin doctor know so much about a lowly PI*, but instead, I decided to goad him just a little. "I don't know if you've heard, but cigarettes are bad for your health."

Mikkel smiled the smile of a German SS officer, right before he executed someone.

"I want you to do a favor for the PM." Mikkel was solicitous, overly so.

I raised my eyebrows.

"The PM would like the Sanne Melgaard case to remain at rest. The killer has been caught. I can guarantee you that no matter what Leila Abadi Knudsen thinks. Justice has been served. An investigation will only rake old coals." When I didn't respond, he added, "This is an election year, and we don't want immigration to be on the agenda as heavily as it was with Sanne. We want to discuss other matters that are important for Danes and the party."

If my eyebrows could have risen any farther, they would have tipped my fedora right off my bald head.

"I'm just asking questions and talking to people. I don't think it'll make the news." I drank my whiskey without revealing my excitement at Mikkel's showing his hand.

"I'll make sure it doesn't." Mikkel was smug again, even a little overconfident. "But you seem to have some connections within *Politiken*, and we wouldn't want leaks to make it to the newspaper as happened with Frederik Vinther and . . . Karina Jensen."

I looked him in the eye and took another sip of my whiskey.

"Yes, we know what you did and why you were fired from the

police." He was still smiling, still being very pleasant. He was giving me the creeps.

"Good for you."

"We also have connections that could affect *your* connections adversely." His eyes narrowed and his mouth turned just this side of unpleasant.

Now he was pissing me off. Here I was, drinking fine scotch and he was threatening Nico.

"Can you elaborate?" I asked coolly.

Mikkel ignored my question. "This is a favor for the prime minister of Denmark. He doesn't ask for favors very often, but when he does, he remembers his friends."

I managed not to be childish and tell him that I didn't vote for a media whore like Elias Juhl, who seemed to go to bed with anyone who would help him retain power, and didn't want him as a friend.

"The prime minister is a powerful man and I'm just a regular PI making a living. I don't think we can be friends."

He nodded. "I was told you have an interesting sense of humor."

"I'm not joking right now."

"Neither am I." He managed to smile and threaten at the same time. "I have just one question. Are you going to stop investigating this ridiculous case brought on by a zealous Muslim lawyer?"

And now he was threatening Leila. *Great.*

"Absolutely not." I finished my drink.

Mikkel didn't say anything for a long moment while he stared at me with cold and mean eyes. If I were a lesser man, I'd have shrunk in size, but since I was fucking Bald Superman, I merely shrugged.

"Let me make this clear with no humor on the side. I'm going to see this investigation through," I told him. "And I have a question for you."

"What's that?" Mikkel asked. He wasn't used to people not falling over themselves to do a favor for his boss.

"Do you know anything about a book Sanne Melgaard was writing before she died, something to do with the Nazi occupation of Denmark?"

If I weren't a trained investigator, I would've missed the flicker in his eyes and the slight tightening of his jaw. But since I was, I didn't, and was tremendously satisfied with myself.

"No." His voice was clipped.

"Thank you." I tipped my hat and left the famous Mikkel Thorsen dying for a cigarette in the garden of Galleri Feldt.

CHAPTER 15

Nico spent the night with me again.

We were having coffee in the morning when she asked if I was free that evening. "At Mojo." I lit my morning cigarette. Sex, coffee, and cigarette. I was a lucky and satisfied man.

"You know, you're multifaceted. You are a PI. A devoted father. You dress like . . . well, you know what you dress like. And then you play the guitar."

"I'm good with my fingers." I winked at her.

Nico smiled. "I can vouch for your fingers."

"I'm the same man no matter what I do."

"Maybe," Nico said on a long sigh. "I can't put a label on you . . . Not that I want to but . . ."

"What labels me, negates me."

"And then there is that." Nico threw up her hands. "You quote Kierkegaard."

"What's your point?" I took a long drag of the cigarette.

She laughed softly. "No point. It's just that sometimes, I wonder what makes you tick."

"What you see is who I am," I said sincerely.

She smiled now, broadly. "I only see a part of you, *mon chéri*, and only the one you let me see." She walked up to me, went on tiptoe, and brushed her lips against mine. "No matter who you are, I'm *very* fond of you."

I kissed her back. She hummed softly.

"This was fun. Let's do this again soon."

"I have my son this week . . . so . . ."

"We'll do it when we can then."

"It's that easy." She smiled.

"Yes," I agreed. "It's that easy."

"Life is not a problem to be solved, but a reality to be experienced," she said with satisfaction.

"Now *you* are quoting Kierkegaard."

"Your influence." As she was walking away, she turned back and said, "Præst, if you're getting serious about Leila, let me know."

I shook my head. "It's not . . . it's nothing."

"That's what they all say before they fall."

I FINISHED AT Mojo at two in the morning. My bicycle was not where I had parked it. This was not an uncommon occurrence. Bicycles got stolen in Copenhagen all the time.

I didn't despair, just picked up my guitar case and decided to walk the two kilometers home. As the month of May was ending, the weather was holding up. It was going to be a good summer, I thought, and whistled Nina Simone's "Sinnerman" as I walked along with the partied-out stragglers.

It happened as I turned onto Eckersbergsgade, my street, named after the painter C. W. Eckersberg. I had walked past the playhouse in the middle of the narrow street and was just about to start looking for my keys when I heard a rustle behind me.

I never saw it coming. There were two of them. The streetlight right above me was busted, so I couldn't see them; I saw only shapes.

One man caught me from behind, trapping my neck in a vise. He smelled like chewing tobacco. My guitar case fell to the ground. The other man punched me in the jaw first, which jarred my brain and then my stomach. His fist seemed huge, like a hammer and just as hard. And then again and then again. After the third punch, I stopped counting as nausea and shock set in, but there were a few more.

The man who smelled like chewing tobacco released me and I dropped to my knees and held back the vomit that was racing up my throat. Hammer Hand kicked me in the stomach, and I fell face forward.

I saw stars.

"Stay away from Yousef Ahmed," Chewing Tobacco said close to my ear. He spoke Danish with an accent, maybe . . . Russian.

A light turned on in the front yard of one of my neighbors and I lifted my head as the men ran. I caught a tattoo on an arm, a skull and crossbones with numbers written around it. I caught only the numbers 77 and 108 before I passed out.

I WOKE UP in the ambulance that was taking me to the hospital. I tried to sit up, but the paramedic, a young woman, firmly told me to lie back down. I did as she asked because my head hurt and I was having trouble breathing.

"Someone squeezed your neck—you'll have marks, like a necklace, for a little bit," the paramedic, a petite brunette, said. She had a tattoo of a butterfly on her wrist, right where her gloves ended. "That's probably why you passed out. You're a bit banged up and have some bruises, but you'll be fine."

"What's the damage?" I croaked.

"You've got some pretty big contusions on your abdomen," another voice said. This was a male paramedic. A big blond guy with a Man U baseball cap.

"I feel like my internal organs have been rearranged."

"Nah," Man U Baseball Cap said. "Just jostled a little."

"And there is a cut on your lip," Butterfly Tattoo informed me. "It's likely you got it when you fell down and hit the asphalt. Your chin is also scraped up. And you probably will have a black eye."

"My guitar." My voice was husky, scratched.

"Your guitar is fine," Man U Baseball Cap told me. "Your neighbor said he'll keep it for you."

I sighed, listening to the ambulance siren. I felt silly lying in an ambulance racing through the roads of Copenhagen even though I was in no real danger of losing my life, just my dinner.

"My throat hurts," I rasped.

"Yeah, that happens when someone strangles you," Butterfly Tattoo said and then added, "You know, it isn't every day we pick up a guy dressed so fancy. That's a nice suit you've got on."

"*Was* a nice suit," Man U Baseball Cap said. "Earlier in the evening we picked up a homeless guy . . . he stank to high heaven."

"No wonder this place smells funny." I tried for humor.

I raised my arm to look at the sleeve of my blazer and sighed. "Damn it, the blazer was vintage."

"Now, it's post . . . vintage," Butterfly Tattoo said.

"Yeah, more euro trash than vintage," Man U Baseball Cap said. We all laughed. My laugh came out like a squawk.

The emergency room at Rigshospitalet wasn't backed up, so I got to see a doctor almost immediately. He was a young man as they usually were in the middle of the night in the ER. Dr. Vilhelm Thomsen informed me when I asked that he'd just started his residency at Rigshospitalet and since my injuries were minor, regardless of how much it hurt, I didn't need to see a specialist.

"You don't have a 'he got beat up' specialist?" I asked, waiting for the young doctor to finish cleaning up my chin.

"I am he." He did the stethoscope, breathe-this-way-and-that-way thing. "You're fine, don't even need stitches."

"Are you sure? I feel like my kidneys are crushed." I touched my stomach gently.

"Yeah, happens when you take a few punches to the gut." His bedside manner needed work. "It'll pass. I'll give you something for the pain. Try not to drink alcohol with the pills."

"I always try not to drink alcohol. I never succeed."

"Yeah, I've heard that about people who get punched in the gut. I'll go get your prescription." He left me with a Politiassistent Anselm, who was patiently waiting to talk with me.

He asked me if I had seen anything.

"It was dark . . . and they were hitting me."

"Yeah, that really fucks up the eyesight," the *Politiassistent* agreed.

"How long have you been on the force, Anselm?"

"Long enough"—he wrinkled his nose—"to know that you got punched because you pissed someone off."

I told him about the men who beat me, the tattoo I had seen, and their Russian accents.

"Russian gang tattoo," the police constable said cheerfully. "You pissed off the Russian Mafia?"

"No," I protested. "I don't ever want to piss off the Russian Mafia or . . . any other kind of Mafia."

"Well, you better find out how you pissed them off, because the next time the guy"—he looked at his notes—"with a hand like a hammer may have a hand like a gun."

"But you're going to protect and serve me."

"Yeah, all the time." He closed his notebook. "You okay to get home?"

"I called a friend." I stood up shakily and draped my now euro trash jacket around my shoulders.

I had used the doctor's phone to text Eymen, asking him to come to Rigshospitalet's emergency room to get me. He had responded that he was on his way. He hadn't asked any questions, as I knew he wouldn't.

Tommy was waiting with Eymen as I hobbled out of the emergency room. In the movies, they always insist people are walked out of the hospital in wheelchairs, but apparently that's not the case in the emergency room if you just got scraped up.

Anselm stiffened when he saw Tommy. "The chief is your friend?"

"Yeah. Now you wish you'd been nicer to me."

The police officer saluted Tommy. "Wait outside for me," Tommy told him, "I'll need a report."

Anselm scuttled away.

"You look like shit," Tommy announced.

"This jacket is vintage." I held up my Christian Dior black velvet blazer, which was torn in several places. My pants were torn too, but they were replaceable. "And my fedora is missing," I added glumly.

"I'll get a couple of detectives on it right away," Tommy said dryly.

"Yeah, it was a Goorin River Gray. Dark gray."

"Sure."

I wavered on my feet then and Eymen was by my side, his arm around my waist, holding me up.

"Someone gave you a beatdown." Tommy looked as pained as I felt.

"You figured that out? You're not police chief for nothing." My voice sounded foreign to me. I was tired. I couldn't keep this up, I realized, and was relieved that Eymen was big, tall, and strong and could hold me up, so I didn't tip over.

"Where do you want to go?" Eymen asked.

"Home."

I didn't want to worry Clara, who *would* worry when she saw me. As things were, I was surprised she wasn't with Eymen. He'd probably let her sleep until he knew what had really happened.

"Clara knows," he told me. "I told her you wouldn't want to come to our place."

"I want my own place."

"And you're going to fucking stay there," Tommy growled, "until I figure out what the hell is going on. Or are you going to tell me?"

"Have mercy on a broken man," I groaned, and I meant it. I was in no shape to deal with Tommy when I could barely keep my eyes open because of the pain and the painkillers the doctor had given me so I could get through the night.

Eymen nodded to Tommy. Code for *I'll get him to talk, and you can come listen . . . later.*

I told Eymen what had happened as we sat in my newly painted living room on my vintage Arne Jacobsen couch, because there was no way I could take the stairs in my condition. I was alternating between sipping a Laphroaig 10 neat and holding a plastic bag with ice wrapped in a towel on my lip to keep the swelling down.

"First Mikkel Thorsen threatens you and now you get beat up," Eymen said. "I'm a finance geek, not a detective, but even I see a connection."

"How would he know Russian gangsters?"

"He knows everyone." Eymen sighed.

"Tommy said he'll keep an eye on Leila. And . . . Nico . . . we need to make sure she's okay."

Eymen nodded. "I'll check in with her tomorrow . . . today . . . in a few hours."

It was already tomorrow, I thought. It was six in the morning; I should be going for a run about now.

"You're just banged up." Eymen eyed me with concern. "I checked. You need some sleep."

I nodded.

"And you're sure you're just banged up?" he asked, and I could hear the fear in his voice.

"Yeah. No biggie."

"Right," he said sarcastically.

I looked through my one good eye and one shrinking eye at him as I took another sip of whiskey. "You think I should stop working this case."

"We'll talk about it later."

I nodded and then groaned. My head felt like something splintered through it.

"Enough." Eymen took the glass of scotch from my right hand and the bag of ice from my left and gently helped me lie down.

I didn't notice when he covered me with a blanket or watched me with a worried look on his face as he sat in my Flag Halyard chair across from me, keeping vigil.

CHAPTER 16

Three days after I was attacked, I met Yousef Ahmed.

It had taken a while for Leila to set up the meet because he was in the hospital, still healing from *his* beating, and bureaucracy took its time. It would've been faster to see him in the prison, where they had a process for it.

By then all that was left of *my* beating was a nearly healed lip, bruises on my stomach, a few scratches on my chin and the palms of my hand, a slightly purple right eye, *and* a sense of fear I couldn't dislodge.

Yousef Ahmed had a black eye that was now yellow and blue, obviously further along in the healing process than mine. His jaw was still swollen. He looked older than the man in the newspaper photos five years ago should. Someone had fucked him up but good, and I knew that played a part, but the other . . . it was something deeper, desperate, like he was a man who had nothing to live for and didn't even want to try.

We met in a secure room at Rigshospitalet. Leila was with us, and she kept throwing me concerned glances. I hadn't told her what happened to me, but she'd found out from Tommy, who had interrogated her to learn what she knew. She'd given him a legalese speech about client-lawyer confidentiality. The subtext, as Tommy put it, was to *go fuck himself.* Tommy had told her that he'd have a constable check in on her on a regular basis, which she told him she wouldn't thank him for because it was his job to serve and protect. As always, Leila was making friends everywhere she went.

"Thank you for seeing me," I said to Yousef Ahmed.

"Leila told me that someone threatened you, beat you." He looked frail but his voice had strength. "You should not investigate this any further. Just leave it. It is what it is."

"If I stopped doing what I do because people threaten me, then I'd need to find a new line of work." It was a rehearsed line and it rolled off my tongue with ease. I was glad it was rehearsed, because the truth was that those Russian thugs who had been sent to threaten me had succeeded in putting the fear of God in me, not just for my vulnerable bones but those of my friends and family.

Yousef smiled weakly. "I didn't kill *her.*" This was his rehearsed line I realized. One that rolled off his tongue with ease, but in his case, I thought when I saw his eyes, honest and determined, despite their state of bruising, he was telling the truth.

"Tell me everything," I said. "Start from the beginning, whatever the beginning is for you."

Yousef took a deep breath. "It was a dark day when they sent Raheem back to Iraq. They would not even let us meet him in the asylum center. We thought because Raheem was a translator for the Danes, they'd want him here. But the days just got darker."

Leila got up to get him a glass of water. She didn't want to hear the next part, I could see. She didn't want to hear about Raheem's death. Well, she had company. Neither did I. But I had to. That was part of the job. And if Raheem could have gone through what he did and this man, his father, had seen what he had, I should have the balls to listen to his story.

"That reporter came to the kiosk . . . from *B.T.* I didn't know. I hadn't heard. He told me about the video. The poor man, he thought I knew. But I didn't. But . . . then I had to see it. I just had to." He took a small sip of water. His hands were shaking as he set the glass down. "They killed my boy." His agony made me reach out to him and put my hands on his shaking ones.

"The reporter . . . he apologized to me again and again. I keep seeing my boy die every time I sleep . . . close my eyes. In my nightmares, behind my eyelids . . . I see it all the time."

Leila went and stood by a window, her hands tucked inside the pockets of her dress pants, her stiff back to us.

"You say someone called you to tell you that Sanne would be in her summerhouse," I coaxed.

He shrugged. "It seems like a dream. No one believed me. The police said that no such phone call came but . . . it did. How else would I know? A man told me that she'd see me in the summerhouse. I thought that she wanted to do it where there was no media. I wasn't sure I would be able to say all that I wanted to say. I was angry and in mourning . . . not sure I could speak in front of her. So, I wrote it all down. Aisha helped me. I wanted to be better than I was. I hated her, but I wanted to forgive her. I lied in that letter and said I did. I hoped that if I said it and wrote it, I *would eventually* forgive her. You understand?"

I would never be able to forgive someone for being responsible for the death of my child. He was a bigger man than I was.

"She wasn't there." He seemed still surprised by that. "I was relieved. I left the letter for her. I was glad I didn't have to lie to her face. I was a coward."

Kierkegaard wondered why forgiveness was so rare and believed that it was because faith in the power of forgiveness is so little. People wonder how forgiveness can help, but Yousef Ahmed knew that it would cleanse him—it would honor his son and at the end be the only justice he could get.

"You might be the bravest man I know," I said sincerely.

He looked at me with tortured eyes. "I couldn't save my son. I feel that Allah is punishing me this way."

"God . . . Allah . . . Jesus, whomever . . . God, is beyond reason and I don't think he *or she* hates us as much as we hate one another." Yousef nodded and I continued, "Did you see anyone around the summerhouse when you went there?"

"No." Yousef shook his head. "No neighbors. The house is on a big plot and is hidden. I couldn't find it at first and had to walk around for a bit."

I had looked the house up on Google Maps. The summerhouse was built in the middle of a large lot surrounded with a thick garden and trees. A long and winding driveway from the main road led to the entrance of the house.

"I waited for a bit after I slid the letter in," Yousef spoke slowly, remembering. "To . . . I don't know why. Then I started to walk . . . to go to the train station. It's about fifteen minutes from there."

"Did you see anyone? Someone walking a dog. A car?" I prompted.

He frowned. "I . . . did see a car in the driveway. It went out. I thought they were lost like me and using the driveway to turn around."

"Do you remember what kind of car?"

Yousef shrugged. "A white car. One of those new cars. The ones that don't make noise."

"An electric car?" I asked.

He smiled. "Yeah."

That, I thought, was what an investigator deemed a clue. Sanne Melgaard used to own a white Tesla. Palle hadn't kept the car after his wife died.

"Who was driving it?"

"I'm sorry, I didn't see," Yousef said. "Is it important?"

"Don't worry about it. What time was this?"

"Around six in the evening," he said thoughtfully. "I took the train and came home. The police came the next morning and . . ."

He finished his story, the way I knew it, the way I had read it, the way Aisha had told me. There were no deviations.

He was exhausted when we finished. A male nurse took him to his room to rest. I was comforted to see the nurse's kindness. Here, at least, they were treating him with respect and care. My heart ached and his sorrow clung to me like the smell of disinfectant in the hospital.

Leila drove me to my office. "He's not getting better. The doctors think there are internal injuries that they didn't catch but he's not strong enough yet for another surgery."

"I'm sorry."

"Do you want to continue with the case?" she asked.

"What?" I asked absently. "Why would I not want to?"

"Because they could kill you."

"I'm harder to kill than most." I winked at her. It was false bravado and we both knew it. The night I was attacked, I had wondered, *What if it were a knife instead of a fist?* Next time it very well could be. What I couldn't understand was why, because I had uncovered fuck all and yet everyone was up in arms about it. The only thing that could be inspiring this brouhaha, I suspected, was the book Sanne had been working on.

"I don't know where to go from here," Leila said forlornly.

I had been thinking the same thing, but I knew what I had to do next. "I think I need to go to Berlin."

"Excuse me?"

I told Leila about the book and how Ulla had told me that Sanne had gone to Berlin to look at archives.

"She probably went to the BArch, the Bundesarchiv." Leila passed a car that was driving a bit too leisurely for her liking. "I worked on some cases, of getting art back to Jewish survivors when I was in London. We used the archives to get information. They're quite extensive. But, Gabriel, I don't see how a book Sanne was writing could be the reason Russian bad guys used their fists on you."

"It's an election year." Mikkel Thorsen had said that to me.

"How does that matter?"

I shrugged. I didn't know.

"Since you already know Bundesarchiv, maybe you could come with me?" I had not planned on asking her. It had slipped out, like something I couldn't control. I decided to think about why I asked her later . . . some other time. Probably never.

The last time we'd been to Berlin together was as a couple. We'd stayed close to Alexanderplatz at a ritzy hotel and had memorably made love on the balcony of the plush room with a view of the city beneath us.

"When do you want to go?"

"I have some meetings tomorrow, but we can leave the day after," I suggested.

She didn't think about it for more than a few seconds. "Okay."

When she stopped her car at my office, she put her hand on mine as I got ready to open the car door. "Gabriel, thank you."

I wanted to turn my hand around and grip hers. But I didn't. I slid my hand from under hers. "No thanks needed. You're paying me for this."

CHAPTER 17

Sophie always called before she came over so it was a surprise when she came the day after I met Yousef Ahmed, unannounced.

"*Hejsa.*" I gave her a hug. She clung to me and broke down crying. I hadn't told her about my attack, but it seemed like she had found out.

"I'm okay," I said, but she kept shaking her head.

"Hey." I lifted her chin so she could look at me; I could see her. "I'm fine."

She nodded. "I . . . that's not it."

"Then what is it?"

She leaned into me, buried her face in my shoulder. When she continued to hug me tight, a small curl of fear unfurled in my stomach. "Did someone hurt you?"

She shook her head.

"Sophie, please, *skat*, you can cry as much as you want, but first tell me why." I tried to keep the panic out of my voice, stay calm.

She sniffled. She walked up to the Arne Jacobsen sofa and picked up her phone, which had been thrown carelessly on top of it. She unlocked it and showed me a picture.

I recoiled.

A dead cat was nailed to Sophie's front door and a note drenched in blood said, "Meow! Say hi to your father, Sophie."

"I thought it was Nina's cat but . . . she was safe at a neighbor's place." Nina was Sophie's apartment mate and was in Ibiza on vacation.

She was shaky. I could see her shiver. I led her to the couch and took a cashmere blanket from the arm and wrapped it around her. I sat down next to her. My knees would buckle if I tried to stand up, I knew. I put my arm around her and kissed her forehead. I exuded the Gabriel Præst calm, but I was a hair's breadth away from having the shakes just like Sophie.

"Did you call the police?" I asked gently.

She nodded. "I left before they came. I needed to see you. Do you know what this is about?"

I nodded. "Yousef Ahmed."

And then I had to tell her about the *little* incident in front of my house a few days before.

She was really shaken up now. "Why didn't you tell me? Does *Mor* know?"

"It's just a few scratches . . ."

"Are you kidding me? Are you going to minimize this?" Sophie pulled away from me, her face drawn in anger.

"No. I'm sorry. You're right, this is serious." I hugged her close, rubbing my hands on her back to comfort her and myself. Fear settled in my stomach, raw and heavy.

"I'm really scared, *Far*."

"I know. Me too. But it's going to be fine. I'm going to stop working on this case. I'll back off and make sure everyone knows. Then they will leave us alone." I had no choice. This was Sophie. I couldn't risk her.

Sophie pulled away from me again. "What?" She was now even more angry.

"I'll make sure you're safe." I held her face in my hands, so she'd look at me. "And you're going to stay with your mother and Erik for a while until everyone knows that I'm done with this case."

"You can't walk away." Sophie removed my hands from her face.

I sighed. "Sophie, they killed a fucking cat and nailed it to your door."

"Does that mean we tuck our tails and run?"

"There is no we, *skat*, there is only me. And yes, I will run if that means you are safe. I feel no shame in doing that."

"Well, you should." All the fear was gone from her demeanor.

"Sophie, *skat*, listen . . ."

"An innocent man may be in prison and you're going to what? Run? And what if someone else investigates? What if Leila continues? You know she will. They'll go after her. How will you feel then?" she yelled.

"She will also stop. I'll make her. And you know what, Yousef Ahmed probably did kill her and . . ."

"If he did then why are they threatening you?" She folded her arms and stood away from me. I recognized that stance, she'd been doing it since she was a child. Her *I want to discuss this matter logically and until I win* pose.

My phone rang then, and I picked it up. It was Tommy. "Yeah, she's here."

"I'm coming over, keep her there," Tommy said.

"You're the police chief, don't you have other things to do?" I asked. But he had already hung up. "Tommy is on his way." I tucked my phone into my pants pocket.

"I told the emergency responders at 112 that Tommy is my grandfather. I lied."

"He'll be flattered." I laughed.

I got some scotch and we both sat down on the bench outside and drank to calm our nerves. I lit a cigarette and ignored her sneer.

"If *they* don't kill you, the cigarettes certainly will."

"It's been a shitty day . . . week." I had good reason to break my rule. Damn good reason.

It took Tommy a little more than ten minutes with lights and sirens to get to my town house. He had probably been at some important meeting in the office, because he was in his uniform. A light blue dress shirt with shoulder slip-ons that displayed his rank and insignia, and dark blue dress pants. He wore black cowboy boots—his attempt at resisting the homogeneity of the uniform.

"First, the cat was already dead before they nailed it to your door," Tommy assured Sophie.

"Well, that's good to know." She sighed in some relief. "I was worried they murdered someone's pet."

Tommy refused scotch but accepted a cup of coffee and agreed with me that I should drop the Yousef Ahmed case like a hot potato and let the police do their work.

"Oh, you mean like they already did?" Sophie asked sarcastically.

"She used to be such a sweet girl." He looked at me accusingly. "What have you done to her?"

Sophie narrowed her eyes. "I'm *still* sweet. And I think it's sad that a police chief and ex-cop are more afraid than I am."

"You have to be protected, Sophie." I used my *it's my way or the highway* tone that never really worked with her.

"Then protect me," Sophie said agreeably.

I held up my hand to silence Tommy. "No cops. I don't trust your guys."

"You can trust me." Tommy was insulted, I could tell. And not just insulted but also a little hurt. Well, he'd have to get over it. This was Sophie we were talking about.

"You can't babysit her, Tommy. And I don't know how far Mikkel Thorsen's reach is." I resisted the urge to run my hands over my face, something I did when I was tired and/or stressed.

"What will you do?" Tommy asked annoyed. "Keep her with you twenty-four/seven?"

I shook my head. "I'm calling Bør."

Tommy snorted. "You'll call an ex-biker and gang member who has killed people and done time to protect your daughter instead of policemen?"

"Bør is a good idea," Sophie agreed with me.

"Bør will put some thugs on her. Some *really bad dudes*," Tommy protested mildly, but he was already giving in, thinking what I was, *really bad dudes* would protect Sophie *really well*.

"I'm okay with that," I said.

"And you, Sophie?" Tommy asked. "You're going to be okay with two biker-gang types walking around Copenhagen with you?"

"It'll guarantee that no one will hassle me." Sophie grinned and then looked at me and said, "Can you make sure they don't have neo-Nazi tattoos? That really freaks me out."

"Unbelievable." Tommy sighed. "But she's your daughter, so why am I surprised."

AS PREDICTED, STINE blamed me for the whole thing, as she should. It *was* my fault. It didn't help that Erik and Sophie didn't blame me but blamed the *bad guys* as they put it.

"You're risking the life of our daughter to do what? Get a murderer off," Stine screamed at me.

We were sitting around the dining table. It had started in a civilized manner with coffee and cake, but as Sophie told her mother *everything*, it had gotten ugly.

"You want to fuck this Leila woman then go do it. But you're not going to sacrifice my daughter because you can't keep it in your pants," she yelled.

"Don't talk about Leila like that. I'm not sleeping with her." I kept my voice calm, even though I had no tolerance for anyone debasing the women I had relationships with. Stine knew this and she was trying to get a rise out of me. I added, "This is not about Leila but about justice." Even to me that sounded corny, but it was how I felt. It *was* about justice.

"They nailed a dead cat to her door." Stine's eyes were wide with fear.

"I know." I put my hand on hers. I understood her fear. I felt it too.

She shook her head. "Why can't you have a normal job like everyone else?"

"I'm a lawyer," Erik pointed out.

"No one is trying to kill you," Stine muttered. "And Gabriel, what if they come after Erik and me? What then?"

I nodded. "You're right. I . . ."

"No, no, no." Sophie stood up, her hands on her hips. "Don't use *Mor*'s fears as an excuse to be a coward."

That stung. I was her father. I was Superman. She had just called me a coward. But to make sure she was safe, I would be whatever I needed to be.

"Stop encouraging him," Stine snapped.

"Stine, he has to see this through," Erik said quietly. "This is not a choice. We do our jobs, and we do what needs to be done."

"Why couldn't I have been married to accountants . . . they have safe jobs." Stine sighed.

The yelling and screaming went on until I left. It probably continued after I left. Sophie had gallantly agreed to put up with her mother and live with them while I worked the case.

Tommy called me as I walked home from Stine's apartment.

"You'll be interested to know that Sanne Melgaard's laptop didn't have anything remarkable on it. Just the usual stuff—documents, emails—but these days people have cloud access and whatnot," he informed me.

"And?"

"She didn't have anything there either," he said. "She didn't even visit porn sites."

"I'm glad to hear that."

"And that's about all I can do with the Sanne Melgaard case," Tommy said wearily. "I talked to Henrik Morck. He says he's sorry about you getting hurt but thinks you should keep at it anyway."

"Good to know."

"Præst, stay healthy."

"Yes." I felt the weight of my Glock 26 in its holster under my jacket. I hadn't taken the jacket off at Stine's because if she saw the gun, she'd probably pop a few blood vessels. I had a permit to carry a gun as many PIs did. I liked the Glock 26; it was smaller than the full-size Glock and was easy to hide.

"Are you carrying?" Tommy asked, as if he could read my thoughts.

"Yes." Tommy knew I had a carry permit.

"Okay. I was worried that you wouldn't."

"I'm too worried not to," I confessed.

I wasn't a fan of guns but in my line of work, it was a necessity at times. As much as I didn't like it, I went to the shooting range at least once a month to ensure that my fingers knew what to do when it was needed. As a policeman, I had been at a raid of a drug house where I had seen and participated in gunfire. I had seen what a bullet does as it goes through flesh. Thankfully, the policeman whom the bullet went through had not been fatally shot. It had put me off guns. Since then, there had been only a couple of cases where I'd felt the need to carry a gun as a precaution; but this was the first time the threat was *this* real. And the only time so far when there was a real risk that I could get killed. The realization was sobering. I was scared. I was not too stubborn or proud to admit that. But a part of me was exhilarated. I was excited about working on something difficult, important, and far, far away from digging through financial records to root out an embezzler.

CHAPTER 18

I met Bør at Duck and Cover on Dannebrogsgade in Vesterbro. It was his favorite bar, and we took our old-fashioned cocktails outside and sat at a small table so he could smoke.

My old-fashioned was with whiskey, while his was virgin. He was a recovering alcoholic who loved to go to bars. The man had ironlike willpower.

"You were missed at my father's eightieth birthday party," he remonstrated.

I nodded. If I went to every birthday party and anniversary I was invited to, I'd do nothing else.

"It was a good party," he told me. "The old man says *hilsen* to you."

"Give him my regards." I had sent him a present to smooth out the edge of not attending his party.

"And he appreciates the bottle of whiskey," he added.

Bør was a large man, and even though he'd left the gang behind, the various tattoos on his arms and bald head ensured that people kept their distance. In his day, he was a dangerous biker with a few murders to his credit, though none could be proven. He had left the life, done time for a drug bust, and had rehabilitated himself. He now had a media company, where he employed ex–gang members and financed movies, and a popular podcast. He had married his long-term and long-suffering boyfriend, Malte, and they had adopted two kids from Africa. They lived in Nør-rebro and had a life that Bør couldn't have imagined a decade ago. He had become a family man, busy with changing diapers, dropping and picking up kids from daycare, and planning date nights.

"I need help," I told him as he finished smoking a cigarette and talking about his kids.

He lit another cigarette. The whole country smoked, I thought irritated, how was someone supposed to kick the habit with temptation lurking everywhere?

"Anything, man," Bør said. I knew he meant it.

I told him about Yousef Ahmed, the attack on me and what had happened with Sophie.

"Sounds like you're tangling with the Russian Mafia. Do you know why?"

"No."

"I'll put two men with her at all times." Bør was resourceful when it came to something like this. "What about you? I can hang with you, man. Still good with my hands and a gun."

I moved my arm uncomfortably at the word *gun* because mine was burning a hole through my conscience.

"You could always just leave the case," Bør suggested. "You don't have to do this, man."

"I can't walk away."

Bør looked at me through a ring of smoke. "You became a PI to do good. I understand."

Bør and I went back a long way and even though he and I were not as close as Eymen and I were, there was, at times, a higher degree of understanding between us.

"I did become a policeman to do good," I agreed. "I quit when I couldn't tell the good guys from the bad. As a PI, I can't always tell the good guys from the bad guys either. I mean, what kind of man hires a private investigator to spy on his wife? And then I do insurance fraud cases and embezzlement. Some poor shmuck robbed a wealthy and morally bankrupt company. But this case, this is different, here I can tell the difference between the good guys and the bad guys."

Bør crushed his cigarette and patted my shoulder. "I'll send some brothers over to your house later today and you all can go see Sophie."

"She's staying with Stine," I told him. "Send them there."

"I like Erik. He's all right."

"That he is."

"Your ex-wife is batshit crazy," he said.

"She's not my ex-wife," I corrected patiently. "We were never married."

We sat in silence for a while and finished our drinks. Then I walked to Stine's apartment, making a note that I needed to either buy or borrow a bicycle as soon as possible.

I did what I normally do when I am working on a case. I thought through everything. The fact was that for all the ruckus this case was generating, I hadn't found any information that should cause trouble for anyone. I had some innuendo from Sanne's sister about a book she had been writing about the German occupation of Denmark. I had the fact that Henrik Morck was drinking himself into a stupor because of guilt. I knew that Mikkel Thorsen's knickers were in a bunch and that the prime minister was asking me for a favor.

It all added up to absolutely nothing.

Then why was I threatened? Why was I carrying a gun? And why had they nailed a cat to Sophie's door?

I thought about Sanne's book again. No one seemed to know she was working on it, but someone had to know. There was something there. I could feel it. I thought again about how Aleksander had said he'd dropped Sanne off in Gilleleje and dropped the car off for Palle to use. But according to the police report, Palle took the train to Gilleleje. Between a Tesla and a train, I'd probably drive the Tesla, but otherwise I did prefer the train; less traffic and all that.

Yousef Ahmed saw a quiet white car. But there were lots of Teslas on the streets of Copenhagen thanks to lower sales taxes on electric cars. It could just be any Tesla. Lots of well-off, Tesla-owning Copenhagen citizens had a summerhouse in Gilleleje. It could mean absolutely nothing.

Even though I was deep in thought, I noticed the man following me. He wore a pair of jeans, a white T-shirt, and a blue baseball cap. He looked like any other Dane in Copenhagen on a pleasant summer evening. It was around eight thirty at night, the light was still out, and there were plenty of people up and about. And still, he managed not to blend in. I noticed him as I stopped in front of a store to window-shop hats. Then I noticed him again when I stopped to window-shop suits. And then again when I stopped to window-shop shoes.

I put my hand under my blazer and felt my Glock. It bothered me that it made me feel safe. The attack on my street had educated me. First, I was aware of my surroundings more than I had been, and second, I knew it would happen again; maybe not today or tomorrow but eventually, as this case wound down, it would happen.

Was Mikkel Thorsen responsible as Eymen thought? Maybe. But then it could just be random white nationalists who didn't like that I was poking my nose in Sanne Melgaard's murder.

It wasn't until we got close to Stine's apartment that I turned around and walked up to the man following me. He stood rooted. It was his tattoos that had given him away.

"Tell Bør I'm not the one who needs protection," I told him. "And you can't follow me for shit. I spotted you all the way on Strøget."

The man shrugged. "Can't do, boss. Bør said that I be with you whatever happens."

I shook my head. "No, you stay with my daughter."

"That's Luc and Big Bo." He gave me his hand to shake. "I'm Small Bo."

I shook his hand. Since this guy was about 195 kilos, 100 of it muscle, I wondered what *Big* meant with Big Bo.

"How big is Big Bo?" I asked.

He smirked but didn't answer.

We looked at each other for a long moment, and then I shrugged. I'd have to talk to Bør. Small Bo was just following orders. I didn't need a man of his size following me around Copenhagen while I was investigating a sensitive case.

Stine surprisingly was not yelling or screaming. Luc and Big Bo had been dropped off by Bør, who hadn't been able to wait for me, because his husband, who worked at an ad agency, had a work dinner, so he had to be home with the kids. The two ex–gang members, Erik, and Sophie were drinking Tuborg beer in the living room. Sophie was showing them pictures of a recent trip she'd taken to London with friends on Instagram. I could talk to anyone, it was part of the gig, but Sophie was better than me; she not only talked to people but also built relationships with them. By the end of this case, Luc and Big Bo would be buddies with Sophie and they would fall at her feet, like all of us lower mortals did.

"They look tough enough." Stine watched Erik and Sophie conversing with the two large men who sported gang tattoos. We stood at the doorway that led into the kitchen from the living room and spoke in whispers.

"They *are* tough," I assured her.

"Do you think they've killed people?" Stine asked me.

"Maybe. But they work for Bør now and all his people are clean . . . you know . . . now."

"No, it's good if they've killed people before," she said and stunned me. "That means that if someone bothers Sophie, they'll take care of her. And Bør loves her. I mean, I never liked the man, but he loves her and right now because you're going to be a selfish prick, I'm happy he does."

I put my arm around her and squeezed. She leaned into me. "I love having her home. Do you think I'm an awful mother that I'm happy she's back home?"

"No." I dropped a kiss on her hair. "You're a loving mother and you're worried about her."

"And you're the shitty parent." She put her arm around my waist.

"Yes." I hugged her close. She may be annoying as hell, but she was the mother of my daughter. She was my family.

After dinner, Sophie came downstairs with me and we stood on the roadside, watching cars go by.

Luc and Big Bo would accompany her whenever she left the house, but when she was home, they would rely on the fact that the apartment was on the fifth floor with a good security system. Sophie had to text them whenever she wanted to leave and wait until they came up to the apartment. They wouldn't walk with her if that made her uncomfortable but behind her. Sophie had told them she had no problem being seen with them.

"Thank you for setting this up." She eyed Small Bo, who was standing across the street, leaning against a tree, waving at me. "Who's that? One of Bør's guys?"

"Small Bo."

Sophie grinned. "I wonder why they call him Small Bo. He seems to be the same size as Big Bo. Do you think it's his shoe size?"

I laughed. "Bør sent him to follow me around. He was supposed to be stealthy."

"I'm happy to see him. Means that when you get jumped next time, there will be someone to save you," Sophie said. "How much danger are you in?"

"For now? None. But if they know I'm going to continue to investigate . . ." I let my words trail away.

"You now believe that Yousef Ahmed didn't do it, don't you?"

I shrugged.

"This is important, *Far*," Sophie pressed. "More important than anything else you've done. Even more important than the Karina Jensen thing. That was corruption; here, an innocent man is spending his life in prison for a crime he didn't commit."

I loved this intelligent and aware child of mine. Stine and I might have many issues, but we'd done right by Sophie. She'd grown up to be morally sound, smart, self-aware, and courageous. She was twenty years old and had just experienced a brutal threat, and yet she was telling me to be as brave as her and fight the good fight. How could I not?

SMALL BO SLEPT on the couch in my living room. He insisted, saying that he wanted to be close to the front and back door. Bør had told him that if anything happened to me, he would beat the living daylights out of Small Bo.

"You know he won't do that," I assured him.

Small Bo nodded. "Yeah, I know. But he wants me to do this and I'm going to do this. It's not out of fear, you understand. It's out of respect. He told me what you're doing. That you're fighting for justice. That's noble, *chef*, and I'm happy to be here for as long as that takes."

I felt like an idiot for thinking Small Bo was a brainless thug. The man had more integrity than many of the cops I knew. The Thug Code! It came with its own rules and morality. Small Bo would think nothing of beating the crap out of anyone and maybe even killing someone if needed, but he believed in justice, not the kind law provided but jungle justice—the raw kind, the kind that gods dole out.

I called Nico as I lay in bed.

"What are you wearing?" I asked.

She laughed.

I told her about what had happened with Sophie and me. I told her that she needed to be careful and stay away from me until I wrapped the case up. As I said that I wondered if I was being a little too overconfident that I could actually *wrap* the fucking thing up.

"Præst, I'm not doing that."

"Nico—"

"Nope," she interrupted. "I'm a journalist. If I run every time something gets hot, I need to find a new line of work. I hear you say the same about your work."

"Mikkel Thorsen mentioned you specifically," I told her. "He isn't kidding."

"Neither am I. And if my kid wasn't at home, I'd ask you to come over and you could find out what I'm wearing."

I sighed. I had known she wouldn't listen. Maybe Tommy would make sure a constable checked in on her.

"Well . . . since I can't come and look under the covers, why don't you help me and tell me what you're wearing?"

"Wouldn't you like to know."

CHAPTER 19

I started my day with a run with Small Bo behind me. I thought he was judgmental about it, which was confirmed when he asked me if I was going to the gym after my warmup because he wouldn't mind a *proper* workout. I refrained from giving him the finger.

I still didn't have a bicycle, so I walked to the office and Small Bo followed me. I listened to a daily news podcast, which was doing a piece on Arne Juhl, the grandfather of the current prime minister, as part of his centennial celebration.

Arne Juhl is a bona fide national hero, Adam Holm, a Danish journalist, said.

Like it was with such shows, Annegrethe Larsen, another famous Danish journalist, had a counterpoint. *I don't know about that. I think we're now far enough from World War Two to see things in a clearer light, not corrupted by the adrenaline of war. I think it's important to keep in mind that even though the Juhl family divested their construction company that made huge amounts of money working with the Germans, they kept that money. It's that money that has made them one of the richest Danish families today.*

Adam Holm wasn't having any of it. Arne Juhl was a key member of Holger Danske. He participated in nearly thirty sabotage acts. And did you know that he was the brains and muscle behind the Forum bombing, so Germans would not be able to convert it into barracks for their soldiers.

The fact is that Arne Juhl was honored with the Presidential Medal of Freedom and the Cross of Honor of the Order of the Dannebrog (Dannebrogordenens Hæderstegn) by King Frederick IX of Denmark.

Annegrethe Larsen chuckled. *There is documented proof that while Arne Juhl was blowing up buildings to resist Germans, Juhl & Bror, the family business, made considerable wealth by building bunkers for the Germans on the west coast until April 1945. It appears they managed to keep both the ill-gotten riches and their pristine pro-Danish reputation.*

The Danish film director Kiel Andersen, who was releasing the biopic *The Peacemaker*, a tribute to Arne and his aspirations and struggle to bring peace to Europe, joined the discussion. It was not coincidental that the timing for the premiere matched the centennial celebrations later in the summer (and in time, I thought cynically, for the election season). It was two against one. Annegrethe Larsen wasn't winning this one, I thought as Kiel Andersen closed by saying, *Arne Juhl's legacy is what we have today, the longest period of peace in Europe.*

I CALLED BØR that afternoon, after leaving Small Bo standing outside my office, his arms crossed, a stance exactly like a movie bodyguard. Big arms, bald head, lots of tattoos, and biceps that stretched his retro METALLICA T-shirt.

"Small Bo is scaring the granny panties off the nice secretaries at Dall og Digman."

"They'll survive." Bør wasn't sympathetic.

"I'm carrying a gun," I told him.

"You?"

"Yes."

I could almost feel Bør's shock through the phone. "Well . . . that's a surprise."

"I'm going to Berlin tomorrow."

"He can fly with you," Bør suggested. "He's a good travel companion."

"I'm taking Clara's Porsche. And Leila is coming with me."

"Why would you drive to Berlin? Safer to fly," he persisted.

"Didn't you hear me? Clara is lending me her brand-new Porsche 911 Carrera."

"Brand-new? Even though she knows how you drive?"

"It's fresh off the production line," I told him with some satisfaction. "And there's nothing wrong with how I drive."

"You drive like a maniac."

"That's a subjective opinion based on one accident that happened in my youth. In any case, I don't have room for Small Bo in the car."

I felt his indecision and finally, he gave in. "Fine. But only if you're going to keep your gun with you. What are you carrying? Your baby Glock?"

"The baby Glock shoots just fine, and an AK-47 doesn't go with my outfit."

I heard him snort.

"And that's another reason I'm not flying. I want to carry my weapon and I'd prefer not to get into trouble with the *Bundespolizei*," I added. "See, how it's all coming together for me?"

"Yeah, I can see that. One trip to the ER, several visits from the police, a dead cat nailed to your daughter's door. If it came together any more, I don't know if you'd make it out alive," he said dryly and then added, "Luc and Big Bo will stay put with Sophie."

"Undoubtedly."

A few hours later, while I was diligently working undisturbed, Erik came into my office and asked about Small Bo; that's how I knew he was gone. He hadn't said goodbye but had taken his marching orders and disappeared.

I had just finished a report on a divorce case for Casper Dall, Erik's partner, and also submitted some paperwork on one of Erik's cases, including a hairy insurance scam that was going to pay for finishing the renovation on my master bathroom, because I had a lead on matching vintage Spanish tiles.

"Where are you staying in Berlin?" Erik asked me as I packed my things in my office at the end of the day.

"I booked a nice suite in a nice hotel on Alexanderplatz on the River Spree with a view of the Berlin Dom." It wasn't the same hotel that Leila and I stayed in before. I didn't want to evoke those memories and maybe it was time to make some new ones.

"Hmm . . . a suite?"

"Yes, with two bedrooms." I had done it in case Leila got the wrong impression. Leila could sleep wherever she wanted.

And where do you want her to sleep? Ilse's voice, which lived inside my head, asked me.

It didn't even take a moment for me to realize that I didn't know. I wasn't sure if I wanted her to sleep with me. I wasn't sure if it was a good idea.

I must be getting old. Sex was sex. It was fun. Sweaty. Sometimes it was a little dull—but most of the time it was pleasant, especially at my age, when I had become more discerning. I liked to like the women I had sex with, which meant I had to know them. Life used to be different when I was younger, shallow but simple.

"Are you getting back together, you and Leila?" Erik wanted to know.

"No."

"No?" The subtext was, Why the suite then, why not separate rooms?

The answer was that I was hedging my bets. I didn't want to tempt fate, but I also didn't want to create barriers. I was as fucked up about Leila as my therapist said I was.

"It's easier to protect her if she's close by. And she's engaged to another man. And how the fuck is this any of your business?"

"You are my wife's ex-husband. You are family," he explained. "Your business is my business."

I sighed. "You know Stine and I were never married, right? She's not my fucking ex-wife."

"Semantics. You say baby mama, I say ex-wife."

"Did you just say baby mama?"

Erik nodded, a broad smile on his face. "Yeah, Big Bo introduced me to hip-hop music. There's a lot of talk about baby mamas in the songs."

That night I slept on the couch in Stine and Erik's living room. I turned down the guestroom. I was standing . . . sleeping guard. Big Bo and Luc would come over at eight in the morning to take Sophie to university. Having known Sophie since she was born, Bør was committed to her safety. The only time Sophie had been arrested, which was during an Earth Day march that turned violent, she'd called Bør instead of me because I'd explicitly asked her not to go and she hadn't listened.

It was a warm evening, so the blanket Stine had given me was on the floor. I was wearing my underpants and a T-shirt; sleeping nude wasn't an option on Stine's couch. I lay awake, watching the sky through the glass wall of their living room. It was June and the sun set later in the evening and rose in the middle of the night.

I couldn't sleep. I knew I should. I had to go to Berlin with Leila the next day, which was a six-hour drive, including a two-hour ferry ride. We were planning to leave late in the evening to get to Berlin early in the morning by catching the last ferry from Gedser in Denmark to Rostock in Germany.

But I couldn't sleep. The case was keeping me awake, as cases sometimes did.

There wasn't one thing about the whole mess that I was comfortable with. The police had done an abysmal job by accepting the framing of Yousef. Tommy wouldn't reopen the Sanne Melgaard case. He'd investigate someone beating me up and scaring Sophie, but even he wouldn't touch the subject of reinvestigation with a ten-foot barge pole—even if it did have a dead cat hanging at the end of it.

I got up and walked into Erik's office to get a writing pad and a pen. I sat at the dining table and began to write down all the names connected to the case. I had just written Ulla Bernsen's name when as if on cue, my phone rang, Ulla's name flashing on the screen.

I WAS ON my third cup of coffee by the time the cops finished talking to Ulla, her neighbors, and me. Thankfully the *Politiinspektør* at Værløse where Ulla lived was Kim Borresen, who knew me and didn't ask too many questions about why Ulla had called me before she called the police when her house was burgled. He knew I was a PI and knew that I was probably there because I was working with Ulla in some capacity. He also knew I wouldn't answer any questions about what I was doing for or with her.

It had happened in the middle of the night, while she was

sleeping. She'd heard a noise and had followed it to the guest bedroom, which was also an office and home to her laptop and printer. The thief had had her laptop in his hand when she'd surprised him and herself. He'd pushed her out of the way and ran but had lost his hold on the laptop on his way out of the house. The laptop had fallen to the ground and had remarkably experienced no damage.

The thief had also rummaged through all the papers and files in the desk cabinets, which were now strewn across the floor.

"Do you want me to take you somewhere?" I asked Ulla after everyone had cleared out. We were sitting at her kitchen table, drinking coffee. Like any self-respecting Dane, she'd served breakfast rolls with butter and strawberry jam. The rolls and jam were homemade, so I had eaten a couple, partly because they were good and partly because I needed the sugar to stave off the tiredness.

She'd refused my help to set the guest bedroom right, not because she had something to hide, I knew, only because she didn't want to go in there yet.

"He was wearing a mask." Ulla was bewildered. "You know, like they do in the movies. You think it's a junkie who wanted to make a quick kroner by selling my laptop?"

I set my coffee cup down and put my hand on hers. "You know what this is about."

She nodded, tears in her eyes. "I'm scared."

You've done it now, Præst, I told myself. You've managed to make your daughter, her mother, your friends, and now this poor old lady scared. I thought then of what Sartre had said, *You must be afraid, my son. That is how one becomes an honest citizen.* I was afraid that something had gone very wrong in the case of Sanne Melgaard's murder; something so wrong committed by people so powerful that they were ready to scare all those in-volved and maybe even kill a few if needed.

"I'm sorry." I really was.

She shook her head. "What happened to your face?" she asked, looking at my now slightly discolored eye and the bruise bloom-ing on my left cheek where it had connected with the asphalt when I had fallen beneath the Russians' fists. I didn't want to frighten her further, but I knew it was my responsibility to tell her the truth, so she could protect herself.

"Some guys beat me up to stop me from investigating the case."

Her eyes widened.

"Oh my God!" she gasped.

And then I told her about the cat nailed to Sophie's door.

Ulla shook her head in disbelief. "Maybe that man is innocent. Why else would someone threaten you?"

"Maybe because I'm ripping open old, healed wounds?"

She didn't believe that any more than I did.

"Look, Ulla, no one seems to know anything about this book Sanne was writing," I said carefully. "No one knows or no one is talking about it. I'm going to Berlin today to see if we can follow her footsteps there."

"Berlin?" Ulla's eyes widened. "Oh, I forgot to tell you but when you said Berlin, I remembered."

She pulled out her phone, opened Facebook messenger, and handed it to me.

"I got this on my Facebook messenger from a Dr. Sommer from Berlin the day after we spoke," she said. "I meant to call you, but it slipped my mind."

The message was from a Dr. Oskar Sommer from the Friedrich Meinecke Institute of History at the Freie Universität Berlin.

Dear Frau Bernsen,

I am reaching out to you about your sister, Sanne
Melgaard. She met with me five years ago, just a few
weeks before she was killed.

Since I don't have your phone number or email
address, I'm contacting you via Facebook in the hope
that this message will reach you.

Frau Melgaard wanted access to certain documents
in the Nazi archives. The documents were restricted
when she approached me but have just been
unclassified for researchers such as me. I have these
documents and as she predicted, they must be handled
with the utmost care.

May I request you to reach out to me by phone or by
email as soon as possible.

My best regards,
Dr. Oskar Sommer

He then had given her his contact information.

I read the message twice and looked at Ulla, who looked more
nervous than before.

"Have you contacted him?" I asked.

She shook her head. "I . . . no. I didn't think anything of it. I
get emails and messages from time to time because of Sanne. I
ignore them."

"Do you mind if I forward this to myself?"

She shook her head. "Did I make a mistake by not telling you
immediately?"

I forwarded the message and handed her phone back. "No." I

didn't add that I had no idea what was a mistake and what wasn't in this case.

She then took a deep breath and burst into tears. I put my arms around her. She cried for a good minute or so and I let her. She seemed relieved after the crying jag was over.

I gave her some kitchen towels to wipe her eyes from the roll on a Trip Trap wooden stand.

"You think the thief was looking for Sanne's book, don't you?"

I told her I couldn't say and then asked, "Have you told anyone else about this message from Dr. Sommer?"

She shook her head.

"You didn't tell Palle?" I asked.

She snorted. "Of course not."

"Have you seen him?"

"Yes, last night. At a mutual friend's house for dinner."

"And you are sure you didn't tell him anything?" I asked, and then held my hands up in defense when I saw her flash me an exasperated look. "Sorry. I have to ask. For your own protection as well as mine, because I don't know who Palle will talk to."

"I didn't tell him anything," she promised. "Not even that you and I spoke. Do you think I'm in trouble?"

"Maybe. I can ask the police to keep an eye on you. Though I'd prefer it if you went away and stayed somewhere else. Just for a little while."

She thought about it for a moment. "A friend of mine invited me to join her at her summerhouse in Norway, by the Oslofjord. I could go there."

"When can you leave?"

Ulla looked panicked. "Do I have to leave right away?"

"Today would be good. Don't you think?" I didn't want to also worry about Ulla. I had enough people to worry about.

I texted Tommy to call me as Ulla planned with her friend and packed. While I waited for Tommy to respond, I used my phone to buy her an airplane ticket for Oslo. I had considered if she should take the ferry but feared she would be followed and vulnerable on the ferry. Airports with all their restrictions made air travel safer. Maybe I should listen to Bør and fly to Berlin with Leila, I thought, but rejected the idea. On an airplane I couldn't take my gun with me, and I felt like I might need it.

"Do you think I'm running a fucking taxi service?" Tommy sounded disgusted when I told him about Ulla and what I needed from him. "Of course, I'll send a car to pick up Frau Bernsen and drive her to the airport."

"And get her through security and all that?" I requested.

"It's a fucking full-service taxi service," he grumbled.

"Thanks, Tommy."

"Where are you going?"

I trusted Tommy, it wasn't that I didn't, but he was a cop and sometimes he couldn't know the things I knew. "Why do you think I'm going somewhere?"

Tommy remained silent.

"A road trip with Leila to Berlin." I tried to make light of it. "Maybe rekindle the old romance."

"I don't think that's why you're going to Berlin. But I also know you're a hardheaded son of a bitch who won't tell me, so be careful and stay the fuck alive."

"That's the plan." I didn't think it was any of his business that I had no plan and was just bumbling around, hoping to fall into some information.

"THERE'S NOTHING HERE." Eymen had used his superior IT skills and gone through Ulla's computer. She'd left it with me and taken the afternoon flight to Oslo. Tommy had arranged for someone in the Oslo police to meet her at Gardermoen Airport and deliver her to her friend's summerhouse. The Oslo police would also check on her there. Good Nordic police cooperation.

"Nothing?" I asked almost pitifully. I had hoped there would be a clue, something that would crack the case wide open.

"Well, her taxes, emails, and pictures of grandchildren," Eymen offered. "Nothing connected to Sanne. And no, no manuscript or even notes on this Nazi book."

I had had dinner that evening with Eymen, Clara, and their kids.

Once the kids went to bed, Clara, Eymen, and I sat on their large balcony, drinking some fine Bordeaux.

"I asked Leila to make an appointment with Dr. Sommer from the Friedrich Meinecke Institute of History and keep the reason vague. I looked him up online. He specializes in social dynamics during Nazi occupation."

"That's specific," Eymen commented.

"Right now, he's doing research on what happened to Nazi collaborators on both sides of the wall and why, the social impact, blah, blah. He's one of those social psychology types," I explained.

"Do you think Sanne was writing about Danish collaborators?" Clara asked.

I shrugged. "Can't say."

"Maybe she was going to reveal something about a Danish collaborator, and they killed her because of it." Her blue eyes were bright, thrilled at the prospect.

Clara was wearing a pair of cutoff shorts and a T-shirt that said FEMINISM (NOUN): THE RADICAL NOTION THAT WOMEN ARE PEOPLE and looked like a princess on R&R. Eymen was the antithesis of her, with his dark hair and olive skin, even though he wore clothes similar to hers, but his T-shirt was plain white with no slogan. He was unimpressed with the whole Yousef Ahmed business. It was always like this. I got into trouble. Clara got excited and then got into trouble with me because of her enthusiasm. Eymen made sure we got out of trouble. It was always a pain in his ass.

"It seems farfetched," Eymen said thoughtfully. "Who cares today if someone collaborated with the Nazis then? It's been seventy-plus years, who is still alive from that time to slander?"

"Maybe it's that person's relatives," I suggested. "Maybe the family wants this kept secret."

"Or you're just poking into a hill of red ants, and they don't like it," Eymen snapped. "Sanne Melgaard's murder was a blow to immigrants in Denmark. Yousef Ahmed proved what Muslim men are accused of being—men full of hate and violence. It was hard enough to be a brown Muslim in Denmark, and that son of a bitch made it harder. Don't you dare sit here and tell me this chase you're on has some moral value. Let sleeping dogs lie, Gabriel. Just let the fucking thing go."

"If we let this go then there is no future that is acceptable for our children, Eymen." Clara didn't wait for me to respond and went on the warpath. This was not a new discussion between them. "They're half brown and half white. Asgar looks like you, he's eleven and soon he's going to be a teenager, and we'll have to talk to him about how he should handle himself if a policeman stops him. We'll have to tell him that he may sometimes not be admitted into a club with his friends because he's brown. You really think that allowing them to put an innocent man in prison because he's Muslim is going to help Asgar or any of the other brown boys growing up in Denmark?"

Eymen put down his glass of wine with some force. "Yousef Ahmed is not innocent. Why do you think he is? The police did their job. There was evidence. I understand his rage. I really do—I don't know what I'd do if I went through what he did. But now . . . I have to carry his sins and so does our son."

They both looked at me and I raised my hands in a *keep me out of your marital dispute* gesture.

Clara glared at me. "Tell me, Gabriel, do you think that Yousef Ahmed killed Sanne Melgaard or was he just convenient?"

"I don't know about the convenient part, but I can't say for sure if he did or did not do it." The fact was that I was biased toward the idea of a frame-up job. It smelled just the way Henrik Morck had said it did.

Eymen shook his head and walked back in from the balcony. When he got to the door, he turned and said, "Gabriel, you're going to get yourself killed and I can't do anything about that because you're a stubborn son of a bitch, but I expect you to have the decency to keep my fucking wife out of it."

"Your fucking wife doesn't care what you think." Clara banged the door shut in his face.

This wasn't the first time they had gotten into a fight because of me.

"Remember how he used to be so concerned about how Muslims were being treated? Now he's all about Muslims staying out of the way and avoiding trouble." She was as annoyed and frustrated as Eymen, just for other reasons. "What the fuck happened to him?" she asked me.

"He had children. Their protection comes first."

"He's being complicit in systemic racism," she said bitterly. "He's being a coward."

"Eymen is a lot of things, Clara, but a coward he's not," I soothed. "He's cautious. We're white, we can get away with what he can't. Remember how he had to be the careful one in university?"

"We're not in university anymore, Gabriel." She sat down next to me.

"No, we're not and the stakes are much higher." I wrapped an arm around her. She put her head on my shoulder.

"I'm still angry with him."

"He's right. I could get myself killed."

"I guess." Her voice was small.

"And this could hurt you," I added.

She lifted one shoulder and then let it drop.

"Your money protects you and so does your last name, but Russian thugs for hire may not care," I said. "And depending upon who the puppet master is, your money might not be enough to stop them."

"Oh please, you're making it sound like there is some movie-like conspiracy here."

"I know." I laughed. "But I did get my ass beat up on the street, just like in the movies."

Clara sighed and straightened. I kissed her on her forehead and rose. "I'll go make up with him and then leave."

She followed me inside the apartment, where I opened the coat closet to get my jacket and my gun in its holster. I had removed the bullets from the gun and left them lose in my jacket pocket.

"You're going to be careful, aren't you?" She was afraid. As afraid as Sophie and Leila and me.

I nodded as I put on my holster and patted my gun.

"I hate that you're carrying that." She pointed at my holster.

"Not more than I do." I decided to wait until I was out of the apartment to load the Glock. It would just upset her.

I found Eymen at the doorstep of Asgar's room, watching his son sleep. When he saw me come toward him, he closed the door and nodded toward his office.

"I'm not angry," he told me before I could say anything. "I'm scared."

"Yeah. Me too."

"You're never scared." Eymen didn't believe me.

"I'm scared all the time," I said sincerely. "They hurt me. They threatened my daughter. I want this to end."

Eymen nodded. "I'm not worried about Clara. No one will come after her and if they did, God help them. I'm worried about *you*."

"I see it all perfectly; there are two possible situations—one can do either this or that. My honest opinion and my friendly advice is this: do it or do not do it—you will regret both." I had used this Kierkegaard quote with Eymen before under other circumstances and he smiled.

I walked up to Eymen and hugged him. We stood together for a moment and then I stepped away.

"If you die doing this, Clara's going to take over the investigation and she's going to drag me in and . . . it will be a clusterfuck," he said, trying for humor and failing. "So . . . try not to get killed."

"I'm going to do my best."

He walked me to the door, and they both saw me off. I was down one flight of stairs when I heard Clara call out to me. She was leaning on the banister.

"Oh, Gabriel, if the car gets a single scratch, you don't have to worry about the Russians, I'll finish you," she promised cheerfully.

CHAPTER 20

Leila was waiting for me outside her apartment building on Nansensgade. I stopped the Porsche in front of her and popped open the trunk in the front for her luggage.

She was wearing a white summer dress, the kind that flowed around her. My chest tightened. She was one of the most beautiful women I had ever known and the decade that had gone by had not changed that or how it made me feel.

She's beautiful, and therefore to be wooed; she is a woman, therefore, to be won.

She had a straw hat with her, no doubt to keep her hair in place, because I had told her that if it wasn't raining, I was planning on driving with the top down regardless of the temperature. It wasn't often that I drove a car and very seldom that I drove a car as fancy as this one.

She had one Louis Vuitton travel bag, which I put in the trunk before settling behind the wheel. It was still light at ten in the evening but not bright enough for sunglasses, which was a shame because the car deserved fancy sunglasses.

"Ready?" I asked.

Leila nodded stiffly. She wasn't happy. I didn't know why and frankly didn't want to know and ruin this drive.

She remained silent as I navigated traffic to get on the E55 toward Gedser, where we'd catch the last ferry to Rostock. Leila had booked a ferry ticket so we could get onto the ferry because she'd not liked my idea of getting there and *figuring* it out.

She wasn't talking and I didn't mind. I liked the silence. I liked the power of the car, the sound, the feel, and even though she seemed annoyed, I enjoyed the presence of the beautiful woman who sat next to me.

We made it to Gedser right on time and got on the ferry without a wait. Once on the ferry, we left the car to go topside, where the stores and restaurants invited passengers to shop duty free and eat bad cafeteria-style food. It took an hour and a half to get to Rostock, and after that Berlin was just another two and a half hours away, considering the light traffic at night.

There weren't that many cars on the ferry and I refrained from remarking to Leila that even if she hadn't bought a ferry ticket in advance, we would've made it. It would've been childish.

At the restaurant, I ordered a beer for myself and a Johnnie Walker for Leila, which I brought to our table. We listened to the announcements and then once the ferry undocked and set sail, I decided to deal with the silent and annoyed Leila.

"You want to tell me why you're so pissed?"

She drank some of her whiskey and set her glass down. "My fiancé and I had a fight."

"About you coming with me?"

"Yes."

"Ah, he's probably worried that you'll do to him with me what you did to me with him," I said, and immediately regretted it. It had sounded a lot more satisfying in my head.

Her eyes went from shocked hurt, which I regretted, to anger, which I'd wanted to avoid in the first place.

"Yes." She was livid. "The men in my life think I'm a promiscuous slut who sleeps around with whomever."

Tricky, I thought. If I said something . . . anything . . . it would be disingenuous. So, I went with humor. "Not whomever, just *sexy* ex-boyfriends."

She didn't smile but she softened. "So, which one of you is sexy, him or you?"

"Obviously, me." I drank some beer and made a decision about Leila. It was time. I was letting her, and the past, go. "Look, I'm sorry this is causing you trouble. If you'd told me I'd have gone alone."

"I didn't want you to go alone." She was flustered for a moment and then shook her head, as if shaking away her thoughts. "Look . . . forget it. I contacted Louisa . . . Frau Weiß at BArch. I didn't tell her the real reason we want to see her, just made an appointment for nine in the morning, when the center opens. I thought it better to explain this face-to-face."

"And you're sure Sanne would have gone to BArch?"

"Yes." Leila was emphatic in her certainty. "Bundesarchiv would be the first stop for anyone who's working on World War Two history. And then we meet Dr. Sommer at one p.m."

We were silent for a moment and then, because I wanted to close out the topic of sleeping with ex-boyfriends, I added, "I booked us a suite with two bedrooms. I'm not trying to start anything up with you."

"I know."

"Tell your English boyfriend. I'm not interested in you."

She looked hurt, which for a moment thrilled me and then made me feel like a colossal ass. "English *fiancé*. And I have told him that."

"And you can also tell him that you're not interested in me."

She licked her lips and didn't respond.

"What?"

She sighed. "Nothing."

"Leila, you're giving me mixed signals and you have to stop doing that." I was suddenly weary. "I'm too fucking old and too fucking bald to deal with this kind of drama."

She looked at me and then smiled weakly. "I *am* interested in you. I . . . *you* left me. I didn't leave you, Gabriel."

"It's been a fucking decade, Leila."

"I know." She looked at me thoughtfully and then straightened, as if preparing to say something important. "Just because it's been a decade doesn't mean I don't feel anything. What I feel is what I feel. It's not an imposition on you and there's no expectation."

"Just fucking temptation." I took my baseball cap off to run my right hand over my bald head to cool it down.

"I'm sorry. I can lie to him and to you; but I can't lie to myself."

"Then why didn't you lie to me?" I demanded. "Damn it, Leila. I'm trying to get through this case alive. I don't have time for something out of a Jane Austen novel. Right now, we're acquaintances and you're my employer."

Leila took a deep breath and nodded. A thin sheen of tears coated her eyes. But she was controlling them so they didn't slide down her face, which was a good thing, I thought, because if she cried, she'd have me exactly where she wanted me, at her fucking feet.

"Did you *just* get over me?" Her voice was shaky. "Was it really that easy?"

I raised my eyebrows. "Leila, cut out the waterworks. I don't owe you answers, closure, or whatever else the fuck you're looking for. Let's do the job and then . . . we can go our separate ways."

That did the trick. If I'd gone with sympathy, she'd have gotten soft. Now she was pissed.

"Fine." Her voice was tight. "Do you think you could get me another whiskey?"

"Johnnie?"

"No."

"What kind?"

"Whatever they have that is the *most* expensive," she said peevishly.

"Of course. After all, you're the boss and you're paying."

THE AIR BETWEEN us was cooler than the wind around us, despite the temperature being in the mid-sixties and us driving two hundred kilometers an hour. I had turned on the heat a hundred kilometers ago, so that my hands wouldn't get cold. Leila had wrapped herself in what looked like a cashmere shawl and had closed her eyes. We didn't talk until we checked in and got into our suite.

"Do you feel like dinner?" I asked her.

"It's three in the morning, Gabriel."

"And?"

She sighed. "Good night." She went inside one of the bedrooms.

I guessed she'd chosen which room she wanted but she'd been hasty. I had the better view, I discovered. She had a view of the Berlin Television Tower while my room faced the River Spree and the Berlin Cathedral.

The suite had a living room and two bedrooms with their own bathrooms. I didn't know about Leila's bathroom, but mine came with a bathtub that I looked longingly at. We were here for two nights, and I didn't know if I'd have a chance to use it. The last time Leila and I had been in a bathtub was in a hotel in Prague, where we'd gone on one of the many long public holiday weekends in May. I shook the memories away. Ilse would tell me that this was normal, and I should remember those times without judging the present. Well, good for Ilse, I thought, but she wasn't in a fucking suite with Leila in the next bedroom. A bedroom with a bathtub. A bedroom with a bed. Leila on the bed.

She'd said she wasn't over our relationship. I had waited ten years to hear that, hadn't I? But now that she had said it, I didn't know what to do with it.

The sex had been amazing. I couldn't remember a lover with whom I had enjoyed sex as much as I had with Leila. Or maybe it was the memory, enhanced because of emotions, of feeling she was the one who got away.

I unpacked. Hung my clothes on hangers; put my underwear and socks away in the dresser. I always emptied my suitcase, even if I was staying for just a night in a hotel. I took a shower and got into bed naked. I checked my messages and there was one from Ulla, telling me she was safe in her friend's summerhouse, asking me to be careful. There was a message from Clara, telling me to have a good night, to take care of her car, and to be careful; and one from Sophie, telling me that she really liked Luc and Big Bo and that I should be careful.

I was sure I'd have trouble falling asleep because of the woman next door, but I surprised myself when I quickly and easily fell into a dreamless sleep.

CHAPTER 21

F rau Weiß, by name, sounded like an elderly stuffy woman; instead she was a flirty woman in her early forties who asked me to call her Louisa. She was tall, slender, and blond, with deep blue eyes and a wide mouth. She was in shape, and I'd guess she lifted weights on a regular basis, because the arms she showed off in a silk blouse didn't come for free. She was attractive.

Louisa hugged Leila and asked her about a case that they'd worked on together in the past.

"They were very happy to find their painting in a museum in Köln," Leila said to Louisa in German. "A client was looking for his grandmother's painting by Max Liebermann and Louisa helped me recover it for them," she added for my benefit, still in German.

I knew of Max Liebermann, a German-Jewish Impressionist, whose *Two Riders on the Beach* was among one of the finest works that the Nazis had stolen. The painting was sold in 2015 by David Toren, one of the heirs of the original owner, for an exorbitant amount of money at Sotheby's. The painting was not as famous as Gustav Klimt's *Portrait of Adele Bloch-Bauer I*, another painting that the Nazis had stolen, but the painting by Liebermann was remarkable, and had made an impression on me when I had read about it some years ago.

Louisa shook hands with me when Leila introduced us. I liked a woman with a firm handshake.

She took us into her office, an airy room with lots of glass and light. I had imagined that the Bundesarchiv would be a dingy place with people walking around like drones, but Louisa's office was beautifully decorated with art pieces and showed off her PhD diploma in German art history from the Humboldt-Universität zu Berlin.

"How can I help you?" she asked after she'd served us coffee from her Nespresso machine. Leila took hers with cream, while I drank it black and missed my morning cigarette. But I didn't smoke when I traveled, so I clamped the desire, or I knew I'd be finding a *tabak* to buy smokes to scratch my itch—and one cigarette would turn into a whole pack.

Leila explained to her that we were following in Sanne Melgaard's footsteps and asked if she could shed any light on her activities at the BArch.

Louisa scrunched her nose. "You say this was five years ago?"

"Yes," Leila confirmed.

"That was before my time." Louisa thought about it for a moment and then picked up her office phone.

"May I request that you join me in my office," she said and then laughed and added, "I will definitely make sure you have a cup of coffee."

She hung up the phone and rose, her wide mouth curved into a broad smile. "*He* likes my Nespresso."

He was Herr Schmidt, a man in his late seventies. He was spry and caught up very quickly on what we were after. He had patchy white hair on his mostly bald head and wore round glasses. The weight of his age hadn't curved his spine. He wore suspenders, which was quirky and old-fashioned. I liked his style.

"A Danish politician." He nodded thoughtfully. He spoke German with a strong Upper Bavarian accent that told me he was probably from Munich.

Leila showed him a picture of Sanne Melgaard on her phone, and his eyes lit up.

"Yes, yes," Herr Schmidt acknowledged. "She came here several times. She wanted some records that were restricted. I couldn't help her."

"Do you know what she was looking for?" Leila asked.

Herr Schmidt nodded. "She was interested in records of Danes who were Nazi collaborators. But I told her most of that data was not with us here. It was probably with the Danmarks Nationalsocialistiske Arbejderparti or in some restricted files somewhere."

Danmarks Nationalsocialistiske Arbejderparti, DNSAP or the Danish Nazi Party, supported the German invasion and occupation of Denmark and received financial and political support from the German Nazi Party. They were not favored by the Danish public, and the story went that when they tried to have a rally during the German occupation, the Danes rose against them and the members of DNSAP had to be protected from physical harm by the Danish police.

However, after the war, the members of the party had not been able to prevent the onslaught of hate that came their way, and neither could the Nazi collaborators. Young men and women from the Danish resistance took to the streets after the Germans left and exacted their anger on whomever they thought had collaborated with Nazis. It had been punishment without due process. I had seen the pictures in documentaries and magazines of Danish prostitutes who had had sex with German soldiers, forced or oth-

erwise, being stripped, shorn of their hair, raped, publicly humiliated, and beaten.

"We gave her access to what we had, but she wanted some *very* specific material." Herr Schmidt screwed his eyes as if trying to remember.

We waited.

Herr Schmidt drank his coffee, and then as if it came to him, he smiled. "Yes, she wanted to know about young Danish men from the resistance who had been covert collaborators. Now, we'd not have that information because double agent archives from Den-mark were handled very discreetly by the Gestapo. I directed her to Dr. Oskar Sommer at the Friedrich Meinecke Institute of His-tory, as he's been doing some research on collaborators."

He sat back, satisfied with himself. "I haven't seen her in a long while. How is she?"

"I'm sorry to say, she's dead. She was murdered," Leila told him.

He gasped. "No! That can't be. I am so sorry to hear that. Mur-dered? By whom? Why?"

"She was a tough politician . . . she made some enemies."

He sighed. "Would you like me to give you the materials we gave her? I probably still have them in a folder on the server. I can give you a USB stick with all of it."

"That would be great, Herr Schmidt. Thank you," Leila said enthusiastically.

When Herr Schmidt went to get the USB stick, Louisa told us, "He has been here forever, and I mean forever. Refuses to retire and we'd be fools to let him go. He knows where everything is."

"We cannot thank you enough for this help. Maybe we could take you out to dinner tonight." I had not planned on asking her to join us, but it had felt right *and* I didn't want to be alone with Leila.

Louisa grinned at me. "As it happens, I am free tonight."

I tipped my black fedora at her, smiled, and avoided looking at Leila. I pulled out my card, which simply had my name, phone number, and email address on it, and gave it to her.

She looked at it and put it down on the table. "I'll make dinner reservations at my favorite restaurant and text you both. And after, *maybe* you can take me to my favorite bar for a nightcap."

She was responding to my invitation with her own.

I nodded with a smile and continued to avoid looking at Leila.

"IT'S LIKE YOU'RE a man whore," Leila accused when we stopped to have lunch at a café close to Dr. Oskar Sommer's office. We had an hour and a half to kill, so we'd decided to eat while going through the contents of the USB stick that Herr Schmidt had given us.

"I was being polite."

"Oh please." Leila snorted. "And what, you're going to bring her into our suite and . . ."

I raised my hand, perversely enjoying myself. "I'm assuming she has her own place and if we reach a point where we want to spend the night together, I'll make sure you're not put in an awkward position."

"Will you sleep with a woman you just met?" she demanded.

When I didn't answer because I didn't think it would be constructive, she turned toward the waiter. "I'll have a glass of the Scharzhofberger Riesling. A big glass. And I'll have the grilled halibut."

"Yes, Frau." The waiter looked at me.

"I'll have a beer . . . whatever you have on tap."

"We have a *hefeweizen* called Weihenstephan Hefe Weissbier, it's very refreshing, made by the oldest brewery in the world, Weihenstephan, which has been making *hefeweizens* since 1040." The waiter knew his beer.

"That sounds great. I'll wait until you're back with our drinks to order lunch."

The waiter took Leila's menu and left to fill our drinks order.

She shook her head. "Sleep with whomever you like."

"It's just a thank-you dinner, Leila," I said softly. "I'm not a hormonal teenager. I don't need to have sex every night or even every other night."

"You're right." She rubbed her temples with her fingers. "I'm being ridiculous . . . even maybe a little like a hormonal teenager."

My laptop beeped then. I had downloaded all the files from the USB onto my computer and backed it up to the cloud using my mobile phone as a hotspot.

"Well, this is interesting." I scanned the titles of the documents. My reading German was less rusty than my spoken German and I opened a document called *Service Record_Hauptsturmführer Fritz Diekmann.*

Leila leaned over to see the document. "A service record?"

I nodded. "Herr Diekmann was a Hauptsturmführer in the Schutzstaffel in Copenhagen. What rank is Hauptsturmführer? I can't keep them straight."

"A captain . . . in the Schutzstaffel, the SS," Leila filled in.

"If he was in Copenhagen, he probably worked for Karl Heinz Hoffmann, head of the Gestapo in Denmark."

Sturmbannführer Karl Heinz Hoffmann, one of the most famous Gestapo officers in Denmark, who also had the distinction of being one of the Germans who was sentenced to death by the Copenhagen City Court. He'd killed hundreds of Danish resistance fighters and tortured them in Shellhus in Copenhagen, which was used as Gestapo headquarters. However, he was pardoned a few years later and then deported to West Germany. He died in 1975, after living a long life, giving interviews and being an unrepentant asshole.

I opened several other service records. "All these SS officers were posted in Denmark from 1944 to 1945."

"All of them?" she asked.

Before I could answer, the waiter came back with our drinks. I ordered a steak, medium-rare, with potatoes and asparagus.

"She was identifying officers who were stationed in Denmark during the occupation." I scrolled through the files and then pulled one up. "This document talks about something called office IV B4."

Leila looked at the document. "This is Eichmannreferat."

"In Danish please?"

"These were the officers who worked on the Jewish problem, as they liked to call it," she explained. "This office coordinated deportation of Jews from all over Europe to concentration camps and killing sites."

I scanned further and read out a report title, "*Storm Afdeling.*"

"Storm Troopers," Leila said. "DNSAP was not successful in Denmark, except when it came to recruiting members for Waffen-SS and Frikorps Danmark. Did you know that nearly twelve thousand Danes fought with the Germans against the Russians?"

"That's a lot of Danes."

Leila nodded. "Waffen-SS recruited nearly half a million non-Germans and Germans living outside of Germany, both as volunteers and conscripts during the war."

"They forced young men to join the German army. A lot of young men who probably died in the Russian winter."

I randomly opened documents and one caught my eye. "This is a list of names of Danish Nazi collaborators. Just a hundred or so. That can't be it."

"No." Leila sipped her wine. "My friend Martin Jäger, he's the head of the History Department at Roskilde University—he's been petitioning the Danish government to open the archives that contain the names of *all* Nazi collaborators in Denmark. He believes there are probably more than two hundred thousand names in the archive; Danes from all walks of life."

"Why are the archives not open?"

"It's under an eighty-year rule," Leila told me. "And this is going to blow your mind. Martin, who is excitable about World War Two Danish history, believes that they won't open these records even after we hit the eighty-year mark because big business and political figures may be compromised. Maybe even the royal family."

"I can't imagine anyone today caring about who collaborated with the Nazis over seventy years ago."

"I think there are many who want justice seen, even if it comes decades late. Do you remember Helmuth Leif Rasmussen?"

I nodded. In 2015, the Danish government decided not to prosecute Helmuth Leif Rasmussen, which caused quite a stir. Granted, he was in his nineties, but during the war he had been a guard at the Waldlager forest camp in Bobruysk in Belarus. Jews too sick, fatigued, or malnourished to work were shot in the back of the head and buried in the graves they had been forced to dig for themselves.

"I don't remember the details. What was the evidence against Helmuth Leif Rasmussen?"

"A Jewish human rights organization, the Simon Wiesenthal Center, presented Danish authorities with a dossier of Helmuth's crimes . . . and it was detailed. Helmuth himself confessed that he was in Waldlager, so it wasn't like a he said, she said situation." Leila sounded a little disgusted.

Our food arrived and we started to dig in. I was hungry, as I hadn't eaten breakfast and was running on less sleep than I was normally used to.

"But they didn't prosecute him." I wasn't asking. It was a fact.

"Because he was old, they said." Leila cut into flaky fish and speared it atop her fork. "Peter Skaarup from the Dansk Folkeparti, Sanne's colleague and good friend, wanted Helmuth prosecuted. According to him, if you have to punish the Islamic State's Danish henchmen for going to war, then you also have to go after people like Helmuth."

"Maybe Sanne also believed that." I wondered. "Maybe she was digging up information about another Helmuth."

"Maybe." Leila drank some wine.

I steadily ate and set my knife and fork down to wash good steak down with good beer. "But he was ninety years old and sure, people were upset, but it wasn't something that anyone would kill over."

"But what if Helmuth was . . . I don't know, the cousin of the queen?" Leila asked. "Or the father of a famous Dane, someone with lots of influence and money. What if Sanne found something no one knew about? A resistance fighter who was a collaborator?"

"And, what? The family is working with Mikkel Thorsen to make sure her book doesn't see the light of day?"

"Maybe . . . just maybe, Sanne Melgaard was killed because of this, and it had nothing to do with Yousef," Leila said, her eyes bright. I loved this Leila. I *had* loved this Leila. This passionate Leila.

Since I had met her again, she'd worn a stiff demeanor, making me forget the carefree and exuberant woman I had known. But here she was, all masks gone, all barriers fallen.

As if underscoring the fall of her façade, she took the hair tie holding her hair away from her face and slid it in a practiced motion onto her right wrist like a bracelet. She wore an elegant dark suit with a snow-white silk camisole; feeling energized, she took the jacket off and I gawked like a teenager. God, she was a beautiful woman with that smooth cinnamon skin, wide mouth, and delicate nose.

I felt an ache in my heart, a dull pain that told me it used to once upon a time beat with great emotion for this woman . . . and given half a chance, still could.

She set her plate aside, having finished her food before me. "May I?" she asked, and I pushed my computer toward her.

Her fingers moved over the keyboard and opened files, scanned them, and closed them. I watched her while I ate, drank my beer, and tried to keep my prurient memories of us together in various carnal positions at bay.

"I am certain she was writing a book about Nazi collaborators," Leila said confidently. "Who do you think she was going to expose? The queen? A politician?"

Mikkel Thorsen's involvement meant that it probably was someone high up.

"In a few years, the records will open, the eighty-year rule will be passed. This is just postponing the grand reveal."

"Be interesting to see what Dr. Sommer has to tell us. Oh, Gabriel, do you think we're getting close to getting Yousef off?" she asked hopefully.

"You're getting *way* ahead of your skis, Leila," I warned. "We have a bunch of hunches and unconnected documents. She might have been writing an innocuous book. Yousef Ahmed might have still killed her. What happened to his son was horrific, I can understand that." But after meeting him I didn't feel it in my gut. The man I had met was a . . . well, he had been a gentle man, an honorable one. But as a PI, I didn't always entirely rely on my gut; trust it I did, but I also verified.

CHAPTER 22

At Koserstraße we found public parking and walked into the Friedrich Meinecke Institute of History fifteen minutes before our appointment with Dr. Sommer. The Department of History and Cultural Studies was a large, modern, imposing building with clean lines and lots of windows. The lobby area was buzzing with life, students with backpacks, men in suits, women in formal office wear, and hives of conversation.

A young woman was sitting at the pristine administration desk and smiled a big toothy smile at us. The nameplate in front of her desk said Petra Fischer. She was probably in her late twenties—blond and blue eyed, with an ample bosom in her tight black knit T-shirt tucked into a body-hugging skirt. Her jacket was draped around her chair. I couldn't see her legs, but they promised to be as delightful-looking as the woman.

"How can I help you?" she asked in German.

Leila told her we had an appointment to see Dr. Oskar Sommer.

Petra looked through her computer and then said, "I'm sorry, he isn't in today."

"We have an appointment with him," Leila asserted.

"We talked to him just yesterday," I told the woman in my rusty German.

She looked again and shrugged. "I don't have access to his calendar. Let me try his mobile phone."

We waited.

She was smiling at us as she called, shifting her headset as she did. "*Hallo, Herr Dr. Sommer?*"

She listened and as she did, her smile faded. She spoke in short sentences that didn't tell us much but by the time she hung up, her face was pale.

"That . . . that was the police," she stammered. "Herr Dr. Sommer is dead."

Leila stared at her for a long moment. "Dead. As in *dead*?"

The young woman nodded and then burst into tears.

"I'm so sorry." I leaned toward her but kept my hands to myself, even though I wanted to pat her shoulder to comfort her.

"Can you give us his address? We'd like to go pay our respects." Leila wasn't feeling like comforting her.

She stared at Leila for a moment and then me. I smiled my best *I'm harmless* smile and then, even though it was against the rules, she gave his address to us. Probably because she was in shock rather than because of my smile. But I decided not to hold that against her.

The dead professor lived on Brandenburgische Straße in the affluent area of Charlottenburg, five kilometers from the institute. I knew Berlin well enough and knew that Charlottenburg boasted big houses, beautiful architecture, and the Charlottenburg Palace. It was the area where one lived to avoid the more bohemian, urban, and progressive neighborhoods in south and east Berlin, such as the Kreuzberg district, which I preferred.

The professor's apartment building, Haus Brandenburg, originally built in 1910, was a designer's paradise and had been completely renovated. The area was lined with snobbish specialty shops, restaurants, and plazas. I hated it immediately.

"It seems like a horrible coincidence, doesn't it, that he's dead right when we come to see him?" Leila sat in the car as if she were waiting for some clue as to our next steps.

"Let's find out. If the police are still in his apartment, maybe we can learn something," I suggested.

Leila nodded, her gaze still unfocused. Then, as if giving herself a mental kick, she shook her head to disperse the uncertainty and got out of the car.

Because I remembered that Leila got claustrophobic in elevators, I didn't pause in front of it and took the stairs with her to the third floor.

Two policemen were standing guard outside the apartment and inside we saw a woman sitting on a sofa crying before the apartment door was closed by one of the policemen, blocking our view.

Leila told the policemen who we were and that we had an appointment with Dr. Sommer. She stressed the fact that she was a lawyer and glossed over the fact that the appointment was at his office and not his home. We looked innocent. I thought we carried it off well enough.

One of the uniformed policemen went inside the apartment and then came out with a man wearing a boring off-the-rack dark gray suit. He introduced himself as Werner Kaiser, a detective from the Kriminalpolizei, or Kripo. We introduced ourselves and all of us shook hands.

"You had a meeting with him here at this time?" Werner asked.

I shrugged. "Well . . . in his office but . . ."

Werner was a tall blond man and looked like he worked out a lot in his spare time, and he clearly had plenty of spare time. He had short military-style hair and his shoes were the kind of black, comfortable, ugly shoes worn the world over by policemen. I had thrown mine out with deep and dark pleasure when I'd given up the uniform.

I was wearing a gray suit like the Kripo detective, but mine was by Giorgio Armani, and my shoes, dark gray Berluti Scritto leather slip-ons, were as far as you could get from cop shoes. I had left my gray Worth & Worth fedora and my Christian Dior tie in the Porsche. I felt adequately dressed.

"Do you have a card?" the German detective asked.

Leila gave him hers.

Werner read the card and looked at us thoughtfully. "Why don't we get some coffee and discuss this? Please wait for me at Park-café Berlin, it's around the corner."

We walked to the café and found an outdoor table. Once seated, I called Tommy and told him what was going on.

"Dead? You kill him?" he asked.

"Yeah, and I'm calling you to confess," I said dryly.

"I'll call my contact at Kripo. Text me the name of the guy you're talking to," Tommy said and disconnected.

I decided to get a beer because coffee was just not going to cut it. A man we were supposed to meet about Sanne Melgaard was dead. Murdered. It didn't feel right to drink coffee to calm my nerves.

Leila ordered tea, something to calm *her* nerves, I presumed.

"Is it me or . . . does it feel like something weird is going on?" she asked.

"Something weird *is* going on," I agreed and took a long swallow of the *hefeweizen* a young waiter had brought for me with some relief.

Leila looked around to see if the detective was coming and then spoke in a low voice. "I think we should drop this case and walk away. People are dying. Let's just leave. Now. I don't want to meet this detective. I don't want to do this anymore."

"He may have died of something innocuous. Maybe a heart attack."

"It's a bit convenient. Don't you think?"

"I don't think Dr. Sommer thought it was convenient." I sighed when she glared at me. "Let's talk to this guy. Maybe we'll find out something." Because as of now I had nothing on the case except a dead person who wasn't going to tell me anything.

I was halfway through my beer when Werner Kaiser found his way to our table. He waved a hand at a waiter and pointed to my beer. The waiter nodded.

"I've been up since four in the morning," he explained.

"You deserve a beer." My phone beeped then, and I looked at the text from Tommy.

Contact says Werner Kaiser is good to go. That meant two things: one, that the detective would cooperate with us, and two, we could trust him.

"My boss got a call from a Copenhagen police chief," Werner spoke in German. "You're a fellow officer."

"Former," I corrected.

The beer arrived and Werner mumbled *Danke* to the waiter.

"What did you want with Herr Dr. Sommer?"

Leila folded her arms. Lawyer mode. "We wanted to talk to him about a case my firm is working on. Mr. Præst is our investigator."

Werner sipped his beer and released a sigh of contentment. "The first sip is always magic," he said in satisfaction, and then proceeded to bring out cigarettes from the inside breast pocket of his suit jacket and waved at the waiter to bring him an ashtray.

We all waited while the ashtray was produced, and Werner lit a cigarette.

I looked longingly at the cigarette and then focused on not smoking. *Two cigarettes a day when you're at home and none when you travel, Præst,* I told myself. *Any more than that and you'll become a chain smoker and die of lung cancer.*

"Can you tell me what the case was about?" Werner took a long drag, and I made an effort not to let my nose get too close to his face.

Leila licked her lips, as if thinking about what to reveal. "We wanted to talk to Herr Dr. Sommer about some research he had been doing on World War Two."

Werner smiled crookedly. "Everyone in the History Department in every university in Germany is doing some sort of research on World War Two, the Cold War, and the Nazis."

"He was doing specific research on Danes who collaborated with the Nazis," Leila insisted.

"Okay," Werner said encouragingly.

"How did he die?" My German was getting a little better as I used it and heard it, but it was far from good.

"He was murdered," Werner announced without fanfare. "This morning, his wife, the CEO of a tech company, returned from a business trip to New York and found him spread out on their blood-soaked three-thousand-thread-count Egyptian cotton sheets. His throat was slit with a sharp knife, expertly. I doubt he made a sound or felt a thing. The poor bastard was dead before he knew it."

Leila's hands shook when she picked up her teacup. I didn't blame her. My fingers, resting against the pilsner glass, weren't entirely steady.

"It was a professional job," Werner continued. "They picked

the lock. The security cameras outside the building might have caught something, but I'm not going to hold my breath. There were none inside the building . . . privacy and all that. The death occurred around one in the morning, according to the medical examiner."

"Anything missing from the house?" I wanted to know.

"Sure. They tossed stuff. Some jewelry, money, things like that are gone. Safe was open . . . not a difficult lock. It was empty, cleaned out."

"But . . ." I prompted.

"But they forgot to take his wife's diamond ring, which was sitting next to her hairbrush." Werner grinned. "Seems to me like the robbery was an afterthought, the killer's heart wasn't in it."

"Or they wanted what was in the safe," I speculated. "Do we know what was in the safe?"

Werner shrugged. "The wife said some papers and such. No cash or jewelry. She may tell us more after she wakes up. She was hysterical. She's sleeping off a sedative at the DRK Kliniken on Spandauer Damm."

"Who was the woman in the apartment?" Leila asked. "The one who was crying?"

"Colleague." Werner didn't explain further.

"Colleague?" I queried.

Werner smiled. "She was visiting the good professor for breakfast. The wife wasn't expected until tomorrow morning, but she came early to surprise her husband—and the *colleague*, thankfully, came after the wife and the police showed up."

"Name of the colleague?" I asked.

"I showed you mine." Werner crushed his cigarette and immediately lit another.

I tamped down my cigarette urge once again and looked

at Leila. She was the lawyer; she'd decide what we should and shouldn't tell him.

Leila cleared her throat and spoke clearly. "We don't know how everything connects."

"I'm taking a chance telling you something I'm not supposed to tell a civilian," Werner observed. "I'm putting my job on the line because I think what you needed from the victim might very well be connected to why he's dead. I mean, he's a boring fucking professor who's diddling a colleague while his wife is away. Why would anyone want him dead?"

"Except the wife," I chimed in.

Werner nodded. "We'll look into that. But I don't think so. Call it a policeman's hunch."

Leila sat up straight. "Five years ago, a Danish politician was murdered."

"Muslim immigrant killed a right-wing politician." Werner drank his beer. "I remember."

"Yousef Ahmed was convicted of killing Sanne Melgaard." Leila licked her lips again. She did that when she was nervous.

"Tommy says he's okay," I encouraged Leila.

She nodded in relief. "Sanne Melgaard was apparently researching Danish Nazi collaborators and writing a book that no one can find or even really knows about. Recently, Sanne's sister received a letter from the dead Herr Doctor that he had found some information in recently unlocked archives."

"We booked a meeting, saying we wanted to talk about his research and were hoping to find out what he knew," I added.

Werner nodded. "Sounds like a Hollywood thriller."

"More confusing than thrilling," I noted.

"Seems possible he was killed because he knew something but . . . what could he know that no one else knows? It's the Wiki era, everyone knows everything. There are no secrets left to hide." Werner finished his beer and stood up. "The woman he was having an affair with is Frau Dr. Monica Franke. Also works at the Friedrich Meinecke Institute of History."

He pulled out a card and wrote something on the back of it and gave it to Leila. "Call me if you find out anything relevant to my case."

After he left, I saw he'd written Monica Franke's address on the back of his card.

I smiled. "I think we have our next lead."

CHAPTER 23

eila took some calls in her bedroom after we came back to the hotel, and I went for a run. The River Spree had a walking, running, and bike path that was popular; I started my run at Marschallbrücke close to the Reichstag and followed the river bank up to Hansabrücke and then back again from there to the Marschall bridge. It was a nice eight-kilometer run; a little longer than the six around the Copenhagen lakes, which I went around twice every morning.

I liked running by the water, especially a river where there were boats and activity. And it was a great way to see Berlin. By the time I got back, I was sweating both from the run and the heat. I could hear a murmur from Leila's room, which meant she was still working. I took a shower and got ready. I decided that the occasion called for a tan Ann Demeulemeester cotton and linen tailored blazer with matching pants. I would have gone with just my white button down, without the blazer, but I had a gun to hide. I paired the suit with a ready-for-summer Fawler Panama hat with a navy band and a pair of navy suede Milano loafers.

I knocked on Leila's door and looked in after I heard her say,

"It's open." She was sitting at the desk, still wearing the suit she'd worn all day, in front of a laptop.

"I'm going to walk to the restaurant." We were to meet Louisa for dinner at a "traditional German restaurant," Lutter & Wegner on Charlottenstraße, a twenty-minute walk from the hotel. I didn't invite her to walk with me. I was giving her a choice. I was only a little disappointed when she said she'd take an Uber, as she still had some work to get through.

She didn't say how handsome I looked. I decided that was probably because she was distracted with work.

I picked up a tail almost as soon as I left the hotel lobby. It was a man in jeans and a T-shirt. I couldn't make out his face, but his black T-shirt had an image of a scorpion in white with the word SCORPIONS, I presumed in honor of the German band that was famous for the song "Wind of Change."

I walked around the streets as an aimless tourist. I had an hour to get to the restaurant. I had time. The man kept pace with me. I went into a men's clothing store, picked up a random jacket, and walked into the fitting room. I put on the new jacket and walked out as if to see how it looked. In the long mirror, I saw the man searching for me. I leaned against a wall to avoid him seeing me, discarded the jacket I had tried on, and walked between the hangers and suits to come up behind the young man. On the way, I picked up a black marker from a counter.

"*Hallo.*" I poked the marker into the small of his back. The man froze. "How's it going?" I asked in German and then slowly pulled out his wallet, which was peeking out of the back pocket of his jeans.

"Steady," I warned when the man moved.

His ID card told me he was eighteen and his name was Marcus Graf. Obviously, the kid was an amateur who couldn't tell the butt of a gun or a knife point from a Magic Marker, but I didn't want to pull out my baby Glock in a clothing store for a teenager.

"Marcus, why are you following me?" I put his wallet back in his pocket.

Marcus was shaking slightly. "Someone asked me to."

"Who?"

Marcus was quiet, so I poked the marker into his back some more. "My cousin. Okay?"

"Name?"

"Sergio," he mumbled.

I pulled the marker away and then turned him to face me. He was pale, and I could see he still had pimples. This kid was younger than Sophie.

"Go home." I moved my jacket just a little so he could see my gun holster.

Marcus stood shocked, his breath coming out in small gasps.

"*Abhauen*," I said in German. *Scram*. And he did as he was told.

As I found my way to Lutter & Wegner, where Louisa promised we would experience traditional German cuisine, I called Werner.

"Do you know a Sergio . . . last name may be Graf?"

"Sure." Werner was smoking, I could hear it. "Volga German . . . German Russians, lots of Russian Mafia connections. Bad guy."

"His cousin, a pimple-faced kid named Marcus Graf, was following me, told me that his cousin asked him to do so," I explained.

"That is not a good thing. Sergio is a *really* bad guy."

"I got that the first time you said it."

"Never heard of Marcus, must have just come from the old country. I have no idea why Sergio would be interested in you,"

Werner said cheerfully. "But then, I don't know what kind of trouble you're in back home. But if Sergio is interested, it could only mean that you've pissed off someone in the Russian Mafia, and they work across Europe. They're collaborative that way. But Sergio is not top tier, he's more your street thug variety."

"I'm a lowly private investigator who mostly takes pictures of people fucking people who they're not married to," I put forth. "The only case I'm working on that's off that beaten path is this one."

And the Christina Hassing case, I remembered. Could this be about that and not Yousef Ahmed?

"And apparently, while the professor's throat was being slit, someone made a mess in his office."

"Define mess."

"All his files were taken . . . and his hard drive was busted," Werner revealed. "The IT geeks think they cleaned out the hard drive before they banged it around."

"I think there might be a connection between his death and the mess in his office."

"No shit." Werner's tone was mirthless. "Did they teach you this stuff in private eye school?"

"You know, I'm probably the best private eye in the world." I was copying the famous Carlsberg slogan: *Probably the best beer in the world.*

"I recommend you use your eyes to watch your back. Better still, get out of Berlin." Werner ignored my Carlsberg comment, which I thought was a superior one and deserved some recognition.

"Great." I beamed. "What does Kripo do besides ask innocent people being followed by hoodlums to leave the city?"

"Sometimes, we investigate. But mostly we sit on our asses and do paperwork." I heard the click of a lighter.

I grinned. I liked Herr Kaiser.

"Let me know what shakes loose when you talk to Sergio."

"What makes you think I'd be doing that?" he asked and hung up.

Lutter & Wegner was all dark wood and large picture windows. It was a wine shop, delicatessen, and restaurant in one and had a large terrace, where I found the beautiful Louisa Weiß, wearing a pair of very tight jeans and high heels with a strappy blouse, showing off those well-toned arms.

"Leila is on her way," I told her as we shook hands and sat down.

She bit her lower lip thoughtfully, a flirtatious smile playing on her lips. "I asked Leila and she told me you're single. How come you're single?"

I laughed. "I need a drink before I answer that question."

She ordered a kir royale while I ordered a dry martini. It was a pleasant warm evening, perfect for a cocktail.

"I could say I haven't met the right woman."

"Leila also told me you have a twenty-year-old daughter."

"Her mother wasn't the right woman," I admitted.

"You must have had her young." Louisa's blue eyes were stunning, and she'd done something with eye makeup to make them even better.

"I was twenty-one and so was my daughter's mother," I explained neutrally. "We were kids with a kid. It didn't last. She's married to a lawyer now. I have my office in his firm and do work for him. I'm married to a town house I've been renovating for ten years."

"Really? I'm renovating a beach house in Rügen." Louisa was happy to change the topic.

"I have been to Rügen," I told her. "It's a lovely island. How long have you been renovating the place?"

We talked a little about the struggles of finding good contractors and other travails we home renovators experienced.

"Do you know why I'm single?" she asked after we had told all our renovation stories and the waiter had brought our drinks.

"*Prost.*" I touched my glass to hers before taking a sip of my drink.

"*Prost.* I'm single because I am waiting for my soul mate."

"That's a good thing to wait for," I agreed.

"Don't worry, you're not my soul mate. At least I don't think so." Her eyes were bright with humor.

"Now I feel cheap."

With that, the conversation moved away from relationships to everything else and we were laughing when Leila arrived. She wore a cream-colored sundress that hugged her lightly in all the right places. The stunning Frau could hold no candle to Leila, who had hardly any makeup on. Her hair was coiled in a loose bun and she smelled like delicate roses.

Præst, you have it bad.

"Murdered?" Louisa gasped when we told her about Dr. Sommer. "I hadn't heard."

"Do you know a Monica Franke?" I asked.

She thought about it and shrugged. "Probably. At the BArch we know most people doing historical research in Berlin . . . but then there are a lot of historians who focus on World War Two."

The evening ended pleasantly. Louisa and I didn't flirt with each other, and I declined her offer of a nightcap in her favorite bar, and she declined my offer of a drink at our hotel bar. The spark was just not there.

Leila was vaguely annoyed with me. She'd have been *obviously* annoyed if I'd gone with Louisa for a nightcap. In any case, I didn't want that. Instead, I had a drink with Leila on the terrace of our hotel bar.

"You look very beautiful," I said to her after the waiter brought our drinks. I got a Laphroaig 10 neat while Leila had Johnnie.

"You don't look too bad yourself. Flamboyant but understated."

"Always." I grinned. "Thank you for coming with me. I don't think BArch would've been as helpful without you."

"I don't know, Louisa seemed to want to be *close* friends with you," Leila remarked and then lifted a hand. "I'm joking, okay?"

"You're not joking," I said easily but firmly. "You're poking at me to see what shakes loose. What are you trying to find out? Just ask."

She looked sheepish. "I'm sorry. I'm behaving like a jealous adolescent."

"Yes." I smiled at her. She smiled back.

"I do have a question." Leila licked her lips and didn't wait for me to agree to answer her question. "Did the end hurt you? It hurt me. It can sometimes still hurt if I think about it."

I sighed. "That was then, and this is now."

"Yes."

"Then we were together, now you're engaged to someone else."

"Yes."

"Are you happily engaged?"

"Yes."

"Well, fuck."

"Now you're joking . . . are you?" Leila was hesitant. The uncertainty in her eyes made me wonder if she truly was happily engaged. But the fact was that she was engaged.

"I am." I wasn't sure if I was joking. I wanted her. But not like this. Not when she was wearing another man's ring. I had rules. Sleeping with a woman who was engaged, married, or in any other form of a committed relationship was against the rules, no matter how tempting the woman.

I changed the conversation, not wanting to dwell. She let me because, I thought, she didn't want to dwell either.

CHAPTER 24

Monica Franke let us into her apartment after we introduced ourselves. Her eyes were red-rimmed, and she looked as if she'd spent the night crying. She was in her early thirties, and when she wasn't disheveled, she was probably an attractive voluptuous woman. Her blond hair was loose around her shoulders, unkempt, and she wore a pair of black yoga pants with a gray T-shirt.

"Oskar was going to get a divorce," she said after we settled on her dark burgundy sofa set. "His wife had money, but they didn't have love. She worked all the time. And that's not who Oskar is . . . was."

She insisted on serving coffee, which she placed on an ornate coffee table in between us. She sat on the three-person sofa, while Leila sat on the two-person loveseat, and I sat on a chair. She poured coffee into cups, declining my offer to do so. It appeared she needed to do something with her hands, which were not entirely steady.

"We're really sorry for your loss." I took the coffee cup she offered.

Her eyes filled with tears as she handed a second cup to Leila. She didn't pour one for herself.

"When I got there, I knew something was wrong. The police were there, and *she* was there. I waited until she was gone and then talked to the police. I had to know what happened. I was in Hamburg last night and only came by train this morning. We were going to spend the day together, as we did when she traveled. On days when we didn't have classes, we got together. Mostly here, but he said he wanted to be in his apartment because he had some papers in his safe he needed for his work. I should've said no, asked him to stay at my place for the night. That's what we should've done. Then they could've burgled the apartment and he'd be alive."

Leila went to sit next to Monica as she cried and put her arm around her. Monica leaned in and wept.

"When you love a married man, you can't grieve openly," Monica sobbed. "I can talk to no one about this. No one. My family will be mortified. My colleagues will judge me. It's just so hard."

"Monica, the police don't think this was a burglary," I voiced softly. "They left a diamond ring that was out in the open. Someone was there to kill him."

Monica looked up at me, horrified. "But why would someone do that?"

"Oskar sent a Facebook message to a woman named Ulla Bernsen in Denmark," I shared. "He said he'd found out something in recently released World War Two documents that he wanted to share with her."

Monica nodded. "Yes. This is about the politician who was killed."

"Yes." I waited as my blood pumped faster.

"She came to see him years ago and she wanted to get records that were not in BArch about Danish collaborators." Monica sniffled. "Specifically, about a collaborator involved in the deportation of Danish Jews."

"To the ghetto in Theresienstadt?" Leila queried.

"Yes." Monica wiped her tears with a tissue. "Jews were hiding all over Denmark and many went to Sweden. The Danish Jews who died, were killed either in Theresienstadt or while they were escaping to Sweden. The Danish politician wanted to know how those Danish Jews who were sent to Theresienstadt had been found by the Gestapo."

"Would there be record of something like this?" I asked.

Monica snorted. "The Nazis were the only army in the world that documented all their misdeeds. Every one of them. Some we can find at BArch and other archives, some disappeared, and some are in other countries, but everything was documented at one time or another."

"What did Oskar find?"

She shrugged. "I don't really know." She then looked at me and asked, "He died because of this, you think?"

"I can't say for sure but it's possible."

"Is my life in danger?"

"If you know about his work, then maybe." I didn't want to lie to her and put her at risk.

Monica's eyes closed for a moment and her voice was tremulous. "What should I do?"

"I know a detective at Kripo," I assured her. "I can call him. They'll keep you safe . . . until . . . we figure out what happened to Oskar."

She digested what I'd said and then she stood up, went to a cabinet, and pulled out a bottle of vodka. She brought three shot glasses to the table and filled them. We all drank a shot.

"I don't know what he found. I have been busy with a conference I had to present at. But I have all his papers at home. He worked here quite a lot, so we could be together during the week."

Monica filled her shot glass again and when we shook our heads, she didn't fill ours. "You can have all of it. Do you want the papers?"

"Yes," Leila and I said in unison.

"Monica, why don't you show me these papers while Gabriel calls Kripo," Leila suggested.

They went through a doorway into what I imagined was an office, and I called Werner.

"I was about to call you," he said. "Guess what, our friend Sergio and a good friend of his were seen on CCTV around Haus Brandenburg on the night of Herr Doctor's death."

"And?"

"And we picked them up to ask a few questions," Werner noted. "They don't know much. Said they were there to look at property and their Realtor canceled on them. Can't find the Realtor."

"Did they kill Sommer?"

"They're thugs but they're not stupid enough to confess to murder . . . during the first interrogation. In any case, I doubt Sergio dirtied his hands. If he hired someone, it was probably his brother Olaf, who's known to be handy with a knife and enjoys his work."

"Everyone should be lucky enough to like their job," I offered. "We're at Monica Franke's apartment. And I think that maybe Olaf might be instructed to find her throat to slit next."

"'Everywhere you go, you bring misery.'" Werner's laugh wasn't amused. "That's a direct quote from your Copenhagen police chief."

"He loves me and sings my praises all the time. It's embarrassing."

"I'll come by, bring some guys with me."

Monica and Leila returned with a plastic Aldi bag filled with what looked like a stack of papers.

I took the bag from Leila and skimmed through the contents. There were handwritten notes that looked like they'd been written during the war and were faded, official records in German, and everything in between.

"What do you think he had in his safe?" I asked Monica.

"Most probably the originals," Monica suggested. "He was excited about the documents he had found in the recently opened archives. He told me he snuck them out of the institute."

"Would he have copies anywhere?"

"Maybe his office," Monica suggested.

I shook my head. The mess *they* made in Sommer's office meant they had cleaned that out as well.

Tears ran down Monica's cheeks, and she wiped them ineffectively with the backs of her hands. "I wish we had talked. He told me he called the Danish politician's husband, a history professor in Copenhagen, and asked him if he wanted the documents. The man said he wasn't interested."

"When did he call the husband?" I asked.

"A couple of days ago. I wish I had asked more questions. I didn't know what he was doing was dangerous. I just . . . I'm so sorry." She burst into tears again, and Leila led her to the couch and let her cry it out.

WERNER WALKED US to the Porsche after he talked to Monica Franke. She was going to stay in her apartment with a police constable for company.

"When will you be back in Copenhagen?" Werner asked.

I looked at my watch. It was around noon now and with breaks we'd be home in six to eight hours, depending upon traffic. "By dinnertime."

"You'll be surprised to know that Sergio Graf is being defended by a top Berlin law firm and not a state defender," Werner informed us. "This is above his paygrade. Especially since he's a lowlife."

"What does that mean?" I asked.

"He isn't talking to anyone. The law firm takes care of . . . ah . . . special kinds of criminals of the financial bent," Werner explained.

When he saw my questioning look, he added, "The law firm specializes in Russians who launder money via German banks."

"Ah, those capitalistic comrades."

"Yeah, they make friends everywhere they go," he said.

"So, your Russian thug is connected to money laundering? Shocked, I'm shocked to hear that."

Leila sighed. "Are you done with your stand-up act?" She was looking at me with absolutely no affection.

"She hides her love for me," I told Werner.

"I'm sure she does." Werner eyed the Aldi bag. "I'm going to pretend you have groceries in that bag and not something vital to my murder investigation."

"Just some apples," I said smoothly.

"Yes, we have good apples." Werner held out his hand and I shook it. "It was a pleasure, Herr Præst. Drive safe."

He shook hands with Leila and then sent us on our way.

I left the top up, because Leila was going through the papers in the Aldi bag as we drove.

"Service records." Leila sifted through the papers.

She pulled out a typed document in German and read through it. "This is interesting. If I read it in German, will you understand?"

"I'll ask you to translate the *really* big words."

"This is a report about bunker construction on the west coast of Jylland."

Nearly seven thousand concrete bunkers had been built along the beaches of the west coast of Jylland during the German occupation of Denmark. I knew because Sophie and I had gone to see a few that had been transformed into pieces of art in the 1990s. Among the most famous were four of the bunkers that were transformed into mules by the British sculptor Bill Woodrow, who attached steel mule heads and tails onto the structures. He'd chosen the mules because they are infertile, and the artist was being symbolic, showing that the evils of World War Two should also be infertile and not be reproduced.

"According to this," Leila slowly read through the document, "several construction companies made bunkers. They were paid by the Danish treasury and IOUs were then sent to Berlin for that amount so the Danish government would be compensated. The report says that there was no time commitment on the IOUs. Millions of Danish kroner were paid to construction companies for the bunkers."

"The construction companies were Danish?"

"Yes, and they didn't just operate in Denmark but elsewhere in Europe." Leila looked at me. "FLSmidth and a business partner, Højgaard & Schultz, used forced and slave labor in Estonia."

"You mean the big cement company that employs thousands of people around the world?" I asked.

"The same. And the construction of the bunkers was one of the most expensive projects of the Wehrmacht in Denmark. Several Danish companies were involved, including Aalborg Portland and some names that are unfamiliar."

"Is this secret knowledge?" I asked.

"I knew about Aalborg Portland and FLSmidth; it's not a secret." Leila read some more. "But we'll have to talk to someone who understands this topic better, knows a lot more."

"Maybe your professor friend at Roskilde?" I suggested.

"Martin Jäger? Oh yes, he'd know."

She made an excited sound. "There is a letter here . . . from a Fritz Diekmann. That name seems familiar."

I thought about it. "One of the documents we got from BArch was his service record."

"Right." Leila scanned the letter. "I'm going to translate it best I can. My Dearest Wife . . . I miss you blah blah. Mail delivery is terrible blah blah. Ah . . . here he says he started to work for Sturmbannführer Karl Heinz Hoffmann."

"He was the head of Gestapo in Copenhagen?"

"Yes. So Diekmann says he's feeling pressure to deliver on orders from the führer. He says they are morally right . . . the Good German nonsense and that Danes are not making it easy, shipping Jews to Sweden. Oh, hear this, *We give chase, and we catch or kill a few but many of them are escaping, right under my nose.*"

"He sounds like a prince," I muttered.

Leila seemed to freeze as she read more.

"What?"

"He says they have a date to round up the Jews and they are going to do it as a surprise. *We have an excellent ally in this effort. A wealthy Danish man who believes in what we're doing, in Hitler, in Germany. He's our way into Holger Danske—he's our man on the inside.*" She put the letter down. "Gabriel, is this what Sanne was looking for? The man on the inside . . . a Dane who was spying for the Gestapo?"

"Could be." I couldn't contain my excitement. "What else?"

"This inside guy agrees with Hitler that Danes are Aryans and superior and he's going to help Diekmann catch many Jews, which Diekmann believes will get him promoted, so he can then move back to Berlin. He says there is a rumor that Otto Bovensiepen will join Dr. Werner Best. He ends with a charming, *Kiss my beautiful girls and remember, I love you all very much*. He wrote this letter on September 28, 1943, at Hotel D'Angleterre," Leila finished.

"Kill Jews, kiss daughter . . . the Good German's checklist." I was disgusted. "Who is Werner Best? His name sounds familiar."

"He testified as a witness at the Nuremberg trials . . . ," Leila began.

"This is the guy who said Gestapo were just police and nothing special?" I interrupted.

"He was also one of the Germans who was sentenced to death by Danish courts after the war . . . but he went home a few years later as part of the Danish amnesty program for Nazi war criminals," Leila filled in. "And Otto Bovensiepen had a special relationship with Denmark. He was sent to Denmark to clean things up and Himmler told him that for every German soldier killed in Denmark, Bovensiepen's unit was to kill five Danish citizens in retaliation."

"Did this Danish double agent Diekmann mentions work with Otto?" For the first time since we'd gotten on the road, I was more excited about what we were discovering than driving the Porsche.

Leila looked through the documents and shrugged. "Who knows. I will have to spend time reading these papers carefully. This is a treasure trove."

Leila continued to browse and then picked up a page. "Look here, we have a *Tagesrapport*."

"Day's report?" I translated.

"Daily report from Staatspolizeileitstelle Kopenhagen, the Copenhagen Gestapo, and it's marked *geheim*, secret. Danish informant, code name Arkitekt has given information of farm in Helsingør. Twenty Jews hiding."

I looked at her and she raised the document for me to see. I couldn't read the typewritten words clearly but caught the word *Arkitekt*.

"Twenty Jews intercepted before reaching Sweden. All twenty Jews sent to Theresienstadt. Two adults, two children shot dead"— she paused—"BOPA member Aage Nielsen arrested. At Gestapo HQ for interrogation. It's certified with a signature in ink . . . which is mostly gone now, by Hauptsturmführer Fritz Diekmann. The report is from September twenty-sixth, so a couple of days before he wrote the letter to his wife."

Aage Nielsen was a famous resistance fighter from the group BOPA, which stood for Borgerlige Partisaner, or Civil Partisans. They were affiliated with the communists and played a key role in the Danish resistance movement against Nazi occupation.

My pulse raced. Was this it? Had Sanne Melgaard found out who Arkitekt was? And why would anyone care?

Leila pulled out another sheet of paper and told me why: "Here is another one from November 11, 1943, Danish informant, code name Arkitekt, has given information about Mokka Café terror attack on 27.10.1943 by BOPA in retaliation for arrest of Aage Nielsen. Terror attack resulted in death of two Wehrmacht soldiers, one German policeman, and one Danish woman. BOPA member has been arrested and is being interrogated in Shellhus."

CHAPTER 25

The traffic got testy, as it always did on the German autobahn around four in the evening, as rush hour started to peak. I noticed the black BMW when we drove past the Rövershäger Ch exit on the A19 and now it was three cars behind us. It wouldn't have been a big deal because this could happen, but the car had also been with us at Kessin, where we'd stopped to get gas and use the facilities.

I didn't say anything to Leila, who was still looking through the papers and offering tidbits of information as she came across something interesting. In this kind of rush-hour traffic, nothing too overt was going to happen, I told myself. They wouldn't pull out an automatic weapon and shoot at us.

I kept an eye on the BMW and memorized the license plate. I'd ask Werner who was following us.

A half hour from Rostock I decided to tell Leila. Now that we were getting close to the ferry, I feared something might happen and I needed her alert. "We're being followed."

Leila sat up with a start and then looked at the side mirror next to her. "Who?"

"Black BMW, one car behind us."

"I can't see who's driving."

"Neither can I."

"Are you sure they're following us?"

"Yes."

I touched my baby Glock in its holster and then gripped the steering wheel tighter.

"I want you to stuff the Aldi bag into your purse," I told her.

"I'll make room." Leila put her large purse on her lap and pulled out a scarf, a bottle of water, a sweater, a makeup bag, a pair of flat shoes . . . and some more stuff.

"What the fuck kind of purse is that?"

"A tote," Leila informed me. "It's Prada."

"It looks like Hermione Granger's magic bag that she could put a fucking elephant inside."

She scattered a few more items onto the floor and stuffed the Aldi bag inside her tote.

"I didn't take you for a Harry Potter fan," Leila remarked.

"I have a daughter." And I needed to get home to her, I thought.

"It's going to be fine." She put a hand on mine, which was holding the steering wheel rather tightly.

"I don't know, *skat*," I said. "They've now started to kill people."

We were about thirty kilometers from the ferry when a white BMW SUV pulled in front of us and slowed. I tried to change lanes, but a Mercedes pulled in next to us. The black BMW was now right behind us. We were boxed in.

Leila was holding on to her seat with one hand and with the other she was holding up her iPhone to take pictures of the cars.

The Mercedes next to us brushed past the Porsche and we felt the scratch of metal against metal, pushing us onto the divider in the center.

"Clara is going to kill me if these guys don't," I tried to joke.

"Hopefully, *after* these guys don't kill you." Leila was pulling out papers and taking pictures of the documents with her iPhone. Smart lady, I thought. If we had to give up the papers for any reason we might still have enough with the photos.

A police car drove past on the other side of the divider and distracted the Mercedes next to us. There was just enough space for me to squeeze through in front of the Mercedes and I took it. I drove as fast as the Porsche would let me on the A19 toward the ferry.

"If I die, Gabriel, I've texted all the pictures of the cars to my partner." Leila stuffed papers back into her Prada bag. "And most of the documents . . . though I'm not sure how well I took the pictures. My hands are shaking."

So were mine, but since I wanted to be the macho savior, I didn't tell her.

"No one is dying." I took an exit.

The BMW SUV, the black BMW, and the Mercedes chased after us. We drove a few meters onto the exit ramp and then suddenly, I made an illegal U-turn, the car screeching as I did it and drove back onto the freeway.

I fought my fear and let my adrenaline drive us to the ferry.

The black BMW was behind us again when we took the exit to the ferry.

"This isn't good, I take it?" Leila asked.

Nah, this wasn't a good thing. I didn't say that to her. It was redundant. "We're going to get on the ferry."

We paid the fare at the ferry post and now the BMW was two cars behind us. I still couldn't see the driver. A part of me wanted to drive up toward the ferry and then make a U-turn to make a run for it, but I didn't know how many cars were following us and where they were.

We parked the car and gingerly got out. I dropped the car keys and bent down to pick them up. The man in the passenger seat of the BMW was Marcus Graf. I didn't recognize the driver.

I held Leila's arm in a tight grip and navigated her in front of me. We went topside and reached a restaurant. We found a table in the middle of the restaurant and sat down.

Leila was shaking. I held her hand in mine. She had her bag held tightly to her chest. "They're going to get this bag over my dead body," she hissed.

"Let's not make statements that might become real," I warned. And then we both let out a short laugh to release some of the tension—we weren't hysterical, but we weren't amused either.

A waiter came by and we both ordered bottled water and whatever whiskey they had, two pours, neat.

Our nerves steadied as we drank the entire contents of the water bottles and our whiskey.

"Are they here?" Leila asked.

I shrugged. "I can't see Marcus Graf but . . . I don't know who the others are, so I can't say."

I texted the license plate numbers of all the cars that had tried to box us in on the autobahn to Werner Kaiser.

Then I texted Tommy.

"I've asked Tommy to have a welcome party waiting for us in Gedser," I explained to Leila.

We didn't dare open the contents of Leila's bag while we were on the ferry. We didn't know who was watching us. We didn't talk much. When we heard the announcement, asking everyone to go to their vehicle, Leila asked, "How do you want to play this? Go first, last, or . . . ?"

I looked around. "We join that family."

We walked up to a Danish family of two parents and three children.

"*Det er en dejlig dag,*" I said to the father, who looked like he was in his mid-thirties.

"Absolutely," he replied in Danish. "It's been a great spring so far. Where are you coming from?"

"Berlin." We started to chat. I kept Leila close, my hand at her elbow as we walked through the door to where the cars were parked. I checked the car: It was too small for anyone to be hiding in the nonexistent back seat, but I looked anyway. I popped open the trunk. I even looked underneath the chassis to see if anyone had left a little blinking light behind. Talk about a Hollywood thriller and a paranoid PI.

Satisfied, I opened Leila's door and watched as she entered, and then I slid into the driver's seat. Tommy texted back as we waited for the ferry to dock and the doors to open.

"Who texted?" Leila asked, her bag in her lap, her arms around it as if it were a child.

"Tommy says all is good."

"What does that mean?"

"Just that. I sent him the license plate number of all the cars following us."

The line of cars snaked off the ferry and onto E55 slowly. We passed through passport control, where we were waved through, and then I saw the BMW, two cars behind being pulled aside for questioning.

I sighed in relief.

I put an AirPod in one ear and called Tommy. "Thanks."

"Hey, traffic policing, that's what I love to do," Tommy responded. "I'm glad that you didn't get yourself or Leila killed."

"Yeah."

"Just a poor professor then."

"I don't know how Dr. Sommer's murder is my fault."

"Everything you touch turns to shit." Tommy sighed. "No one I know can take chicken salad and make chicken shit out of it like you can."

"I'll take that as a compliment," I quipped. "I'm going to drop off Leila and then I'm coming to you. I need help."

"Come home. I'll keep the porch light on in case you're scared." He hung up.

I drove Leila home and she gave me her Prada bag.

"You can give me my bag afterward." She put all her many things that were on the floor of the Porsche on her scarf and tied it up into a makeshift sack. "You be careful with those papers."

"Yes," I promised.

"Or maybe we should take them to my office and put them in the safe after we digitize them," Leila wondered, when I parked in front of her apartment building.

"I need Tommy to look through them first and then he can put them away safely," I said. "We're in over our heads. It's time for lights and sirens."

"Someone is going to come after you for those papers," Leila warned. "And this time they may not believe it's enough to beat you up."

"I have a gun, and I even managed to get us back from Berlin with no more than an ugly scratch on the Porsche."

She looked at me then. "This turned out very differently than I thought it would."

"What did you think?"

She smiled and then shook her head. "Never mind."

"Did you think we'd end up in bed?" I asked.

Her smile widened. "Something like that."

"Did you want that to happen?"

"Maybe." She nibbled her lower lip with her teeth. "I'm glad it didn't happen, because now I can walk upstairs to my apartment without guilt."

"Okay."

"On the other hand, I'm sad that it didn't happen, because I bought new La Perla underwear." She winked at me.

I laughed. "You tell me that *now*. Maybe next time."

"Yes. *Definitely*, maybe next time." She laughed and added, "You'll be careful, won't you?"

"No one can save me from Clara, but I'm not going to get mugged outside the Copenhagen police chief's house."

CHAPTER 26

What the fuck happened?" I asked.

I had a splitting headache, and I couldn't see very well.

"Someone hit you with something harder than your head," I heard Tommy say.

"Fuck me."

"Well, they certainly did."

I couldn't focus on what was around me. I knew I was lying down, and I tried to sit up but couldn't.

"Tommy?" I asked.

"Yes?"

"This isn't like in the movies where you're the corrupt cop friend who's going to kill me?"

I heard Tommy laugh. "I'd do it because you're a pain in the ass, not because I'm corrupt."

I sat up gingerly after a moment and touched the back of my head, under the towel Tommy had wrapped around it. I could feel the blood there, some dried and some still wet.

"They got me in front of your house," I almost whined and then, as if that had sapped all my energy, lay back down.

"I believe they did. But everyone on Svanemøllevej has a fucking security camera, so we'll get something," he said. "I have some guys asking questions."

I heard the front door open and then the gasp of Tommy's wife, Nadia, "Oh my God, is that Gabriel?"

"Yes." Tommy walked up to her and kissed her lightly on her mouth. "He got mugged."

"Where?"

"In front of your house." I closed my eyes.

"Really?" she asked her husband.

"Yes," Tommy admitted.

I smiled when Nadia said, "And I thought we were safe here because you're such a big shot policeman. This is embarrassing, Tommy."

"Tell me about it," Tommy swore. "But it's Gabriel, so can I really be blamed?"

"Let me take a look at you." Nadia was an ER physician, and I'd be just as fine lying on Tommy's couch as I would in an emergency room.

After she cleaned me up, gave me a couple of stitches, and bandaged me, I was able to sit up and drink the whiskey Nadia told me not to drink with the painkillers she had given me.

"What the fuck happened?" Tommy asked.

"I messed up your couch." I looked at the blood stains on the tan suede fabric.

"I can buy a new couch," he growled.

"Good, because I can't afford your designer shit." I almost whimpered when I took a sip of whiskey as the alcohol sanitized a cut on my lip. "Was there a bag next to me?"

"Bag?"

"A tote."

"What is a fucking tote?"

"It's a woman's large bag," Nadia hollered from the kitchen.

"Why would you have a woman's large bag?" Tommy wondered.

Nadia came into the living room with what looked like a chocolate cake. "Dessert? I promised Tommy cake for dessert since I didn't eat with him."

"The papers were in the bag. Now Leila is going to go after me. It was a Prada bag . . . tote . . . whatever. First, I get Clara's car scratched, and now I lose a designer bag. My life is soon not going to be worth living."

"This bag had the papers you got from the dead professor's mistress and wanted to show me?" Tommy inquired.

"Yes, those papers," I confirmed.

"Well, that sucks." Tommy picked up a plate with a large slice of chocolate cake. Just looking at it made me nauseous.

"I better call Leila." I looked around for my phone. "Do you have my phone?"

"No." Tommy cut a small piece of cake and took a bite.

"Seeing him eat makes me want to throw up," I told Nadia, who nodded sympathetically.

"You probably have a concussion. Lots of throwing up and misery coming your way."

"Gee, thanks," I said.

"It could be a lot worse," Nadia soothed.

"It could be a lot better," I grumbled.

Tommy released the security lock on his phone and gave it to me. "Her number is in my contacts."

I called the number, but no one picked up. Maybe she was screening her calls, so I texted her.

"Something isn't right." I was certain now and kicked myself for not thinking about it earlier. If they came after me, they might have gone after her.

Tommy didn't discuss it. He took his phone and started making calls.

LEILA LOOKED FRAIL as she lay in an ER bed at Rigshospitalet. I watched her from the glass window on the door.

"I'm Edward Clarke." A man, not as tall as me, but tall enough, came up to me.

I nodded vaguely at him.

"And if you didn't look like you'd just had your skull cracked open, I'd punch you in the face." He spoke in English and his accent was British. *Ah, the fiancé. The guy she'd cheated on me with.* And *he* wanted to punch me? Please. If I didn't feel like shit, I'd punch him for years of fucking misery.

Tommy came up to both of us, two cups of coffee in hand. He gave one to me and kept the other for himself and looked keenly at Edward. "You are?" he asked.

Edward told Tommy and they shook hands.

"The police constable says that someone was waiting for her on the stairs," Tommy spoke in English to include Edward.

"I should've walked her to the door." I wanted to kick myself . . . hard.

"You bloody well should've," Edward retorted. "What the fuck were you thinking? She told me a guy was murdered, and you just let her wander off on her own?"

"It was a mistake." I had thought the danger had passed. We were in Copenhagen, and no one would come after her. They'd come after me, but not her. And I had dropped her right in front of her apartment door. I should've walked her up, but I hadn't because I hadn't wanted to bump into Mr. British Fiancé. The irony.

"And in his defense, he was also mugged," Tommy reminded him.

Nadia came to us then. "She's fine. She's sleeping it off. She was in shock, so they gave her a sedative."

I started to translate for Edward as Nadia had spoken in Danish, but he held his hand up. "I understand enough Danish."

"Oh, I'm sorry." Nadia immediately shifted to English and introduced herself.

"I talked to the constable who was first on scene," Tommy informed us. "She was carrying some stuff in her scarf."

"Yeah, she emptied the stuff in her bag into the scarf," I explained.

"Well, they yanked it, and she lost her balance and fell. The scarf and all the items spilled everywhere. She didn't see anyone. It was dark." Tommy was looking at his phone, where he'd probably received the report by email. "The man she lives with"—he pointed his chin toward Edward—"came running out as did a neighbor. The perp ran. No one saw anything."

"Did they say anything to her?" I asked.

Tommy shook his head. "She fell hard down the stairs and screamed, so she didn't even see if it was one perp or two or . . . And no, no security cameras in the building."

"No, because nothing like this happens." Edward was belligerent. "It's his fault." He pointed at me.

"It always is," Tommy assured him.

"With friends like you . . ." I sighed.

"Let's leave the patients and their caregivers in relative peace and take this elsewhere," Nadia suggested calmly, and we walked to the hospital's cafeteria. It was empty and the chairs had been upended onto the tables. Tommy and I pulled four chairs down and we all sat. Tommy and Nadia on one side and Edward and me on the other.

For a moment, none of us spoke. The enormity of the situation was starting to sink in. Something was rotten in the state of Denmark, I thought and sighed at the cliché.

Is *anxiety the dizziness of freedom*, as Kierkegaard would say? No, I thought, this wasn't anxiety, this was fear. I was afraid and I couldn't remember the last time I had been this scared.

Well, Præst, this is what separates the sheep from the goats. It's like Proust said, "To be an idealist in imagination is not at all difficult, but to have to exist as an idealist is an extremely rigorous life-task, because existing is precisely the objection to it."

"I want you and Leila to—" Tommy started.

"She's Yousef Ahmed's lawyer, Tommy, she's not going to run from that," I interrupted him. "And I can't just stop doing what I'm doing. Not now. We need to resolve this."

"And what is *this*?" Edward demanded.

I shrugged. "I don't know. But I'm going to find out."

"Can you try and not get my fiancée killed in the process?"

I glared at Edward.

"Do you ever say her name?"

"Excuse me?"

"*Do you say her name?*" I enunciated each word. "You keep calling her *fiancée*. Yeah, we got it the first time that you're fucking engaged to her." I ignored Nadia's look of amusement and Tommy's look of concern.

"I'll call her whatever the fuck I feel like," Edward barked in that snotty English way of his.

"You know, she never says your name either." I smiled coldly. "Calls you the guy she cheated on me with."

Edward leaned in until his face was close to mine. "You have some balls."

"Big hairy ones," I taunted.

He pushed me then and that was the excuse I needed, because I was in a crappy mood and spoiling for a fight. It happened as I watched it. I turned into the Gabriel Præst of my early twenties, when I got into every bar fight I could get myself invited to.

I pushed back hard, so hard that his chair—granted it was one of those weak plastic ones made to look like wood—toppled and him with it.

I stood up, as did Edward. "Are you crazy?" He was incredulous that this was happening.

"Yeah, what're you going to do about it?" I crowed.

"Præst," I heard Tommy say in warning, but I didn't acknowledge him. Son of a bitch British dumbass stole my woman and was now asking me for explanations.

Edward punched me. In the face. I saw stars. It wasn't a strong punch but a lucky one, because it connected with my nose and immediately blood started to pour out of it. I staggered and then found my balance. In my misspent youth, I had trained mostly out of self-defense because I was getting into so many fights. I knew that delivering a stomach punch was an effective way to knock the wind out of my opponent and if I aimed at their sides or lower abdomen, they would go down. I threw an uppercut to connect with his lower abdomen; it was a direct punch, and even though I pulled it a little, it was enough to take us both down, stumbling over his toppled chair.

Tommy sighed. Nadia rummaged through her purse and threw me a tampon. "Do something with that nosebleed before you ruin your shirt." She then helped Edward up.

She glared at Tommy. "Thanks for your help."

Tommy raised his coffee in salute and continued to drink.

I took some napkins from the metal holder on the table to wipe the blood off my nose, but it was a losing battle. I gave up and unwrapped the tampon, broke it in half, and stuffed each piece into my nostrils. I wiped blood off my mouth and then realized that his fist had connected with my nose via my lip, because I had a cracked upper lip to top it—it matched with the crack on the lower lip I got from the guys who mugged me a few hours ago.

Edward was still wheezing, hunched over, but he at least wasn't bleeding.

"I think you can't say you should see the other guy in this case, Præst. You look worse than he does," Tommy reflected. "You both feeling better now?"

Nadia shook her head in disgust. "Tommy, I'm going to take the car and go home. You can come with me or find alternative transportation."

"You both going to behave or am I going to have to put you in a jail cell for property destruction?" Tommy asked and when neither of us said anything, he added, "Because I'd like to go home with my beautiful wife."

"We're fine," I mumbled.

"I can't hear you," Tommy said.

"*Der er ingen ko på isen,*" I said sharply in Danish, which was the silly idiom that translated to "there is no cow on the ice" and meant "there is no problem."

"And you?" he asked Edward.

"Yeah," he said sulkily.

"Stop behaving like you're a headmaster on the playground." I patted my nose gently to feel the damage.

"I will if you stop behaving like fucking hormonal teenagers,"

Tommy chided. "Him, I know. But you, you're British. I expected more stoicism."

On that parting remark, Tommy left with his wife.

I wanted to say, *He started it*, but the hormonal teenager remark stung. I was forty-one years old, and I was behaving like a moron.

"I'm sorry." I tried to be the bigger man.

"Yeah, well, I'm not." Edward was having none of it.

I laughed and then winced, because my lip hurt like a bitch. "Neither am I," I admitted.

He then grinned and held out his hand.

"You're all right, Clarke." I took his extended hand.

CHAPTER 27

The next day, after she was released from the hospital, Leila officially stepped away from the case, transferring it to a colleague who was now the lawyer on record for Yousef Ahmed. I had forced her to do it, saying that if she didn't, I would walk. Officially she was off the case; unofficially, she was hounding me.

She called the day after. "I have a plan. Want to hear about my plan?"

I was riding a bicycle I had borrowed from Eymen as he had given up on being a good environmental citizen and drove everywhere. "No. I'm concussed. I'm taking it easy for the next couple of days."

"Concussed? If you're so concussed, what are you doing on a bicycle?" she demanded.

"How do you know where I am?"

"I can hear the wind around you. And you can't take it easy for a couple of days, time is, pardon the cliché, of the essence. Are you crazy?"

"No, just concussed." I hustled past a father on a Christiania bicycle with two kids giggling in the box in front. "Leila, you need to let me do this my way, which means there's no *we* and there's no *your* plan."

"What's that supposed to mean?" She shrieked into my Air-Pods.

"Did your fiancé tell you what happened in the cafeteria?" I turned left onto Sølvgade.

"No. What happened?"

I was so sure the weasel would've weaseled. "We got into a fight."

"A fight?" She sounded genuinely shocked. "*You* got into a fight?"

"What's that supposed to mean?" It was my turn to sound a little shrill, but I was manly, so I tempered it to a *shrilly* growl.

"What do you mean by *fight*?"

"You should see the other guy." I turned right onto Kronprinsessegade. "I am the other guy."

"What?"

"He punched me in the face. I punched him in the gut," I explained.

"I thought Tommy was in the hospital with you."

"Yeah, he and Nadia watched."

I heard her breathe slowly as if she were counting from one to ten. Good for her if that crap worked.

"Why did you fight?"

"He was pissed off at me and I was pissed off at the world. We let out some steam."

"I'm confused."

"About what?"

"You're not the brawling type of man."

"*Skat*, you should've seen me in my youth." I stopped in front of

Pastis and took off my bicycle helmet. "Is your fiancé the brawling type?"

"Don't be preposterous, he's British."

WERNER KAISER CALLED me a day later to tell me that the black BMW was registered to a friend of a friend of a Russian thug.

"I saw Marcus Graf in the car." I was sitting at Pastis, drinking a kir royale to kick off happy hour, which started at 3:00 p.m.

"Good for you." I heard his lighter. The fucker was smoking again.

"Are you going to pick him up?"

"For what? Sitting in a car and being seen by you?" Werner asked.

"When you put it that way."

"But you'll be pleased to know that we do have a known burglar in custody for your Herr Doctor's murder." Werner sounded like he was taking a long drag, enjoying his cigarette. "A small-time crook called Anton Buch. His fingerprints were on the scene. He says he only robbed and didn't do the murder. We think we'll get him for both."

"That was fast."

"German excellence," Werner confirmed dryly. "Everyone's happy, we're done investigating, and Frau Franke is in her apartment feeling safe."

"She shouldn't."

"That's why I've asked a constable to hang around her building," Werner assured me. "You have anything?"

"A concussion." I told him about Leila and me losing the documents.

"What will you do next?"

"I think I'm going to meet a professor of history." I emptied my glass of Champagne cocktail.

"Educating yourself is a noble thing," Werner said and hung up.

I MET MARTIN Jäger, Leila's friend and professor of history at Roskilde University, at Jazzhus Montmartre on Store Regnegade. I was playing with Johnny C's band as their guitar player had come down with a cold. I looked like shit, with a fading black eye, a healing cut on the lip, and a bruise that was a little blue, a little purple, and a little yellow on my nose. But since my hands were just fine, I had agreed to play that night. I think I brought a little extra to the band with my busted-up face. Johnny C had disagreed and said it didn't matter once the lights were dimmed.

Martin was a jazz fan and had been pleased to talk to me for a free ticket to Jazzhus Montmartre and a drink. After we played "Bang Bang (My Baby Shot Me Down)" we took a thirty-minute break, and Martin and I walked up to Mo'Joe coffee on Gothersgade and sat at an outdoor table with two beers we'd brought along with us from the Jazzhus. The café was closed this late in the evening, but they left their furniture outside, albeit nailed to the ground.

"That was fun," Martin said. "You're really good."

"Thank you."

"Did you have an accident?" he asked, looking at my face.

"Yeah. My face met someone's fist once and the asphalt of the road in front of my house once. And the back of my head met with an unidentified object thicker than my head. And then it met yet another fist. I've had a busy few days."

He nodded gravely.

He was a lanky man, not too tall, about 187 or so. He didn't look like a professor but a student. He wore a pair of jeans and a polo shirt, with sneakers. His voice matched his appearance, adding to his boyish charm.

People were milling around the hot-dog stand right next to Mo'Joe and I watched intently to identify anyone who looked like a Russian thug. I thought about the Glock 26 that fit neatly into my ankle holster, which I was wearing because I found it uncomfortable to play the guitar with my shoulder holster. The gun felt heavy around my right ankle but reassured me.

"Do you mind?" he asked as he pulled out a pack of King's Blue cigarettes.

Fuck me, I thought. *Everyone fucking smokes. Does no one care about their health anymore?* I ignored that come-hither feeling my fingers felt to hold a cigarette and shook my head.

"Leila said you're an expert on the Nazi occupation of Denmark." I watched him light his cigarette.

"Yes, I am. I am working on a paper about retribution during that time—how Danes turned against Danes right after the war," he said sincerely. "What is your interest?"

"I want to know more about collaboration between the Danes and Germans."

Martin laughed. "That will take all night. Collaboration was rampant in Denmark, across all walks of life. In the beginning, the politicians who worked with the Germans did it to ensure Danes would have an undisturbed daily life. But as the occupation continued, the communists set up the Danmarks Frihedsråd. You know what that is?"

I nodded. The Danish Freedom Council was a clandestine organization set up to resist German rule.

"You see, there were several small groups and people who were resisting the German rule. The Danish Freedom Council brought together all the factions across Denmark. The communists organized the council and were very successful. They helped save many Jews by getting them into Sweden, attacked German troops, and when the time came for the Germans to leave, it was this council that made sure there wasn't anarchy. The Germans had dismantled the Danish police, we didn't have an army, so the council set up soldiers, waiting for the Germans to leave so they could restore law and order and . . . ultimately democracy in Denmark."

"How did they feel about collaborators?"

"They wanted them all tried. But the irony is that once the Germans left and we had elections, the communists were voted out and the politicians who had been working with the Germans were back in power," Martin explained. "Why do you think so many of those records are still under seal? It was the politicians and their friends who were Nazi collaborators, and they didn't want that information to be seen by the Danish public. Imagine, you're the president of a famous cement company that established a small sister company, and that company did business with the Germans and profited off coerced Danish labor, maybe participated in collective punishment, and your sons and grandsons are now running the company."

I drank some beer. "As a Dane I feel defensive. I don't recognize this. We're a great country. We're not corrupt. We're all about taking care of the people. There is equality in Denmark." Even as I said it, I knew it wasn't entirely true. After all, wasn't I talking to Martin because a brown Muslim man had been railroaded by the politicians, the police, and the media?

"The rich, the über-rich, in every society are exempt from following the rules. Denmark is no different."

I nodded. "There are two ways to be fooled. One is to believe what isn't true; the other is to refuse to believe what is true."

"Who said that?"

"Kierkegaard."

"Right. Leila mentioned that you are a pseudo-intellectual."

"Pseudo?"

Martin shrugged.

"Leila would know," I agreed. "Back to the point, what happened to Nazi collaborators?"

"They were lined up and executed. But it was the little people. The prostitute who slept with German soldiers to feed herself, the young Danish girl who fell in love with a German soldier, the union worker who had no choice but to work for the Germans or starve, people like that," he told me. "You should read this journal entry I found as part of my research. It's very revealing. I'll send it to you. It's about *Tysker piger*."

"*Tysker piger*. German girls. Their heads were shaved, and they were beaten and raped."

"The resistance turned mean. Some collaborators who saw the writing on the wall after Germany lost to Russia changed their tune during the end of the war; some snitched for both the Germans and the Danes, profiting from all sides. And even today we don't know the extent of that because the records, as I mentioned earlier, are sealed." Martin crushed his cigarette and thankfully didn't light another one. He drank his beer.

"A historian told me that the Germans are the only army in the world that recorded all their crimes." I remembered what Monica Franke had said.

Martin nodded.

I looked at my watch. "Time for me to go back. Will you stay? I can take you for dinner to Rio Bravo."

"Sure. It's been a long time since I was there."

Rio Bravo had been a Copenhagen staple for four decades and was one of the few restaurants where the kitchen was open until the early hours of the morning; perfect for those in the entertainment and hospitality business. The ambience was western saloon, but the cuisine was old-school country-style Danish.

I ordered the most Danish thing on the menu, *stegt flæsk med persillesovs*, fried pork belly with parsley cream sauce, which was served with potatoes. Martin ordered *stjerneskud*, fried plaice fish with French fries, shrimp, asparagus, and béarnaise sauce. This was not the kind of food you paired with wine so we both got the full-bodied Grimbergen Double-Ambrée beer the restaurant had on tap.

"I have a question for you." Martin looked serious.

"Shoot."

"You dress . . . very . . . provocatively. As in, you're noticed," he explained, a little uncomfortable.

I smiled. "It's a uniform. Today, I wanted to feel like a jazz musician, so I dressed like one."

I wore an Ermenegildo Zegna shirt paired with Etro pants that I'd once seen Herbie Hancock wear in a magazine and a Worth & Worth by Orlando Palacios fedora.

"Very interesting. When did you decide that clothes are a uniform?"

"After I stopped being a policeman and gave up the formal one," I told him. "That was many years ago."

"I know men are not supposed to do this, but I'm going to ask anyway. Can you help me shop?" He expelled a breath after he spoke.

I raised a questioning eyebrow.

"For clothes. I . . . I just started dating this . . . very chill and very cool woman. Look, I'm thirty-four years old and look like I'm twenty-four," he stammered.

"I'm not going shopping with you . . . I don't have the patience.

But I'll hook you up," I offered. "My friend David has a men's clothing store. I'll take you there."

After dinner, we sat at the tables outside and this time I did take a cigarette from Martin. It was my second and last cigarette of the day.

Since Martin was a professor at his young age, it was no surprise that he was über-smart and knew his stuff.

"Look, the big construction companies got away with it. They made a shit ton of money off the Germans and on the Danish taxpayer dime and nothing happened to them. They were protected by the politicians whom they owned. Small construction companies were penalized and shut down. They gave a woman in Esbjerg who did laundry for German soldiers fifteen years in prison, like she had a choice," Martin said in disgust.

"What revelation would cause the biggest scandal?" I asked.

Martin thought about it for a moment as he smoked and then said, "The royal family, of course. But I don't think so, not the main family. Christian the Tenth was openly against the Nazis. Many politicians helped the Jews escape. The story goes that Georg Ferdinand Duckwitz . . . he was a German naval attaché . . . leaked the Nazi plan to deport Danish Jews to some Danish politicians. That news spread like wildfire across the city and Danish authorities, Jewish community leaders, and many citizens got together to hide the Jews. When the Gestapo did the roundup of Jews on October 1, 1943, they didn't find many. The Danish police refused to cooperate and didn't let Germans enter Jewish homes. That's when the Nazis fired all the policemen. Imagine that? They sacrificed their livelihoods to protect Jews. This is also who we are. This is also what it means to be Danish."

I remembered something Monica Franke had told us. "But some Jews were rounded up? Some of them were deported to . . ."

"Theresienstadt in Czechoslovakia," Martin finished for me. "Some were found by accident, and some were given up by Danish informants. There is anecdotal evidence that a member of the Danish Nazi Party who was also working with the Danish resistance, Holger Danske if I remember right, revealed information about Jews hiding on a farm to the Germans. The Gestapo went to the farm and killed the Danish owners and their two children, and then deported twenty Jews, some of them children, to Theresienstadt. Most Danes survived Theresienstadt, but I don't think it was a picnic and there were many who perished. Many Danes lost their lives helping Jews and fighting in the resistance."

I remembered the document that Leila had read aloud, the daily report about Arkitekt.

"Is there any evidence, anecdotal or otherwise, about who this Danish double agent was who worked for both the Gestapo and Holger Danske?"

Martin shook his head. "There are probably records somewhere. But I don't think even the Danish Nazi Party documents will reveal a double agent. Someone who was working for both the resistance and the Germans, that information would probably be in German documents. But who knows what is in the documents that are sealed under the eighty-year rule?"

"Won't those documents come into the open soon?"

Martin scoffed. "They won't let them. You asked what would cause scandal? If we found out that some Danish citizen from a prominent family snitched out those twenty Jews and caused the death of Danish citizens . . . well, that family is toast. They'll have to leave the country. Just saying someone collaborated won't be enough. Say, if we found out that someone had snitched on Danes who were involved in one of the bombings against Nazis in Copenhagen. Or gave up Danish resistance fighters who were tortured and killed in Shellhus. If a collaborator participated in that popular sport that the Germans called collective punishment . . . clearing murders, well, *that* would be a scandal."

I crushed my cigarette morosely. I immediately felt like smoking another. That was how nicotine addiction worked. I resisted the temptation.

"What is a clearing murder?" I asked, only vaguely familiar with it.

"Oh, the Germans loved to do this. They also called them revenge killings. Say, the resistance bombed a German facility and a German died. The Nazis would round up five civilians at random and execute them in front of everybody—five citizens for one German. It was brutal. They did this all over Europe," Martin explained. "What makes my skin crawl is that people who participated and helped commit acts of atrocities on Danish citizens held senior posts in the government after the war. That's not who we are."

"No," I agreed. "But it did happen."

"Yes." Martin nodded. "Kai Henning Bothildsen Nielsen was convicted of fifty-seven murders and nine murder attempts and given the death sentence. He was executed by firing squad. He was just twenty-seven years old. He was punished but, in my opinion, too many escaped any kind of punishment or even censure. They went about their lives as if nothing happened. Those people and their families are still in power. Do you know that nearly half of the so-called Danish financial elites have that position because their fathers and grandfathers made money by working with the Germans?"

"I know that Sanne Melgaard was researching Danish collaborators who were also part of the resistance." I thought about all that I had learned from Martin, and that's when I felt that jab of epiphany an investigator waits for. A gut feeling that I couldn't deny.

"What would someone do to protect themselves if they were playing both sides, getting Danes killed?"

"World War Two was a long time ago; that person would be in their nineties now."

"What about that person's family?" I asked.

"Depends, doesn't it," Martin said thoughtfully.

"How about if we find out today that a Dane who is revered as a hero was actually a collaborator? And that Dane's family is powerful and influential today."

"That would be a scandal," Martin agreed.

"Enough to kill someone to keep it secret?"

Martin shrugged. "Depends upon who's doing the killing. Just because you're paranoid, doesn't mean they're not following you."

And Mikkel Thorsen was a paranoid son of a bitch, wasn't he? Coming after me long before I had uncovered anything.

Ah . . . a clue, I thought. Finally, a clue.

Præst, you're not as much of a loser as you thought you were a minute ago. I could only hope that the clue would lead me to another and then another until the puzzle fell into place. As Kierkegaard said, *Hope is passion for what is possible.* And Kierkegaard was no fool.

CHAPTER 28

The next morning when I bicycled back from my run at Fitness World on Vester Farimagsgade (I had started to go to a gym to reduce the risk of getting shot), Politiassistent Freja Jakobsen was waiting for me at the gate of my town house.

"What did I do?" I asked as I parked the bicycle in its metal stand in my stamp of a front yard and locked it.

I was sweaty and thirsty. I couldn't help the sweaty part, but I took the water bottle from its holder on the bicycle and drank.

"We need to talk." Freja was all business. "And I have a long and busy day, so I wanted to catch you now before my shift starts."

"Sounds serious. Is it?" I walked past her to my door. I punched in the code to open the smart lock and held the door open for her.

"I don't know." Freja seemed uneasy. "I heard a rumor that you got your head bashed in because you're picking a fight with some bad people. Is that true?"

"I'll make you coffee." I walked up to the kitchen area.

"You're done with the house," she exclaimed.

The first floor was finally done. It was a combined living, dining, and kitchen space—what they called *samtale køkken*, an open conversation kitchen. And yes, it was *finally* fucking done.

"Just this floor."

"It looks fabulous." She sounded surprised, but I understood that. No one thought there was a method to my madness, sometimes even I wasn't sure but now . . . I could see the fruits of my labor. It looked damned good. I hardly had any furniture, but I had what I needed, my blue Arne Jacobsen swan sofa, the Flag Halyard chair by the window, the antique (and hauled from Amsterdam from a private seller) blue-and-white ceramic-tiled coffee table designed by Severin Hansen Jr. for the SAS Royal hotel in Copenhagen, and my prized possession atop a simple stereo console, the Victrola Jackson turntable and my records stacked within. I didn't have a dining table, yet, but I had very comfortable barstools by the kitchen counter. I didn't know if I would get a dining table. I liked the empty space—the gleaming hardwood shone.

"Thank you."

"You took your time." She looked around, inspecting.

"It's the destination, not the journey."

As the coffee machine gurgled, I opened the door to the backyard and pulled out a cigarette from a drawer. I poured myself and Freja a cup of coffee and went outside. I sat on the table of the bench where I had my ashtray. I would have to eventually figure out my backyard, I thought. It needed some plants. Some proper furniture and not this bench that had been here since I was a child.

She hummed as she drank the coffee. "You make good coffee, Præst."

"But that's not what you're here for."

She shook her head. "Rumor has it that PET is investigating some Russian investments in Denmark that may not be entirely legal."

"They never are, those fucking Russians."

"And you won't be surprised to hear that these investments are being protected by some politicians."

"There is corruption in the Danish government? I'm shocked to hear this." I drank some coffee.

Freja grinned. "It's one thing to move funds here and there to buy a pair of Gucci shoes like that PM did, but this is money laundering."

I took a long puff of my cigarette. "And how is all this connected to me?"

"Apparently, your name was discussed during some conversations between unsavory people, which was picked up on a wiretap."

"I'm just a lowly PI," I said, but my nerves jangled a little.

"Right."

"How do you know this?"

Freja made a frustrated sound. "I can't tell you how I know. I just know."

"You know you can trust me," I coaxed.

Freja set the coffee cup down. She came up to me, leaned down, and took a puff from my cigarette. "Someone may have mentioned something to me."

"Where did someone mention something to you?"

"In bed, postcoital." A flush ran up her face.

"*Ah.*" I smiled.

"Exactly."

"I've got to ask, why were you talking about me . . . ah . . . postcoital?"

Freja made a face. "We weren't talking about you. He was talking about what he's working on, and he knows that you and I are friends. I may have mentioned you to him."

"Because I was the best lover you ever had."

Freja rolled her eyes.

"Whatever makes you feel better about yourself."

"Would these unsavory people be Russian?"

"Yes," Freja agreed. "They certainly would be."

"Who can I talk to about this?" I asked.

Freja drank coffee as she thought about it. "Nico?"

I shook my head. "I don't want to drag Nico into this when they're beating people up."

"Let me find out who would be a good contact," Freja offered. "I'll ask my . . . *friend*."

"Thanks, Freja."

"You owe me dinner at Pastis."

"Bring your *friend* along, we'll make it a *ménage à trois*."

I CALLED PALLE Melgaard once I got to my office. He didn't answer, so I sent him a text message asking him to get in touch with me, indicating it was urgent.

I then called Aleksander Ipsen to find that his phone was disconnected. I called Mikkel Thorsen's office.

"Mikkel Thorsen's office, Pernille Lauridsen speaking," a perky female voice answered the phone.

"Hello, Pernille, this is Erik Tuxen." I sounded like I was an elderly man, at least seventy. Erik Oluf Tuxen was a Danish jazz band leader who died in 1957.

"Hello, Herr Tuxen." Pernille was polite.

"May I speak with Aleksander?"

"I'm sorry but he doesn't work here anymore."

"What? He never told me. Did he get fired?" Erik Tuxen sounded worried.

"No, no," Pernille assured me. "This is good news. Aleksander got a new job at KBM."

KBM was an architecture firm in Copenhagen that had recently bagged large contracts across the world. It was an old Danish firm with roots in construction, where KBM stood for *konstruktion*, *bygger*, and *murer*, construction, builder, and mason.

I googled KBM and called their main location on Islands Brygge. I dug in some more and saw what we PIs called a clue. A Josefine Thorsen was on the board of KBM. A few more searches told me that Josefine Thorsen was married to Mikkel Thorsen. They had two children, a girl and a boy, and lived in Charlottenlund.

"KBM Architects, how can I help you?" a polished female voice asked me.

"May I speak with Aleksander Ipsen?" I asked.

The woman asked me to hold, and I heard her type on her keyboard. "I'm sorry, but Mr. Ipsen is in Greece. Can I take a message?"

"Can you give me his mobile number?" I asked.

"I'm afraid we don't do that. But if you leave a message for him, I'll make sure he gets it and calls you back," the woman explained.

"Thank you." I hung up.

I then walked up to the white board in my office and got to work. It was time. Usually, I didn't need a board. I could figure a case out without it. But this was getting convoluted.

I put a picture of Sanne Melgaard from my files on top and then started to build her family tree. I put Yousef Ahmed as the convicted killer with a large question mark. I then started to put up pictures that I could find and those I couldn't were empty circles.

Denmark. Mikkel Thorsen: PM's spin doctor. Aleksander Ipsen: former secretary of Sanne Melgaard.

Germany. Oskar Sommer: contact of Sanne Melgaard. Sergio Graf: Russian thug. Marcus Graf: Sergio's cousin.

Twenty Jews: taken to Theresienstadt Ghetto. Four Danes: dead.

Collaborator called Arkitekt.

Hauptsturmführer Fritz Diekmann.

Who collaborated with the Nazis? Everyone.

Then I started a new chain of connections. Prime Minister: Elias Juhl. Relation with Russian thugs?

No, that didn't make sense. Mikkel Thorsen, maybe? His wife, who was on the board of a construction company?

Freja called me then. "There is someone you can talk to. Toomas Reznikov." She spelled the name. I wrote it down on a notepad on my desk.

"Where will I find him?"

"Ask your friend Bør," Freja said and hung up.

I called Bør.

"What's hanging?"

"Who would I talk to about Russian gangsters?"

"Safely? You'd talk to Siri on your iPhone."

I remained silent.

"These are not people you fuck with," Bør added.

"I don't want to fuck them; I just want to talk to Toomas Reznikov. A friend of mine suggests that he is a friend of yours."

"That's a bad suggestion."

"But not an inaccurate one?"

He remained silent for a long moment. If I didn't know him better, I'd think he would not help me. But I did know him and knew he would. "Come by My Brother's House tonight around nine."

I went back to my board and stared at it. I had a convicted Muslim man. I had a dead white politician. I had a live politician's creepy spin doctor. I had an unknown Nazi collaborator, code name Arkitekt. I had a dead Herr Dr. Sommer. I had the Russian Mafia. I had many dots with nothing to connect them.

After ten minutes of staring at the board I was no wiser than when I'd started.

I made myself a cup of coffee and began to read what Martin had sent me. It was a journal entry by a woman called Esther Madsen.

May 1945, Nørrebro, Copenhagen

When they dragged her to Axeltorv after the Germans left in May 1945, they called her a German Girl, a Field Mattress, a German Slut, a German Mare, and worse. They had called her and other Danish women who were in relationships with German soldiers such names even before the Germans left. Then, Aase Petersen, my best friend, hadn't cared. She was in love. And why shouldn't she be? There was no law against falling in love with a German.

She met Captain Fritz Diekmann at Mokka Café in the town center, close to Dagmarhus, where the German embassy had set up its headquarters for the German civil administration of Denmark. Fritz found her a secretarial job at Dagmarhus. She became his girlfriend. He took her to restaurants and showered her with presents and attention. She didn't care that he had a wife and children back in Berlin. Here, in Copenhagen, he was hers. She would meet him at his room in the Hotel D'Angleterre.

She became friends with his friends, soldiers, and even met with Danish Nazi informants he handled. She was thrilled to be part of the powerful Third Reich.

She met one such informant in Hotel D'Angleterre in late September of 1943. The young Dane, who had a code name because they never used real names, joined Fritz and her for dinner in their suite. It was all hush-hush—no one could know he was there. He had come into the hotel through the service entrance. It was exciting.

Fritz told her the man came from a wealthy Danish family. Fritz trusted Aase implicitly and this wasn't the first time she met an informant. Fritz used to be a member of the IV B4 and worked directly for Gestapo head Karl Heinz Hoffmann. His trust in Aase was for her a measure of his love for her.

This Nazi informant was different, she told me, because she told me everything. Why wouldn't she? That's what happens when you've been friends since you were babies. We'd never kept secrets from each other back in Odense, and we weren't going to start once we arrived in Copenhagen at the onset of the German occupation, looking for employment. We shared a small apartment in Vesterbro. I worked in a bar and since I made less money than Aase, paid less rent. Aase didn't mind.

When I think back on what happened, how she became sucked into the lies, I clearly remember one of our most disturbing conversations:

"This man is both a Danish resistance fighter and a Nazi informant?" I asked, surprised, when we met for a cup of coffee at Café Petersborg in Bredgade.

"Well, he is pretending to be in the resistance so he can get information for the Gestapo," Aase said. "He comes from a very wealthy family . . . something in construction. He has this rich-man air about him. And he's on our side."

I shook my head. "Our side is not the Nazi side, Aase."

Aase sneered. "They're here to stay, Esther, and the sooner you accept it, the better. Anyway, he told Fritz that there were twenty Jews hiding on a farm. Fritz found them before they could escape to Sweden."

"What happened to them?" I asked.

"They were sent to Theresienstadt," Aase told me.

"Really? I've heard terrible things about these Jewish camps," I said.

"Stories! The Danish Red Cross has been there, and they say it's very nice. The children are healthy, and people are taken care of," Aase protested. "They're being sent away for their own safety."

What Aase didn't know, and the world found out later, was that the Danes were fooled. The Germans did permit representatives from the Danish Red Cross and the International Red Cross to visit Theresienstadt camp but what they saw was theater. The SS had made the Jews beautify the ghetto, forcing them to plant gardens, paint barracks, and present cultural programs for the entertainment of the visiting dignitaries.

Once I asked Aase how she could continue to work for Nazis. "I love Fritz," she told me.

She paid for that love . . . how she paid for that love. When the Germans left, Aase was just another German Girl with no protection. She was one of the women dragged by the mob onto Axeltorv in May of 1945. The mob used a black marker to draw the Nazi swastika on her naked back and thighs and used scissors to forcefully cut off her beautiful blond hair. They beat her, spit on her, and humiliated her. I watched. I couldn't save her or help her.

It went on for hours.

The next morning, Aase's body was found in front of Dagmarhus. She lay naked, half her face missing. She'd been beaten to death.

The police didn't even bother to investigate. It was impossible to identify the culprits. The fact was that those who came onto the street after liberation were deemed heroes while those who slept with the Germans and sympathized with them were villains who deserved whatever violence came their way.

I stopped wearing a scarf after the Germans left so I wouldn't be misidentified as a German Girl, hiding crooked short hair. I felt disloyal to Aase but a part of me, a part I can't forgive even years later, felt Aase had deserved what had happened to her.

I called Martin and left him a message. I wanted to know everything he could find about this Fritz Diekmann. I could feel my blood hum. I was getting close to the truth; I could smell it.

The truth is a snare: you cannot get it without being caught yourself; you cannot get the truth by catching it yourself but only by it catching you.

CHAPTER 29

My Brother's House was a bar close to the main train station. It was divided into a main bar by the entrance and three rooms with couches and seating areas as if they were living rooms. Bør and I sat at the very end of one of the back rooms marked *privat*. The room had a bartender and enough seating for about eight people. Two or three comfortable leather chairs per table. The place smelled of booze and cigarettes.

Bør told me that we'd be meeting his friend Toomas Reznikov, formerly of the Bratva and, more important, of the secret Brother's Circle, for a friendly drink.

"That's the organization no one admits exists," I prompted.

"That would be it."

"I shouldn't mention the Brother's Circle to Toomas then."

"Don't joke with Toomas," Bør warned. "The man has no sense of humor."

"Okay."

"They make a good drink here." Bør turned to the waiter. "An old-fashioned for him but with the good scotch, not the Canadian Crown Royal crap."

The bartender nodded. "What about you?"

"A virgin mojito. That's the one without the good rum."

The bartender brought our drinks. Mine looked manly while Bør's had a green umbrella in it.

"You okay with the tiny umbrella?" I asked Bør.

He twirled the umbrella with his thumb and forefinger. "Sure. It makes my hands look big."

TOOMAS CAME SOON after we got our drinks. He was round like Santa and had a big white beard like Santa, but unlike the jolly man, he wore a pair of jeans with a button-down white shirt. He didn't have a full head of hair, but what he did have stood up as if to make its presence felt. The combination was teddy bear of a grandfather meets Einstein. Except for the tattoos peeking from under his folded sleeves and the gun he had holstered to his ankle, he could be just any nice old guy who spoke Danish with a Russian accent.

He shook hands with me. "Yes, yes, Bør said you were someone I must talk to."

"Emil, get me a Stoli," he said to the bartender before sitting down. "You have to ask here for the specific brand, or they give you shit. I'm okay drinking Russian Standard but I draw the line at Moskovskaya Osobaya. That's just horse piss."

I didn't know vodka the way I knew wine and whiskey, so I just nodded as if I believed that Moskovskaya Osobaya was horse piss, though I had tasted neither the vodka nor horse piss and couldn't say for sure.

As soon as the bartender put his drink in front of him, Toomas asked him to bring "some of those nice canapés."

"The ones with caviar?" Emil asked.

"Yes, those are the *nice* ones," Toomas said, then turned to face me. "Can't drink good vodka without caviar, can we?"

"I agree." The man had good taste and I wasn't going to contradict him. In fact, I was thinking of ordering a Stoli myself to go with the *nice* canapés.

"I hear some Russians gave you a tune-up." He spoke softly, as if he didn't want anyone to hear, even though it was just us and the bartender, Emil, in the room.

"It wasn't a fair fight. There were two of them. Actually, it wouldn't have been a fair fight with even one of them unless I had a gun."

"Is he being funny?" Toomas asked Bør.

"Yes," Bør sighed.

Toomas looked at me. "You're not funny."

"My feelings are hurt," I beamed.

Toomas raised his hands in disbelief. "What the fuck is wrong with him, man?"

"I told you, Toomas doesn't have a sense of humor." Bør glared at me.

"I had to find out for myself," I confessed with a broad smile. "Toomas, my apologies for being funny."

Toomas looked at me for a moment, trying to see if I was insulting him in any way and then, deciding I wasn't, he looked at me gravely. "You understand that I would be betraying my people if I told you anything about the men who gave you the tune-up."

"That's not betrayal. That's helping a friend, helping Bør."

"*They* are also my friends," Toomas pointed out.

"You should keep better company."

Toomas leaned back and looked at Bør. "Man, he's full of it." Bør shrugged.

"Look, I sympathize with your situation, but nothing I tell you will help your situation." Toomas sounded bored, almost dismissive. Many people talked to me like this. It didn't deter me.

"I don't want help. I want information. One of the men had a tattoo." I described the tattoo to Toomas.

"That's a Russian gang tattoo; means he kills, no big deal." Toomas shrugged.

"I need to know how tattoo guy is connected to Mikkel Thorsen."

Toomas's eyes narrowed. He held up his hand as he heard Emil get closer with his tray. "Leave it here and get out."

Emil did as he was told.

"We don't work with politicians." Toomas was serious now. So serious, he even ignored the *nice* canapés. "Makes it messy and gives us problems with Moscow. You understand?"

"Maybe these guys don't mind messy."

"Maybe," Toomas speculated. "Why do you think Thorsen is involved?"

I told him how Mikkel had threatened me right before the Russian thugs had tuned me up.

"Could be something else," Toomas suggested. "What else you involved in?"

I told him. One insurance fraud, two cases of embezzlement, and one divorce. All small potatoes.

He drank some vodka and ate a canapé.

Bør didn't move, didn't say anything, just silently sat there like he was deep in thought.

"Bør trusts you," Toomas finally said. "Then I must trust you too."

"Yes, you must."

"And you must trust me," he advised.

"No. I don't know you."

"Bør trusts me." Toomas was insulted.

"Good for Bør. I just want to know how the Russian Mafia is involved with Danish politics."

"It's not." Toomas was exasperated. "There's nothing to tell you, you understand?"

Bør cleared his throat then and Toomas sighed.

"Fine. There may possibly have been some investments made by legitimate Russian banks in some construction projects in Denmark. That's all."

"How does that connect to politics?"

"Do you know who runs the construction companies?"

I shook my head. "Tell me."

"You have a Danish construction company all legitimate and clean. They set up a subsidiary in Estonia. That company gets money from the Russian Mafia that is invested into construction projects around the world, sometimes maybe in Denmark also," Toomas explained.

"Does everyone know about this and is okay with it?" I asked.

Toomas laughed scornfully. "No, and it's not okay that Russian Mafia money is being laundered through construction projects. They'd shit their pants."

"But you know."

"Knowing is knowing; can't prove anything," he whispered.

"Are the guys who beat me up soldiers?"

Toomas nodded. "Sometimes there are problems when there is construction. Someone doesn't want to sell land, sometimes it's something else with, say, the unions. There is always something that can go wrong. Then the construction company may hire some consultants to help. In some countries, they can eliminate certain problems with no issue from the law and in some, like Denmark, they maintain balance with . . ."

"Tune-ups?" I asked.

Toomas smiled and nodded.

"Are they based in Denmark or do these *consultants* work here but live elsewhere?"

"Depends upon the consultant," Toomas said. "I will ask around, *carefully*, because I like my head where it is. And if I hear something, I will tell you, because I owe Bør my life. He asks me to help you, I can't say no."

"And you'll be doing the right thing as well."

"And who is to tell me what's right and what's wrong?"

"Good point." I raised my glass to him, "*Nazdarovya.*"

"*Nazdarovya.*" Toomas drained his glass of Stoli. "Let's eat."

We all left the bar together after half a bottle of Stoli and all the caviar and blinis were gone. Toomas went his way and Bør asked to walk with me, so I walked Eymen's bicycle toward his apartment near Halmtorvet.

"How is Sophie?" he asked.

"Getting along well with Big Bo and Luc."

"They're fond of her," Bør said. "How are you?"

"Scared."

Bør nodded. "What are you doing about it?"

"Nothing. You know how it is. You just accept it and keep doing what you have to do."

"Always liked that about you. You appreciate fear, but you don't let it rule you."

"'Fear is the mind-killer.'"

"Kierkegaard?"

"No, Frank Herbert."

"I don't know who he is," Bør said.

We walked awhile and then as we got closer to Bør's apartment he faced me. "I'd feel better if there was a man on you."

"No." I shook my head. "If I can't do my job, then I need to find something else to do, and I only know this and playing the guitar. And playing the guitar won't pay my bills."

"This has become something else," Bør noted.

"It was always something else, even before I started to poke around."

Bør nodded gravely. "Look, Præst, if you get killed, your daughter will hate me for the rest of my life."

"Not my problem. I'll be dead."

"Toomas may talk to someone about you talking to him," Bør cautioned. "He's not what you call trustworthy."

"I know. I'm hoping he will. Then maybe something will shake loose."

Bør took a deep breath. "You play a dangerous game."

"You're wrong. I'm not playing, and this is not a game," I said sincerely, without my trademark humor.

CHAPTER 30

Nico invited me for dinner at Restaurant l'Alsace on Ny Østergade. Her treat she'd said. She had good news.

When I got there, I was in my work uniform—a charcoal gray suit with a white shirt, no tie, gray-and-black Dior Timeless Derby shoes, and my favorite Nick Fouquet black fedora.

She wore a little black dress with high heels that had bows on top of them, like presents to be opened. Her blond hair was scattered around her face. She'd obviously just had her hair done. She looked *très chic*.

"I'm celebrating," she told me when she ordered a bottle of Henri Giraud Champagne.

"Tell me."

Her blue eyes were bright. "My stories about rape and justice have been nominated for a Cavling Prize."

"Oh my God." I pulled her across the table to kiss her on the mouth. "Congratulations. This is terrific news. I'm proud of you."

The Cavling Prize was the most prestigious journalism award in Denmark, which commemorated Henrik Cavling, the founder of the Danish Journalists Confederation.

"I don't even care if I win." She laughed with unrestricted joy. "Of course, I care. But . . . no, I don't. Being nominated is amazing. And I couldn't have gotten here without you. I started this journey with the Christina Hassing case, and you helped at every step."

The waiter brought our Champagne and did the theater of showing and then opening the bottle. He filled our glasses and we toasted to Nico's fabulous career in journalism and that one day she'd be the editor-in-chief of *Politiken*.

The waiter took our orders. I got the halibut while Nico ordered the tournedos served with a truffle sauce.

"I'm curious about the discoloring around your nose . . . and your cheek . . . and I think there's a cut healing on your lip, which I hope won't hamper your post-dinner performance." She touched my cheek gently and trailed her fingers to my lips. "Did you get into another fight?"

I kissed her fingers. "My face is a regular punching bag. I'd barely healed from the last beating. But this one was a proper fight. He punched me in the face, I punched him in the gut. *We both fall down.*"

"And who is this *he*?"

"Leila's fiancé."

Nico burst out laughing. "*Nooooo!* That's too delicious."

"He started it."

"He did not."

I shook my head. "You're right. I did. He may have been the first to lay a hand, but I was goading him. I was in a bad mood and shit happened."

"The indomitably controlled Gabriel Præst loses it with an ex-girlfriend's new fiancé." Nico grinned brightly.

"We weren't fighting over Leila," I emphasized. "We were behaving like hormonal teenagers, as Tommy said. You know, men behaving like boys, trying to behave like men."

After dinner, we walked to where our bicycles were parked.

"Præst," Nico said as I was about to say good night. "Come home with me tonight."

I shook my head. "I don't want any of this to touch you."

"I want you home with me tonight."

I wanted that too. A warm body, the comfort of arms, a friend.

We bicycled together to Østerbro. We locked our bicycles in the courtyard of her apartment complex and then walked up the two flights to her apartment.

She unlocked the door and I pushed it open. "Do you mind?" I asked.

"Really, Præst, now you're being ridiculous. You're not the PET and I'm not the queen." She sighed when she saw I was resolute. "But go ahead."

I walked around the apartment and looked in the nooks and crannies. It was a small apartment. Two bedrooms—one was Nico's and I'd slept there with her and the other was her son's. There was a living room and a dining room plus a kitchen and one tiny bathroom. Standard Copenhagen fare.

"Happy?" she asked.

"Yes," I admitted. "But I could be happier."

She took my hand and walked me to her bedroom and made me happier than I had been in a long while.

The next morning, I told her to be careful about a hundred times before I left. And what was I going to do the next day and the next and the next? I wondered. I couldn't get her into her house every day and stay every night. I couldn't ask Bør to have someone follow Nico around; she was a reporter, she'd throw a fit.

This needed to end.

As if the universe heard me, I got a text message from Palle Melgaard.

>   Today. 11:00 a.m. Restaurant & Værtshus Sankt
> Peder, Hellerup.

CHAPTER 31

Restaurant & Værtshus Sankt Peder was a Hellerup staple that offered authentic Danish cuisine from the heart-attack collection. They served a variety of *smørrebrød*, open-faced sandwiches, including pickled herring, potato with bacon, chicken salad soaked in mayonnaise, and the famous *stjerneskud*, Shooting Star, a filet of plaice with shrimp, trout roe, asparagus, and mayonnaise. I loved the food, but I worried that eating at Rio Bravo and Sankt Peder a few days apart might make me susceptible to a coronary event.

I was there a little before eleven and found a table in the corner. I ordered coffee, which came in a French press. The place had just opened a half hour before, so there weren't too many people. It would start to fill up during lunch around noon.

Palle arrived ten minutes past eleven and looked more haggard than the last time I saw him. He sat across from me.

"Good morning," I greeted him.

He frowned at me, his eyes looking like they hadn't seen sleep in a while.

I poured him a cup of coffee, because he looked like he needed it. He drank some and then set the cup down.

"Look, I don't know what's going on, but something is," he blurted.

Since I had similar thoughts, I remained silent and merely acknowledged what he'd said with a nod.

"What do you know?" he asked.

"About what?" I asked.

"Don't play games, Præst," he warned. "What do you know?"

"About what?" I asked again. "I suggest you be a little more specific."

Palle's nostrils flared. "A few days ago, a professor from Berlin called me. He said he'd found some documents that Sanne wanted. I told him that she was dead, and I didn't care. Next thing I know that man is murdered. I read the German papers online and this guy was killed in his own house."

"Yes."

"Yes, what?"

"Yes, I know," I said. "Herr Dr. Oskar Sommer was killed in his house. Someone slit his throat ear to ear. I was in Berlin when it happened. And I know it looks suspicious, but it wasn't me."

"You think this is funny?" Palle's voice was sharp, and I saw a few of the waiters turn toward us. I smiled at them, the *this old man is just excited, nothing to see here* smile.

"I think that you know a lot more about what's going on than I do. You know about the research your wife was doing. The book she was writing," I contended.

"Of course," he ground out. "I was her husband. She tried to hide it from me, but I knew."

"Why was she hiding it from you?"

Palle breathed deeply. "Because she knew that I didn't agree with her work. It was wartime, everyone did what they needed to do to survive. I'm not a moralist and I didn't agree with her point of view," he said and then added, "I need to know what you know."

"I know very little," I confessed. "I know that she was doing research on Danish Nazi collaborators and that she contacted the dead Herr Doctor. And that she did research in Berlin at the Bundesarchiv. I also know that the computer geeks found nothing of interest on her computer."

Palle looked guilty then.

I raised my eyebrows. "Do you know something about her computer?"

"I deleted her fucking book, okay," Palle gushed, a little with pleasure and a little with fear. "I deleted it before anyone else could find it."

"Why?"

"Because she was going to hurt a lot of people." Palle's voice was high-pitched now. "She was planning to release information about some very important Danes and their families. She was going to tell the world how the lives of these people were . . . how did she write it, *covered in the blood of Danish citizens and Jews killed by the Germans*. I told her not to do it. She didn't listen. She was going to talk to an editor at Gyldendal. She went to the summerhouse that weekend to edit the book, finish it before she talked to this editor. She said she was waiting for some last documents from somewhere and then she would have all the proof she needed."

I waited a beat and then asked, my throat dry, "Palle, did you kill your wife?"

He looked at me with such confusion at the question that I had my answer. In my gut I already knew he wasn't the type to murder anyone, and especially not in the brutal way Sanne was killed. No, that felt more like the Russians.

"What is wrong with you?" he demanded. "Yousef Ahmed killed her."

"When did you delete the manuscript from her computer?" I asked.

"I'm not telling you anything," Palle declared with a wave of his hand.

"Then why did you want to meet with me?"

"I think my life is in danger." Palle looked around like one of those paranoid old men from the movies.

"Then let me take you to the police chief, and we can make sure you're protected." I poured myself another cup of coffee. An old couple came into the restaurant and sat down at a table. A waiter went up to their table immediately and chitchatted with them. These were regulars, locals who came for lunch.

Palle shook his head. "Then everyone will find out about that book. Journalists will poke into the research. No. No. That cannot happen. The fabric of Danish society is at stake, can't you see?"

"No, I can't see," I retorted. "Danish society is not based on protecting those who conspired with the Germans, our society is built on honesty and integrity."

"You don't know what it was like," he quavered. "I've heard the stories from my parents and aunts and uncles. My father was a union worker, and they told him he had to go work in Germany. What was he supposed to do? If he didn't accept the job that they gave him, he wouldn't get unemployment benefits, so he had to go and work in Germany, or he and his family would starve. When he came back, he had to run away, or they'd have beaten him on the streets for being a collaborator, maybe even executed him like they did others."

"Palle, did you at least read the book before you deleted it?"

He shook his head. "That filth? No. I skimmed but it was garbage. She was angry with everyone. They'd stripped her of her power. She was losing the party. She was losing everything, and she wanted to give a big fuck-you to everyone."

"Or maybe she was trying to right a wrong," I suggested.

He scoffed. "That man's son died, and she was suddenly sorry. Do you know she was going to apologize? Stupid woman. Mikkel and I talked her out of it. We told her that no good would come of it. She had to stay strong and be the face of—" He stopped speaking.

"Of what? Of racism? Of intolerance?" I asked.

Palle sneered at me. "You think you're some liberal hotshot, don't you? Wait until they take over our country and bring Sharia law here. *We* won't let that happen."

By *we*, I assume he meant the white supremacists like him, but I decided that was a discussion that would get me nowhere.

"When you say Mikkel, you mean Mikkel Thorsen?" I asked calmly.

He looked confused for a moment. "Who else?"

"Did he know about the book?" I asked.

Palle shrugged.

"You told him?"

Palle looked at me. "Yes. She listened to him, and I thought maybe he could convince her to stop working on it."

"Did he talk to her?"

"I don't know." Palle shook his head in despair. "It was all happening so fast, and then she died. I told Mikkel at the funeral that I'd deleted everything and there was nothing to worry about."

"Who was she writing about, Palle?" I asked.

"I don't know," Palle moaned. "She used code names. When I was deleting the book, I saw that there were no names. Just ABC and DEF. Like it was some spy thriller."

"Did you know what she was going to reveal?"

"Names of collaborators."

"But which ones?" I asked.

Palle was getting irritated with my questions. "How does it matter?"

"Because she was looking for a specific collaborator, someone who was part of Holger Danske and was also working for the Gestapo. Someone who was to blame for the death of four Danish citizens on the night of October 1, 1943, when the Germans rounded up Jews in Denmark; someone who revealed the identities of Holger Danske members to the Gestapo."

Palle had a blank look on his face.

How could he not have read the manuscript? How could he not have at least been tempted?

"Palle, I think this is what happened, and you can interrupt me anytime you think I get it wrong." I decided to go for it. Tell him what I knew and see where it took me. I didn't have much else. "Aleksander Ipsen dropped Sanne off at the summerhouse. He drove back into the city and left the car with you. On the day she died, you drove to the summerhouse in the afternoon. You probably killed her or found her dead, I'm not sure, but you deleted the manuscript from her computer. You knew that the police would get suspicious if her computer went missing, so you left it there. And you probably found the letter Yousef Ahmed left for her and took it with you. Then you drove back to Copenhagen and returned that evening by train."

"You have no proof." Palle's voice shook.

"The only reason I can think you took the train that evening is that the Tesla didn't have enough charge to get you back to the summerhouse," I surmised.

He looked so surprised by my assessment that I knew I was right.

"Like I said, you have no proof."

"Why did you take Yousef Ahmed's letter with you?" I asked. I couldn't see Palle as a killer. Someone else had killed Sanne, but he'd taken advantage of it.

"What if there was a letter? It was nonsense. *I forgive you*, like we need that asshole's forgiveness." Palle was panicked now. "And there was no book. I have told everyone that I have deleted it. *There is no book*."

"Who is everyone?" I asked.

Palle got up then. "I should never have come to see you."

"Palle, who did you tell that you deleted the book? Who did you tell about Dr. Sommer's message to you?" I insisted. "They'll kill you for knowing too much, so tell me so I can do something about this."

Palle swallowed. "Elias Juhl."

CHAPTER 32

O f all the people I had thought would be involved, I'd never thought it would be the Prime Minister.

Elias Juhl was a statesman. I hadn't voted for him, but he was very popular. He came from a political dynasty. The Juhls were who you saw in the dictionary when you looked up Danish political royalty. His father, Gert Juhl, had been the prime minister in the eighties. His grandfather Arne Juhl had been a member of Holger Danske and fought against the Germans. There was a novel, a movie, and a television series based on his exploits of saving Jews by getting them to Sweden. Arne Juhl had been awarded the American Presidential Medal of Freedom for his work in the resistance and the Cross of Honor of the Order of the Dannebrog. He was a political god—a Danish hero.

It looked like the book I thought no one knew about was the book that everyone knew about. Palle. Mikkel Thorsen. Ulla. Goddamn Elias Juhl.

I bicycled home from Hellerup and immediately took a shower. It was a warm June day and the cycling had made me sweat. Also, meeting Palle had made me feel dirty, even though I wasn't the sentimental type.

Who killed Sanne Melgaard? I wondered as I got dressed. Elias Juhl? Could he have had it done and framed Yousef Ahmed? Or did Mikkel Thorsen do his dirty work? Or this had nothing to do with the Juhl family and it was something Mikkel Thorsen was involved in.

I felt like I was carrying a very large unexplained piece of the puzzle and needed to understand it better.

I texted Martin and asked him if he was interested in a drink in the city.

Martin was waiting for me at Bootleggers at one of the scarred tables in the back where a candle was stuck into a beer bottle. Bootleggers served cocktails with a 1920s twist, which meant that they served absinthe the right way and made an excellent old-fashioned. But they also had twenty different beers on tap and my favorite was the Aktien Original 1857 lager from Bayreuther Bierbrauerei, a malt that was light, balanced, and spicy.

"What would you like?" I asked.

"Oh no, it's my turn," Martin protested. "You paid last time."

"Don't worry, I'm going to make you sing for your supper," I assured him. "I have more questions."

"And I have some answers about Fritz Diekmann." He looked at the board with the list of beers. "I will have an iStout Affogato. That sounds like it'll put hair on my chest, and I desperately need that."

We sat down with our beers. It was five in the evening and the crowd was the postwork happy-hour lot.

"I've never been here," Martin said and then added, "But I like it. It's . . . very . . . you know . . . rough."

Their prices didn't say so, I thought.

"First things first. Let me tell you what I found out about Fritz Diekmann." Martin opened his bag and pulled out an iPad. He flipped screens and then settled himself. "Fritz Diekmann was a captain and worked in Dagmarhus for Gestapo head Karl Heinz Hoffmann."

I drank some beer.

"Do you know about Operation Carthage?" he asked me. I held my hand facedown and rocked it in a *más o menos* gesture.

"Okay, let me tell you," Martin continued, and read out, "On March 21, 1945, the British Royal Air Force raided Copenhagen. Shellhus was the target, probably because it was where the Gestapo imprisoned, tortured, and killed Danish resistance fighters. Eighteen prisoners were freed but the raid killed fifty-five German soldiers, forty-seven Danish employees of the Gestapo, and eight prisoners. All in all, there were one hundred twenty-five civilian deaths, which included eighty-six students from the nearby Jeanne d'Arc School." He paused and added, "This was the beginning of the end of the German occupation. Captain Diekmann left right after Operation Carthage. And from Esther Madsen's journal entry, it looks like he was sleeping with this Aase chick, who died."

"And this Aase had met an informant. A wealthy Dane," I added.

Martin nodded. "Now, I'm not sure how any of this connects to anything, but the Juhl family is political royalty. Both father and son were elected as PM. Arne was a big name in the Danish resistance, in Holger Danske. He saved a lot of Jews."

"And how did they become political royalty?"

Martin drank some beer and then browsed through his iPad and nodded thoughtfully. "Well, they had money, that's obvious. The Juhl family had had a large construction company since the 1800s. They were masons; two brothers started the business in Jylland. They moved to Copenhagen during the roaring twenties to take advantage of all the money being spent on construction and built luxury homes, renovated palaces, things like that. The older brother, Halfdan, was rumored to have a mistress in Berlin, and he went back and forth between there and Copenhagen. Arne was a teenager when Hitler came to power after the Reichstag adopted the Enabling Act of 1933, and a year after that Hitler became führer."

"So, this Arne guy was in his twenties during the occupation." I felt a twinge inside me. The *this is a clue, Præst* twinge.

"Yeah. Staunchly against the occupation but . . . he did business with the Germans like everyone else. In the beginning at least. You have to understand, Hitler seemed invincible, and the Danish government and business leaders were thinking that this could go on for years; and maybe Denmark would become a German state like Bavaria," Martin explained.

"But then the Germans lost to Russia and people started to think that Hitler could be defeated."

"Right." Martin nodded. "That changed everything. A lot of people then joined the Danish resistance."

"And Arne was one of them?"

"Holger Danske was founded in 1942 . . . so in the middle of the occupation, and he probably joined them around the same time." Martin skimmed through some documents. "Dates are foggy . . . It's not like they gave out ID cards with initiation records."

I drank my beer and enjoyed the spicy flavor.

"What was the Juhl construction company called?"

"Juhl and Bror . . . Juhl and Brother," Martin told me. "The name has changed and now it's . . ."—he closed his eyes as if the computer in his brain was doing its own Google search— "K . . . B . . . M."

I smiled. "KBM. The architecture company?"

"Well, they do both architecture work and construction," Martin informed me. "They did that building in Qatar and they also were involved in those towers in Shanghai."

"Does the family still have financial interests in KBM?" I asked. Martin did a search on his iPad.

"No, not since right after the war. *But* Mikkel Thorsen's wife sits on the board."

"Yes." Another clue? Præst, you're floating in them now. If only you were smart enough to cobble them together.

"What's up with Elias Juhl?" Martin asked.

"I'm not sure. For a private investigator, I'm unsure most of the time."

"Leila thinks you're a good investigator."

I didn't respond. I didn't want to talk about Leila. My lip still throbbed, as did my pride.

He smiled at me. "It's none of my business, but she's a friend, so I should tell you that she and Edward broke up."

I hummed in acknowledgment and didn't say anything, because I didn't know how to feel about it. She was single. I was single. We were both single at the same time. That could mean something if we wanted it to.

Love does not alter the beloved, it alters itself.

I wasn't sure what it had *altered* into for me.

"She's staying with a friend," he went on. "It really pissed him off that she went to Berlin with you and that . . . well, you know, she got hurt."

"Yeah, pissed me off too."

"But it isn't your fault," Martin insisted. "That is the job, right? Well, at least that's what Leila told me when I spoke to her."

I finished my beer. "You ready to upgrade your wardrobe?"

Martin nodded excitedly. "Yeah, absolutely. I'm taking this girl to the opera. She's a big fan of *Tosca* and I want to impress her."

I handed him over to David in his store and as I was leaving, I heard David say, "No, you cannot wear a blazer with a T-shirt, it's blasphemy."

I smiled.

CHAPTER 33

The day after I spoke to Martin, I found out where Aleksander Ipsen lived from his city records and bicycled to his apartment building in Vesterbro. Since it was raining, I went to the café across the street from his place. I sat by the window, keeping an eye on his building while I drank coffee.

After I paid for the coffee, I put on my Burberry raincoat and my Melin Trenches Hydro cap, designed for the never-ending, nagging, needle-like Danish rain, and walked across to Aleksander's building. I saw his name and pressed the buzzer next to it. There was no response.

A woman was leaving the building then, harried with a big bag, rain gear, and a dog. I held the door for her. I was a gentleman after all.

"*Mange tak.*" She did not pay me any attention as she thanked me and left.

I entered the building. Gabriel Præst supersleuth doing some breaking and entering.

Aleksander lived on the third floor. As quickly and quietly as I could, I used my trusty lockpick to open his door. I had all the required PI skills at my fingertips.

I went inside the apartment and closed the door behind me. I took my shoes off so I wouldn't leave a trail of dirt across the floor. That would be a dead giveaway when he came back. It was a small apartment with a kitchen, one bathroom, a bedroom, and a living room that was full of furniture, including a dining table, which was too big for the space.

He had some good pieces, I noticed, an interesting African sculpture of a woman with her head thrown back, a Native American rug in the living room, and Philippe Starck dining chairs that must've cost him a pretty penny.

It looked like a single man's apartment in Copenhagen. He used his dining table as his desk, because there were several piles of papers and files on it surrounding a MacBook Air that looked like it had seen better days. Why hadn't he taken his computer with him? I wondered. Maybe this was his private computer and he'd taken a work laptop with him.

I sat down on a Starck chair and opened the computer. Of course, it was password protected, but confirming my suspicion that this was not his "regular" computer, there was a yellow Post-it on the screen with the characters *AlPha55%#* written on it; probably to remind him of the password on the occasions he had to use the computer. This was what an investigator called getting a break. Considering how hairbrained this case was, I was due one.

I typed the characters and the image of a sand dune, standard Mac issue, came up on the screen with various programs on the bar at the bottom.

The universe was smiling at me.

I browsed through the computer and then did some searches.

One of the searches I did was for the word *SANNE*, and several files came to life, including some from his email program. These were emails from Sanne. He had forwarded them from his work email to his personal email. Some of them were saying thank you for his great work and things like that; two were about some speech-related stuff and one was about her traveling to Berlin.

Aleks,

I will be in Germany most of next week. Text me if you need and I'll call you back. Please remember to book an appointment for Thursday, any time, with Dr. Hannah Krause from the NS-Dokumentationszentrum in Munich. She's staying at the Hilton Berlin and she'd like to meet in her hotel. And update my calendar accordingly.

Regards,
Sanne

I took a photograph of the email on my iPhone. His computer had the usual stuff, photographs, his CV, emails from family and friends. I also learned that he liked interracial gang-bang porn and his favorite porn site was XHamster.

I rifled through the papers and didn't find anything of interest except his appointment letter as senior director of corporate communication at KBM, signed by a Jesper Bohr, the VP of HR for KBM, confirming his six-month expat gig in Greece, followed by a full-time job in Copenhagen. I took a picture of that as well. I was just about ready to leave after having wandered through the apartment when I saw a picture on one of his bookshelves. It was of Aleksander, Sanne Melgaard, Mikkel Thorsen, and Elias Juhl. They were at what looked like a party, holding Champagne flutes, and they were smiling.

I looked at the picture for a long moment and then walked out of Aleksander Ipsen's apartment.

I CAME BACK to my office and called Dr. Hannah Krause at the NS-Dokumentationszentrum, the Documentation Centre for the History of National Socialism, which, according to Wikipedia, was attempting to address the dark Nazi period in German history.

I had found her email address and phone number on the website of the museum. It was a miracle, but the phone call did not lead to a secretary who'd ask me to make an appointment or leave a message; Dr. Krause answered.

"Frau Krause, I'm Bruno Henriksen from Gyldendal Norsk Forlag." I used the name of a Danish musician who had played jazz underground to protest the German occupation. Considering the case I was working on, it seemed apt.

I explained to Dr. Krause that I was Sanne Melgaard's editor and was reviewing her book so we could publish it posthumously and wanted to ask her some questions.

"That's wonderful that her work continues," Dr. Krause gushed. "Frau Melgaard was a remarkable woman and a great historian."

I was going to have to take a chance here, and if it went south, I could always hang up.

"Sanne said she was looking for proof about . . ." I paused. "Well, about a . . ."

"Collaborator," she finished. "Yes. Code name Arkitekt. Recently several records were unsealed in Germany, and I have to confess I haven't looked at her request lately but let me check."

I heard her type on her keyboard for a while and then she said, "Ah, here are the documents I put together for her. Now, I remember, she was looking into a construction company called Jylland

Murer. They were paid nearly ten million Danish kroner at that time to build several bunkers on the west coast of Denmark."

I started to take notes as she spoke.

"Jylland Murer was also involved in using slave labor to build Nazi facilities . . . I believe they were concentration camps in Estonia and Czechoslovakia—and they were paid very well for this," she continued. "Would you like me to send all this information to you?"

"Yes." I gave her my Gmail account. I worried for a moment if she'd ask me for a Gyldendal email address, but she didn't seem to care one way or another.

"I look forward to the book being published," she said.

"I'll make sure to send you a copy," I lied.

We thanked each other and I hung up.

I called Martin as I waited for Hannah Krause's email.

"Can you look through some documents for me and tell me what the fuck is going on?" I asked him.

"What kind of documents?" Martin asked.

"World War Two kind."

"My favorite kind. Send them over. When do you need a report by?"

"Yesterday?"

"Sure, I'll see what I can do for you in a couple of days, depending upon the amount of information you send."

"And if you find anything about Arkitekt, flag it."

"Aye, aye, sir."

CHAPTER 34

Sophie hugged me when we met for Saturday breakfast at my place. I'd gotten baked goods from Emmerys down the street. I spread the cinnamon snails, croissants, slices of fresh rye bread, butter, and cheese on the kitchen counter. It was raining again, a nagging rain that just kept on going without a break. It was damp, cold, and windy, so we decided to eat inside.

"You're tired." She broke open a croissant.

"Yes."

"And Leila?"

"What about Leila?" I asked.

"How is she?"

"She broke up with the guy . . ."

"Who punched you in the face," Sophie finished.

"Yeah, that guy." I resisted the urge to touch my lips, which still stung a little.

"The coast is clear," Sophie sang.

"I don't think it's going to happen," I said honestly.

"Why?"

"Because I already know it won't end well. There's too much baggage. We didn't treat each other well. I don't think we can get past that."

"Why not?"

"Because that's who we are, *skat*," I said gently. "Instead of discussing an old man's love life, let's discuss your university life."

Sophie knew better than to push me.

"I'm in love with Daniel Kahneman," she declared.

"You could do worse. But why is an economist part of a psychology curriculum?"

"Because he's a psychologist . . . who won the Nobel Prize in Economics. Isn't that something? His economic theories are based on how people think. You have to read *Thinking, Fast and Slow*." She was excited now and passionate; I loved Sophie when she was in this space where she was curious and wanted to learn and teach.

"He says that people assess the importance of issues based on how easily they can remember the issue, so if you keep hearing something on the news, then you think it's important."

"Our brains are inherently lazy and want to use the minimum amount of energy, so we take the path of least resistance," I offered.

"Exactly," Sophie exclaimed. "We trust our gut because it takes less effort than actually looking at data and basing our decisions on that."

"Gut instinct is . . ."

"Bullshit," Sophie announced. "You'll do better if you use data to make decisions rather than your gut."

"Come on. Being human is all about gut instinct."

"What you call instinct is based on a lot of data your brain has accumulated and processed," she protested. "Now, let's take what happened with this rape case thing. You know from experience, having done many investigations, that sometimes rape cases cannot be proven in a court of law, so you take it to Nico because you know the press will be on it like bees on honey. That is not because of your gut; it's because you know how the system works because you have experience with it and have collected data. So voilà, the bad guy who's in his hospital bed with a broken jaw is probably going to face more allegations because of the story Nico did. By the way, did you beat him up?"

"No. I'm not that kind of guy."

"Sure, you are," Sophie said without hesitation. "You don't want to be that guy, but you are."

"And what does Kahneman say about that?"

"He says that you're more likely to learn about yourself by finding surprises in your own behavior than by generalizing behavior into types. When you say, I'm not that type of guy, you're saying there are these guys who have a type, and they don't beat people up. You're you and you're not any type. You can't generalize. Your individual behavior is yours and defines you."

"And who am I?"

"My father."

"And a thug?"

I leaned over and brushed my lips against her forehead.

I got up and brought out two shot glasses and a bottle of Gammel Dansk, a Danish bitters that I sometimes enjoy with breakfast on weekends.

"None for me. I had a hangover incident from Jägermeister a few weeks ago and now I'm off bitters."

I poured myself a shot and sipped it, letting all that spice and flavor warm me from the inside. It was old-fashioned to drink it during breakfast, but I was that kind of a guy.

"You're not a thug," she concluded. "You have experience to know where thuggery is warranted and where it's not. You're carrying a gun because experience tells you that the guys who beat you up and nailed a . . . cat to my door . . . I still can't believe that happened . . . but you know these guys are dangerous and you must protect yourself. That's not instinct. That's experience."

"Maybe I should read Kahneman."

She smiled. "You'll love it. And you should . . ."

My phone rang. It was Tommy, so I picked it up.

"I need you to come to Rigshospitalet."

"Good morning to you too," I joked.

"It's Yousef Ahmed, Gabriel." My antenna went up. He used my first name, which he rarely did. "He's dead. He was bleeding internally, and they couldn't do anything for him."

I stood still for a long moment, my eyes filled with tears, of anger, of shame, and of helplessness. This man didn't have to die. Or maybe death was the ease he needed, the place he needed to go to rest and not to relive the horror of his son being tortured and murdered, not to feel the pain of being a convicted man whose legacy would taint his children.

"Gabriel?" Tommy prompted.

"I'm here," I said hoarsely.

"Leila is on her way," he told me. "I thought you should be there too. Don't tell Nico fuck all. Okay?"

"Okay." I disconnected and let my weak legs give and sank my body onto a barstool.

"*Far?*" Sophie asked, concerned.

"Yousef Ahmed died."

I dropped my face into my hands. Sophie wrapped her arms around me. We stayed like that for a long while before I went to the hospital.

I CAME HOME alone at midnight.

It had been a circus. I helped get Aisha Ahmed, her brother

and mother into a hotel with police security. They were being hounded by the media, white supremacists, and their own people, who wanted to use them as the poster children for injustice. I kept Leila away from the media as well, because she was too emotional to speak coherently.

I sat in my backyard, in the cold mistlike rain, without a raincoat. I smoked one cigarette after another and went to work on a bottle of Lagavulin. I was too late to do anything. He died unhappy and without justice, not for his son and not for himself. His whole life had been one injustice after another; I'd been party to the last one, where we'd all as a society accepted his culpability.

I heard my doorbell but ignored it. I had turned my phone off and left it in the kitchen. I wanted to be alone.

"*Hej.*" Eymen joined me in the rain.

He had his own key.

"*Hej.*" I slurred a little. My throat hurt because of the cigarettes and the cold air.

Eymen sat down across from me at the picnic table in the rain. He picked up my glass of whiskey and drank it. He put it back on the table and poured in some more. He asked me for a cigarette and lit it. Eymen used to smoke a long time ago. Now it was on special occasions only.

We sat there quietly, drinking and smoking, until the bottle was empty and the cigarettes were all gone.

It was nearly morning, not that the sun was going to peek through the angry clouds. It seemed right that it should be raining, cleansing the Copenhagen filth on the day after Yousef Ahmed was murdered by its citizens.

We went inside the house and Eymen made coffee while I took a shower. He showered while I drank coffee. He put on a pair of my jeans and a T-shirt and came downstairs.

He drank coffee and left. We didn't talk.

We had mourned together, grieved, and as we had, we had also healed a little.

I went to bed and slept until I heard my doorbell go nuts around three in the afternoon.

Groggily, I came downstairs in underwear I had hurriedly put on to find Leila at the door.

"Why are you here?" I demanded roughly, my throat hurting, every bruise on my body making itself known.

She walked past me, straight into the kitchen, and opened the fridge. She pulled out two bottles of Carlsberg and opened one for herself.

"Where the fuck have you been?" she asked angrily.

"Sleeping."

"Your phone?"

"Turned off." It was charging on the counter, so I picked it up and turned it on.

There were missed calls and messages from Stine, Erik, Sophie, Bør, Tommy, Nico, Freja, and Leila.

"I think everyone I know in Copenhagen has tried to reach me in the past eight hours," I declared.

She drank some beer. I opened the other bottle of beer and sat down at the counter.

"We need to keep working the case." Leila was charged, full of energy.

"There's no we, *skat*," I said. "After you finish that beer, get out. I want to be alone."

"We have to keep—"

"You know, you have this nasty habit of repeating yourself," I taunted. "You don't listen. You just keep talking over people. You're not part of this case. Get out of my house."

"No." Leila drained her bottle of beer.

"Leila, I'm not feeling particularly civilized." I walked up to her and took her arm and started to pull her toward the front door. She resisted and as we got to the door, she pushed me hard, and I lost my grip on her.

"Damn it, Gabriel. I'm hurting too."

"Frankly, my dear, I don't give a damn," I said in my best Rhett Butler imitation.

And then something happened. I wasn't sure how it happened but an hour later we were naked in my bed and if I could, I'd have kicked myself *very* hard.

She turned to look at me. "Don't make this more than it is."

"I think that's my line."

She smiled at me. "The sex is still good."

"The best." I smiled back. When you couldn't change what had happened, you might as well enjoy it.

"I see you have a really nice bathtub." She rolled on the bed, nodding toward the master bathroom.

"Yes."

Maybe it was okay, I told myself as I filled the bathtub and watched her watch me. She was naked and I loved watching her lean against the bathroom door, waiting for the bathtub to fill. She stepped into the water, and I joined her.

It was sex. It was adrenaline. It was fun. It was also comfort. It was just the thing I needed to get out of my slump and get back to work.

CHAPTER 35

When Sophie was little, we had come up with an equation for what constituted a decent, good, and very good day. A decent day was a day when it didn't rain or snow. A good day was when it didn't rain or snow and there was no wind. A very good day was when it didn't rain or snow, it wasn't windy, the sky was blue, and the sun was shining. This had nothing to do with the temperature.

The days after Yousef Ahmed died, succumbing to injuries he'd received during the assault in prison, were bad days. It rained relentlessly. It was blowing half a pelican, as they say in Danish. The sky was covered in dark clouds. The trifecta had descended upon us as if the universe was mourning for Yousef Ahmed.

The newspaper headlines screamed about his death. Some talked about how justice had been done in a country where the death penalty didn't exist. Some talked about the condition of prisons in Denmark. Few talked about the treatment of minorities and especially Muslims in Denmark.

I met Martin at L'Education Nationale on Larsbjørnsstræde for lunch. He said he'd pay for lunch, and I told him he should knock himself out. I had been coming to L'Education for years to get my fix of cassoulet and coq au vin.

But it was lunch, so I ordered the frisée salad with bacon vinaigrette while Martin ordered an omelet. We got a carafe of coffee and water to wash our lunch down.

"This material you sent is a lot of fun." He drank some coffee and added, "I hope they bring the food soon, I'm starving."

He was wearing a pair of Levi's with a blue striped buttondown shirt with the sleeves rolled up to his forearms that I knew he'd bought at Herrernes Magasin by David K. He was still wearing sneakers but looked more like a budding professor than a college student.

"I put together a report." He pulled out a thick envelope and gave it to me. I put it in my messenger bag. I'd read it later.

"Give me the skinny."

"First, I'm sorry about Yousef . . ."

I nodded hastily.

He could see this wasn't something I wanted to discuss, so he let it go. "Let's get to business then. Looks like your Dr. Hannah Krause did not look through what she had. Some documents are from Sanne to her, asking her to confirm provenance and authenticate, and some are just research materials that Hannah put together. It's not clear."

He opened his iPad and went through his notes. I didn't interrupt and waited.

"So . . . in this letter from 1938, Arne Juhl writes to his uncle Halfdan Juhl, who lived in Berlin," he said and looked up at me. "This was even before the Germans occupied Denmark. His father had already started the paperwork to create Jylland Murer as a subsidiary of Juhl and Bror. He writes that by doing this it will *protect the Juhl family from any consequences if Hitler by some* chance loses the war. *I believe that the more we work with the Nazis, the better our future will be.*"

I took a deep breath. "And Arne was also part of the resistance and helped Jews escape the gas chamber."

"Yes. As a historian, I can't begin to tell you what a great find this is." Martin's face was wreathed in a big smile.

Our food arrived and we ate without speaking, thinking about the bomb he'd detonated; I was trying to figure out if it was a small firecracker bomb or the big one, and I wasn't sure.

"Let me get this straight. Arne was a resistance fighter and made money by building bunkers for the Germans."

"He did," Martin said on a mouthful of omelet. "Until nearly the end of the war, Jylland Murer was collecting money from the Germans for services rendered. But that's not all."

I raised my eyebrows.

"I found gold." He sounded almost giddy. He pulled out a sheet of paper from his bag as if it were delicate parchment. "I think this is a page from Sanne Melgaard's manuscript. She sent it to Dr. Krause to verify the information. I looked at everything, but this was the only page from her book."

I looked at the page. The page number was 57 and the header read: *NAZISYMPATISØRER: DANMARK'S BESKIDTE HEMMELIGHEDER. Forfatter: Sanne Melgaard* (Nazi Collaborators: Denmark's Dirty Secret).

In the German headquarters in Copenhagen, pursuit of the fleeing Jews was assigned to a small group of men in the German security police's department IV B4, which dealt with the Jewish question. They were completely dependent on Danish informers.

Upon the liberation of Theresienstadt in 1945, only

17,320 prisoners of an estimated 140,000 remained in camp; all others had been shipped to death camps or died from disease within the walls of the camp. Nearly 400 of the 450 Danish Jews originally sent to the camp in October 1943 survived.

The Danish Nazi informant who revealed the location of Annemarie Erskinsen and her companions to the Gestapo, which led to the death of 4 Danish citizens and the arrest of 20 Danish Jews, has never been identified.

Until now, I thought, my blood humming with excitement.

Sanne had highlighted the figures and made a note on the side of the page: "Verify numbers."

My heart was thumping loudly. "Do we know if this Annemarie actually existed?"

His eyes shone with excitement. "Annemarie Erskinsen was one of one hundred ninety-eight Jews arrested on October 1, 1943, in Copenhagen. She and her parents and seventeen other Jews were found hiding on a farm in Helsingør. She survived. Came back home in a Swedish White Bus."

These Swedish White Buses were part of the Bernadotte Operation, a collaboration between the Swedish Red Cross and the Danish resistance that brought home Danes arrested by the Nazis.

"I tracked down Lotte Christensen, Annemarie's granddaughter," he continued. "And guess what, she spoke to Sanne Melgaard about her grandmother. She did an interview with her. Sanne told her it was for an article she was writing to celebrate Danes who saved Jews."

I touched the page reverently. "This is just one sheet of paper. Just one page out of a whole book . . . but . . ."

"But what?"

"I think Arne Juhl is Arkitekt."

Martin grinned. "Yeah. I think so too."

"We have no proof."

"But if it is true, Elias Juhl will have to . . . well, he'll have to resign. He's built his career on Arne's and Gert's legacy. I mean, they're releasing a movie about Arne to celebrate his centenary."

"Mikkel Thorsen would want to shut this down," I speculated. "It's an election year."

"What are you going to do?" he asked.

"With what?"

"With this." Martin pointed to the page of Sanne's manuscript that lay between us.

"I have a plan."

"Will you tell me?"

I shook my head.

"Because it's a really dumb plan?" he asked.

I nodded.

"It could get you hurt or killed?" he asked.

I nodded again.

"Then maybe you should conceive a new plan," he suggested.

"If anyone on the verge of action should judge himself according to the outcome, he would never begin," I quoted Kierkegaard.

"I think philosophers quote in abstraction; there's no consequence to their words . . ." Martin paused and then laughed softly, "But Sartre did say that words . . ."

". . . are loaded pistols," I finished.

I realized I couldn't finish my salad; there wasn't enough room for food because I was filled with anxiety, fear, and excitement. I took the page of Sanne's book he had printed out and put it inside my Tumi messenger bag.

"Martin, I need a huge favor."

"Anything."

"You can tell no one about any of this."

Martin looked at me uncertainly, and then he nodded. "Never?"

I shook my head.

"Why?"

"Because I don't care about this Arkitekt or Elias Juhl or fucking World War Two."

Martin continued to nod. "You care about freeing Yousef Ahmed . . . even though he's dead."

"Yes."

His voice was small. "I understand. You can trust me. But if I find this information some other way and then can tell this story . . ."

"You do what you want with it."

Martin grinned. We rose and shook hands.

"You'll have to excuse me; I have to go see a man about a book. And thank you. You've been very helpful."

As I was leaving, he called out after me, "Stay alive, Præst."

CHAPTER 36

That night everything went to hell.

"What the fuck happened?" Tommy asked as he walked into what was left of my living room and kitchen.

"I think it's called a Molotov cocktail," I said grimly.

"Don't be a smart-ass." Tommy looked stunned when he saw the scorched floor of the living room around the base of a blue bottle, probably the one that had been thrown into my house filled with gasoline and lit on fire. He snapped his fingers at a police constable. "Take that into evidence."

"And where were you?"

"Smoking out in the back," I revealed. "Saved my life."

Tommy waved to the detective police constable who was going to oversee the Molotov cocktail bombing of my town house. When the detective, a short, stocky blonde with a lot of muscle, came to him, he asked for a report to be sent to him ASAP. The detective nodded and went her way.

The damage was centered on the first level of the house, which I had just finished fixing up. The floor was going to have to be replaced, I thought with a pang. The original fucking floor was destroyed.

The kitchen would need to be renovated, *again*, because the granite counter was cracked. My much-loved Jura coffeemaker was history. The walls would have to be redone entirely. I'd have to find an Arne Jacobsen sofa that I could afford. There was no way I could buy another Flag Halyard chair; I had barely been able to afford it the first time. The antique tiled coffee table was now wood splinters and broken ceramic tiles in blue and white, covered in soot. Insurance would help some but how would I replace the memories?

What hurt the most was that the Molotov cocktail had decimated my Victrola Jackson turntable and all my records, painstakingly collected over the past three decades.

What the cocktail didn't fuck up had been destroyed by the water from the fire truck.

"I'm going to take him with me," Tommy told the detective. "You get this cleaned up and report to me."

The detective nodded but looked at him quizzically. Why was the top Copenhagen cop interested in something like this?

"He's my father," I said to the detective.

"I'm not that old."

"Well, he's like my father." I patted Tommy's shoulder.

The detective grinned. "Maybe your father will bring you to the police station tomorrow so we can get your statement. We're going to have questions."

"Where are we going?" I asked Tommy after we stepped out of the house.

"Home." He used his this-is-nonnegotiable tone. "You can't sleep here."

I shook my head. "I'm staying."

"You can't . . ."

"Upstairs is fine," I protested.

"It smells like a barbecue pit."

"They're not driving me out of my house." I was adamant.

Tommy took a deep breath. "I'm leaving a cop outside."

"Why? The damage is done."

"They weren't after the house, Præst," he thundered. "They're after you."

I ignored his anger and hitched my Tumi bag over my shoulder. I had taken the bag outside with me when I went for a smoke. It was a stroke of luck. My friend Marcel had said, and this proved it, *But sometimes it is just when everything seems to be lost that we experience a presentiment that may save us*.

The neighbors had long gone back inside their homes. The fire truck had left. The police would leave soon, after collecting evidence or whatever the fuck they were going to do.

"You know, the bar down the street is open all night," I suggested.

Tommy and I walked down Øster Farimagsgade to Stue 11.

We sat outside with beers, and I realized my hands were shaking as I lit a cigarette.

"If the Russians don't kill you, those cigarettes will," Tommy said, but there was no heat in his voice.

"They just saved my life," I objected. "But for them I'd be toast in my living room along with my Arne Jacobsen sofa."

"Walk me through it."

I told him I'd met Martin for lunch. Then I'd gone to the office to work. I came home around ten in the evening. I went outside for a cigarette as soon as I got in, and that's when it happened. I didn't see who threw the bottle. I had my phone with me, so I called 112. I used the outside hose to contain the fire, but it was the fire trucks that made the difference.

"I just made the house wet. And then they made it wet too," I drawled. "At least the rooms upstairs are fine. Damn it, Tommy, I'd just finished working on the living room and kitchen."

"This, whatever this is, needs to stop," Tommy announced.

"Yeah." I crushed the cigarette I'd just finished smoking and lit another one. My hands were still shaking but less than they had been a half hour ago.

"How will we make this stop?" Tommy asked me.

"There's no *we* and I don't think you want to know how *I* will make this stop," I asserted.

Tommy nodded. There were limitations to what he could do. He could try to catch the people who had thrown the Molotov cocktail, but ultimately, I had to find a way to stop the people who'd given the order to throw the Molotov cocktail.

I called Eymen after I came back to the now-empty house that was stinking of wet smoke, not exactly a scent waiting to be bottled by a candlemaker. There was no way I could spend the night here. But I also didn't want to go to Stine's or Eymen's. I could stay in a hotel, but I wanted privacy.

"You still have your old apartment in Vesterbro?" I asked Eymen.

"Yes."

"Anyone living there right now?"

"No. I'm getting it ready for my cousin, who's going to go to university here. Gabriel, what happened?" he probed.

"I need a place to stay," I said flatly. "They crapped my house out."

"What?"

"Yeah. They threw a fucking Molotov cocktail in and . . . it's a mess. I need a place. I need to be alone."

"I'm on my way."

I packed some clothes in a suitcase along with the hardware I had at home and waited for Eymen.

"CLARA, I'M POOR company right now," I told her when she came over to Eymen's old one-bedroom apartment, where she and Eymen had lived when we'd been in university.

I had slept in and woken up around ten in the morning; I was still groggy, tired, and feeling hungover, even though I hadn't drunk much.

"Like I give a shit." She barged in. She looked behind her and ordered, "Bring it in."

A man carrying a box followed her. She'd brought a Jura coffee machine along with coffee and a bottle of Laphroaig. She had brought some clothes with their tags still on—a few pairs of pants and T-shirts, socks and underwear, and a pair of sneakers from Illum.

"Why don't you set the coffee machine up while I bring breakfast in."

I took a deep breath and stared at the machine and clothes. I leaned against a wall and bent my head down and waited for the storm of emotion to pass. I had just lost my home—the home that I had been building for myself for the past decade was trashed. It would need to be cleaned out, fumigated, and renovated. It wouldn't be that house again. It was just *stuff*, I knew that in my head, but my heart hurt. It was my stuff. The things could be replaced but not the love and care with which I'd built that place with my own hands.

Clara came back, saw me, came up to me, and hugged me. We held each other and stood for a long while. She then sent me to take a shower and got coffee ready for me.

We sat at the small table on the small balcony with coffee and croissants.

"Do you have a plan?" she asked.

I nodded.

"Will you tell me?"

I shook my head.

"How can I help?"

"I need Mikkel Thorsen's private number. The one he doesn't use for business."

Clara picked up her phone from the table and tapped her fingers. She set it down and waited. Her phone pinged and she picked it up.

"I'm forwarding the information to you."

"Thanks."

"Gabriel, I can help," she cajoled.

"I know and I'm grateful," I assured her. "But I need to finish this my way. Do you understand?"

"No, I don't understand," Clara remonstrated.

I smiled and leaned over to kiss her on her cheek. "Yes, you do. You don't like it, but you understand."

"Oh, Gabriel." Clara leaned her head on my shoulder. "Try to not get yourself killed, will you?"

"I'm going to be fine."

"I'm sorry about your house."

I nodded.

She looked up at me and then laughed. "Your fucking house, Gabriel, it's never going to be finished, is it? I mean, you were getting close, and the universe didn't let it happen."

"I think the universe needs to give me a break."

CHAPTER 37

After I spoke with Mikkel Thorsen and made an appointment with him, I called Bør.

"Where are you meeting him?" Bør asked.

"At Fermentoren in Kødbyen."

"Fancy bar."

"He's a fancy guy."

"You going to talk to him?" he asked.

"Yes."

"Will you tell me what you're going to talk about?"

I told him.

"Okay." Bør gave a long-suffering sigh. "And I can't stop you from doing this stupid thing?"

"No," I confirmed.

"Tell me again how you think this will work." This time he wasn't going to judge; this time he was going to follow my plan and make it better.

I did so while I cleaned the weapon I had been trained on, the police standard issue in Denmark, the carry size SIG Sauer P320. I had a license for both the Glock and the SIG Sauer. I also had a gun without registration, but I didn't think I needed it. Bør, on the other hand, would make sure his weapon was untraceable.

"You need someone to follow you . . . and someone to cover you when you go into the bar and especially when you leave the bar," he told me. "I'm coming over. Let's draw a map and nail this down."

"Can you get me a bicycle? The one I borrowed from Eymen got toasted by the Molotov cocktail," I requested.

"You lost one and you blew up the other?"

"Yeah, I'm not having much luck with bicycles."

"Not having much luck, period." Bør grunted.

He came a half hour later with a brand-new Taarnby bicycle. "I bought you a new one. Try not to damage it."

"You didn't have to."

"I know." He put his hand on my shoulder. "We'll make this right."

I nodded and covered his hand with mine.

We checked the route I would take to the bar and back on my laptop and marked the points where I was most likely to get ambushed.

"You sure he's going to hit you on your way back?" he asked.

"I don't know. But, yeah, I think so."

"Not on your way in?"

I shook my head.

"What if he doesn't hit you today?"

"Then I live to fight another day."

"And I keep someone to cover you," Bør said; he wasn't asking.

"Yes."

"Let's hope you finish it tonight then."

After Bør left, I tested my shoulder holster with the SIG Sauer in front of the full-length mirror in Eymen's old bedroom and it felt fine. I put on a dark gray concealed-carry jacket I'd had tailored for just this purpose. It smelled like smoke but there wasn't much I could do about that at this point, so I ignored the smell.

I would carry the baby Glock in the pocket of the jacket for easy reach. I finished the look with a Lock & Co. Hatters James Bond trilby hat in the same gray.

I took the letter I had written to Sophie once I decided what I was going to do and left it sealed on the kitchen counter. In case I didn't make it back, I wanted to apologize to her and remind her to live her life without compromise and get on with it. I was sincerely hoping I could throw that letter out later that night.

Leila called me as I left the apartment. "The funeral is set for next Friday."

"Thanks for letting me know."

"You'll be there?"

"Yes." If I'm alive.

"Gabriel, are you—"

"I have to go, Leila," I interrupted her. "I want to once again say I'm sorry about how it ended between us. I regret it. I missed you for many years and sometimes still do."

I was getting maudlin, probably because I felt like I was walking to my death and needed to say my goodbyes. Præst in confession mode.

"Why are you telling me this now?"

I paused for a moment and told her what I felt in my heart; what I had known from the minute she'd walked into Mojo on that May night. "Because we can't be what we were, Leila."

"I hope not, because what we were was terrible." She let out a short humorless laugh. "But we can be better."

I tried to be as honest as I could. "Yes, I think we can be, but I don't know if I want that."

There was silence on her side.

"Okay," I heard her say, her words full of emotion. "But I want you to think about it before you say no."

"I have to go."

"I love you, Gabriel."

"Yeah, I know. I love you too." I disconnected. Where had that come from? Ilse would have a field day when I told her that I had said the L word to Leila.

I stepped out into the rain and raised my jacket collar to protect my neck from the cold. I bicycled against the wind all the way to Halmtorvet. I wasn't even a bit tired when I reached Fermentoren, the bar where I was meeting Mikkel Thorsen. Adrenaline was a potent drug.

CHAPTER 38

got to the bar a half hour before the appointment with Mikkel Thorsen, which was at seven in the evening. Even though the sun hadn't set, the clouds painted the city gray. Lots of desolate streets, I thought, for Russians with gang tattoos to come after me.

I knew that they wouldn't touch me until after the meeting with Thorsen. He knew what I had—or what he thought I had—and he wanted to talk it through, negotiate with me.

I ordered a Whiskey Tango Foxtrot Smoke beer and sipped it slowly. I wasn't going to get drunk on one beer, but I wasn't going to do anything that could diminish any of my capacities, mental or physical. I sat inside the bar, facing the entrance. I could feel my shoulder holster and the SIG Sauer. It comforted me. And for added comfort, my hand often touched my jacket pocket to make sure the baby Glock was still there.

I waited patiently. I didn't let fear touch me. I didn't let the what-ifs bother me. I was here to bring justice to Yousef Ahmed. That was my endgame. The rest was gravy.

Mikkel Thorsen showed up five minutes after seven.

I got a text on my phone from Bør: **Beer this weekend?** It was his way of saying, Mikkel was here. I had hoped Bør would not risk himself by being around when it went down, but he would have it no other way.

Mikkel nodded at me. He removed his dark raincoat and hung it on a hook by the door and walked up to me. He wore a dark suit with a blue tie and a stupid grin on his face. His eyes were not smiling. He looked tense. I enjoyed seeing that. I knew that my face showed no emotion. I had learned the skill as a policeman and had honed it further as a private investigator. People didn't like to spill their guts to someone who showed empathy, sympathy, or antipathy—they wanted genuine emotion and when those emotions were contrary to what I knew the person I was talking to wanted to see, I put on my silent mask.

He held out his hand. I stood up and shook it.

"What's good?" he asked as he sat down and looked through the beer menu. He waved at a waiter who came by immediately and asked for a pilsner.

"You said you have the manuscript," he said without preamble. "Have you read it?"

"Cover to cover," I lied. "She was a hell of a writer."

"Yes, that she was," Mikkel agreed.

His beer arrived and he didn't touch it, just let it sit there.

"Yousef Ahmed is dead. This case is dead," Mikkel told me. "Why are you still persisting?"

"That's the kind of guy I am."

He grinned. "Yeah, I've heard. You're one stubborn son of a bitch."

I didn't respond. I knew the fact that I was expressionless was freaking him out a little.

"What do you want?" he asked.

"The truth."

Mikkel laughed then. It was genuine. "What the fuck is wrong with you?"

"Who killed Sanne Melgaard?" I asked.

"Yousef Ahmed."

I shook my head. "Let me tell you what I think happened. Palle told you about the book. He told you *and* the prime minister. He told you that she was going to expose the Juhl family. Not just for making money off Danish taxpayers while working for the Germans, but also for using slave labor in other countries."

"Many companies did that." Mikkel shrugged. "It's old news."

"But what's fresh news is that good old Arne, who went about killing and humiliating Danish collaborators with others from the Danish resistance after the Germans left, was a Nazi collaborator himself and responsible for the deportation of twenty Jews and the death of four Danish citizens, two of them children, and God knows how many more. They'll take away that Medal of Freedom, take away the royal honors and there will be no movie, no nothing . . . just scorn and disgust and delicious news for the twenty-four/seven media hounds," I narrated calmly. "They'll do more research, open more restricted files, find more evidence. Elias Juhl will not run for office . . . he will be run out of the country."

I watched Mikkel as I spoke. His lips tightened. He was paler than he had been when he came into the bar. It was satisfying.

"And now five years later, it's once again an election year," I continued. "Sanne wanted to hit Elias hard for making her irrelevant. She was vindictive that way, wasn't she?"

"There is no proof," Mikkel murmured. "Just because she wrote it doesn't make it true."

"But Oskar Sommer found documents."

"Oskar Sommer is dead."

He wasn't even pretending anymore. He could've said, *Who's Oskar Sommer?* but he hadn't. The gloves were off.

"Even without those documents, she put a good case together," I said pleasantly. "It may not be substantiated right now, but I'm sure once the book is out there, researchers will do whatever they can to find the proof. Can't kill all the researchers, can you, Mikkel?"

Mikkel took a deep breath and sighed, like he was bored. "Is this all you have to say? Because I'm busy."

"Palle, the idiot, deleted the manuscript before you could read it." I ignored him, spoke over him. "But she made a copy. I have the copy and the source documents . . . most of them. It's compelling."

His nostrils flared and his blue eyes simmered with anger. "Fucking Ulla."

"By the way, the documents we got from Oskar Sommer's mistress didn't have anything valuable in them. Your goons nearly cracked my skull for no good reason," I chided. "Oh, and can I have the bag back? It's apparently a Prada tote and you know how women are about their bags."

"Cute." Mikkel leaned back. "They say that you have a sense of humor."

"In spades."

"Show me the proof," he demanded.

"Oh, come on, Thorsen, I'm not *that* stupid," I crooned. "Who killed her? Was it you?" I saw something flicker on his face. "So, one of the Russians. You know the media is going to love that Russian connection. Maybe Elias Juhl can get cozy with Putin, and we can slot him away as a nut job like that old U.S. nut job. He'll never see the light of day after that, and the king you made will fall so hard that not all the king's men will be able to put him together again."

"What do you want?"

"The man who killed her has to confess."

"Are you mad? Then all of this will come to light. Not that there is anything to come to light," he hissed.

"They'll find the guy who beat me up, the guys who threw the Molotov cocktail into my house . . . the cops will find your thugs," I drawled. "And do you really think they're going to stick their necks out for you? There's no honor among thieves, Thorsen. You know that."

"This is nonnegotiable," Mikkel said with finality.

"So, what you're saying is that you won't clear Yousef Ahmed's name?"

"Yes. We can't."

When he said "we" I wondered if he meant Elias Juhl and him or if he was using the royal *we*.

"Does your boss know how deep you're in this?" I asked and from his expression, albeit fleeting, I saw that maybe Elias Juhl didn't know all of it.

"What else can we do for you?" he asked. This was now a negotiation for him.

I leaned back and looked at him thoughtfully. "Money."

Mikkel smiled. Greed he understood.

"Five million Danish kroner to the Ahmed family." I had thought of a number before the meeting, just in case.

Mikkel shrugged. "We can make that happen."

"And no one from my family, my friends, or I ever see a Russian man with a gang tattoo . . . actually any Russian . . . ever again," I continued.

"Okay," Mikkel agreed.

"If you back out, the manuscript goes out on all social media for everyone to see."

"Where is the manuscript?" Mikkel asked.

I took the single page of Sanne's manuscript I had made a copy of and put it in front of him. Mikkel read the page; when he was done, the remaining color from his face was gone.

"Did you know that Annemarie was one of the Jews that Arne Juhl betrayed?"

In response, he crumpled the page in his hand and squished it into a ball.

"That's okay." I smiled. "I have a USB stick with the whole book on it."

I pulled out a USB stick and put it down between us.

Mikkel looked at it and then at me. A part of him wanted to grab it, but he knew that wasn't going to solve his problem.

"Who else has seen the book? The lawyer? The reporter? Who?" he asked.

"No one," I assured him. "No one but me."

"How do I know there are no other copies?"

"You don't," I said lazily. "You *only* have my word."

Mikkel watched me for a moment. "I have been told you keep your word. But I will need time to make arrangements."

"Of course." I took the USB stick back and dropped it into my jacket pocket.

"You know, you're blackmailing me. That is illegal," Mikkel ground out.

I laughed. "Thorsen, of all the things we've talked about this evening, settling your debt with the Ahmed family might be the least illegal one."

Mikkel took a deep breath. "I don't understand you. What's in this for you?"

"I don't care about what someone's grandpa did during World War Two. I was hired to clear Yousef Ahmed's name. If I can't do that, then I can at least make sure his family is taken care of."

I kept my voice flat and enunciated every word, speaking slowly and clearly.

"You'll hear from me. Until then, don't do anything stupid." Mikkel pulled out a lighter from his pocket and burned the page and let it drop in his full glass of beer. The beer turned dark. He stood up then, took out his wallet, and threw two hundred-kroner notes on the table. "My treat."

I watched him leave the bar.

I texted Bør that I was going to go home. I got no response, but I didn't need one to know that he would be watching me as carefully as a lioness does her cub.

THEY DIDN'T COME for me until I had reached the area of Istedgade frequented by drug dealers, people on crack, hookers on crack, and enough used needles on the street to spread the most infectious diseases in the world.

The first bullet whizzed past me. When it did, I wasn't sure what it was but the speed, the heat, and the near miss made my heart stop, and I stopped with it. I immediately dropped the bicycle and backed into a shuttered storefront.

I heard the next shot but didn't see it.

I pulled out my Glock.

Someone cried out. I couldn't make out if it was a man or a woman. It was raining, so there weren't many people on the street, and no one on Istedgade would call 112 because they heard gunshots, not in this part of the street.

Footsteps ran toward me. My heartbeat kept pace with those steps. With my gun in hand, I waited.

A bullet shot through the air, making my eardrums rattle. No matter how many times you've heard a gun go off, you never got used to it. I never had. It was probably Bør discouraging the men after me. I had given explicit orders to dissuade but not hurt or kill, unless unavoidable.

Morc footsteps. More gunshots.

A man raced past the storefront where I was taking cover. He was large and he turned with his gun pointed at me. We both fired at the same time. The man went down, his gun discharging one time as he collapsed on the wet street.

The junkies cleared out like a bomb had gone off. Istedgade had never been this desolate before. I heard two more shots and then there was silence.

I stayed put and texted Tommy with shaking fingers. I gave him my location and told him I was under fire.

It felt likc a lifetime before I heard the sirens.

But when I looked at the time on my phone, it had been only two minutes. It hadn't sunk in yet that I had killed a man. But I had. I waited until a police car stopped by the body. I put my gun in my pocket and, with my hands up in the air, walked out.

"Gabriel Præst," I shouted. "Private. Ex police."

A police constable came up to me, holding his gun on me.

"I have a gun in my right pocket, a Glock. I have a SIG Sauer in a holster under my left shoulder," I told him, my hands up in the air.

The constable was young and looked scared. His partner, an older guy, came out and sighed. "Put your hands down, Præst, you look like an idiot."

It was an old colleague of mine, Jon Husum. I let my hands and shoulders fall.

"You okay?" he asked, and then looked at my left shoulder and added, tension creeping up in his voice, "Damn it, Præst, are you shot?"

I turned to look at the hole in my beautiful handmade one-of-a-kind concealed-carry jacket, which was quickly turning scarlet, and sighed. "Fuck, my jacket is ruined," I grumbled and then everything went dark.

CHAPTER 39

Tommy and Eymen were talking as I came to. The smell gave it away. I was in a fucking hospital. Again. Twice in as many months. And my left arm hurt like a motherfucker.

"Did he tell you he was doing this?" Tommy wanted to know in that gruff demanding voice of his.

"I'm not his mother," Eymen responded, equally gruff. "Clara knew he was up to something, but we didn't realize he was going to shake down Thorsen and then get shot in the process."

I was too tired to open my eyes, so I closed them. I was floating in and out. At one time I heard a rustling sound.

"Hey, *skat*." Eymen's voice was soft. "He's still sleeping."

"He's not going to if you both keep fighting. Tommy and Eymen, give it a rest," I heard Sophie say.

I smiled. She was one tough cookie, my daughter was.

The next time I came to, I heard laughter.

"Bør, that's not a real word," Sophie was saying.

"It is." It was Bør.

"It's German." I recognized Nico's voice.

"Why can't we use German words?" Bør wanted to know.

"Because it's Danish Scrabble," someone said, and I heard Sophie laugh.

It lightened my heart as I drifted back into darkness.

I was alone when I finally managed to wake up for longer than a few moments. Everything was a bit fuzzy. My eyes adjusted to the room; it was dimly lit but I could make out a sleeping figure on a chair next to my bed.

Eymen.

"Hey," I said hoarsely.

Eymen woke up suddenly and then I heard his breathing stabilize. "Let's get you some water."

I sat up and felt a cold straw near my mouth and grasped for it. I thought I'd drunk the whole glass but when I looked at the glass it was three-quarters full.

I sank back into the pillow because that had taken all my energy. "What's the damage?"

"Bullet tore through your left arm. You'll have a nice scar to impress the ladies with. Besides that, you're fine."

"Don't feel fine," I complained.

"That's a direct consequence of being in a shootout."

"You should see the other guy," I said weakly.

"He's dead."

"See." I closed my eyes. I waited for him to tell me.

"His name was Boris Labazanov."

"Boris? Really?"

"I know, right." Eymen laughed softly. "Couldn't get more obviously Russian."

"Bør in trouble?" I asked.

"No," Eymen assured me. "He didn't hit anyone. He did disperse them, so they didn't all come after you. He wasn't there when the police arrived."

"Good. That's good." My energy was leaving me.

"They've given you some nice painkillers, so you should rest," Eymen informed me.

"Yeah," I mumbled. "I'm tired."

"You did good, Gabriel." Eymen took my hand in his. "You did good. Let that brain go silent. And sleep."

"What happened to Thorsen?"

He said something but I couldn't hear him.

"Eymen," I called out in panic when my head swirled again, and the world tilted.

I went back to darkness.

As EYMEN HAD predicted, I was fine except for the bandaged left arm; so, they let me leave the hospital two days after I got there. Eymen and Sophie drove me home and didn't badger me to stay with either of them. The house still smelled like wet burned wood—but Clara had had it professionally cleaned, so it wasn't as bad as it could have been. She had installed a coffee machine and small fridge with beer and water in my office. She had also left a few bottles of good Bordeaux next to new wineglasses and made sure the mini fridge was stocked with cold cuts, a loaf of rye bread, a big bowl of strawberries, and butter. All the basics.

The morning after I came home, I went for a run, one arm in a sling. My speed sucked and at times I walked, at times I wheezed, but I managed to go around the lake once.

I was exhausted when I came home. I made myself a cup of coffee, went downstairs to my backyard, and smoked a cigarette.

I started to feel normal again.

I bicycled to Københavns Politigård, the Copenhagen Police Headquarters, on Polititorvet in the afternoon for a meeting with the police officer in charge of the Istedgade shooting. It took me twice as long as it normally would, because bicycling with one hand slowed me down. I was also at about 50 percent of energy. I should've taken a taxi, but I wasn't going to let anyone change my life—I was going to live in my house and ride my new Taarnby bicycle, the hell with a bomb in my living room and a bullet wound in my shoulder.

I met Politibetjent Embla Poulsen in Tommy's office. We both sat across the desk from Tommy, who seemed calm as a lake, which made me uncomfortable and suspicious. He hadn't talked to me about the case since I had been shot, and every time I'd asked, he'd told me to get better. After I was released from the hospital, he'd requested this meeting.

"You met Mikkel Thorsen at Halmtorvet," Embla began as she looked through her notebook. "Can you tell us what the conversation was about?"

"We talked about the Yousef Ahmed case."

"What about the case?" Embla asked.

Embla was a serious-looking woman with a buzzed haircut. She showed her whimsy with crawler earrings that went all the way up her ear and sparkled. She wore no makeup, and she didn't need to, because she was a beautiful woman. She stood a couple inches over my six feet two and made me want to sit up straight.

"Nothing special."

"We've talked to Mikkel Thorsen," Embla cautioned me. "He says you were blackmailing him."

"About what?"

"He said that you made up a story about the Russian Mafia," Embla informed me and watched for my response. There was none.

"What story?"

"He didn't say."

"No story, no blackmail," I smiled.

"Be straight with us, Præst," Embla insisted, "and this will go easy."

"Or what?" I asked with a smile. "What's this? Bad cop, silent cop? And you think doing it in Tommy's office will make it seem less like an interrogation? And where is Thorsen?"

"In a room in this building that's a little less comfortable than this one," Embla bit out.

I hadn't known that, but didn't let my surprise show. There was nothing about Thorsen being arrested or questioned in the news either. There had been a story about the shootout on Istedgade but there had been no follow up on it. Nico had checked with the reporter who wrote the story and found out that the police had put it down to yet another incidence of gang violence.

"Oh, did you think we wouldn't track down the known associates of Boris Labazanov and find out who called them about you leaving the bar?" Embla asked flatly. "You do understand, we know how to do our jobs."

"Good for you."

Embla put her notebook down on Tommy's desk and turned to face me.

"I don't think you understand, Præst, you killed a man, and we need to understand why." Her tone had gone from good cop to mean cop.

"That's simple. He was shooting at me."

"Why was he shooting at you?"

"You could ask him if he were alive. I'd also like to know."

"*Chef*, you said he'd talk if we did it like this. He isn't talking," Embla complained to Tommy.

Tommy nodded but didn't say anything.

"If you can tell me what the fuck is going on, maybe I can be more forthcoming," I suggested.

Tommy took a deep breath and nodded at Embla.

"Large amounts of money have been transferred from a Danske bank subsidiary in Estonia to an account in Denmark," she explained. "Both accounts are in the name of KBM Architects and under the authorization of a board member, Josefine Thorsen, Mikkel Thorsen's wife. The original source of the money is a bank in Moscow, which KBM says is for a construction project in Sochi. The money cops have been looking into this for about two years now . . . because there is no construction project in Sochi."

"Wow. I am shocked to hear that money laundering is going on." I didn't exactly jeer but it was close.

Embla ignored me. "Both Mikkel Thorsen and his wife claim they have nothing to do with this bank account where money was being funneled from Moscow. They allege that you set this up to frame them."

"Am I the one on drugs, or is she?" I asked lazily.

"Do you know a Toomas Reznikov?" Embla continued.

"I have met him," I admitted. "Once."

"Yes, we know about that time because it was in public," Embla said and smiled. "We keep an eye on My Brother's House. The bartender is undercover there."

"Emil." I remembered the name of the bartender.

"Toomas Reznikov is one of Boris Labazanov's known associates," she continued.

"If I was so smart at setting this up, why would I end up getting shot in the arm and killing a man?" I asked.

"Well . . ."

"I'm going to need a lawyer before I talk to you anymore."

Tommy nodded, as if he was hoping I'd say exactly that.

"You're making this unnecessarily adversarial," Embla admonished. "No one is accusing you of anything. We just want information."

"I've gone from victim to someone who's trying to blackmail and frame Mikkel Thorsen in fifteen minutes," I remarked. "*This* is fucking adversarial."

"I repeat, you're not being accused by the police of anything. We're trying to get to the truth." Embla was struggling to stay calm.

"Here are some truths for you." I rearranged my thoughts to decide how much to say. "Mikkel Thorsen killed Sanne Melgaard . . . or had her killed. You should question the Russians you have in custody about that."

I held up my hand to silence Embla's questions after that controversial statement.

"Let me finish," I requested. "I don't know why he did that but I'm sure you can get him to tell you. He framed Yousef Ahmed because immigration is always a nice line item in the political shopping list in an election year, as that year was. It gets people riled up, and Yousef Ahmed became the poster child of the bad angry Muslim who slits the throats of nice old white women."

"You're making no sense," Embla said.

"Talk to the Russians," I insisted. "Track a payment from Mikkel Thorsen five years ago and you'll find it."

Embla picked up her notebook and scrawled hurriedly in it.

"How much are you not telling us?" Embla asked.

I shook my head.

"Præst," Embla warned.

"Find out who killed Sanne Melgaard, and this time let's make sure we don't try and pin it on someone convenient." I stood up. "And next time, don't try and trap me with a conversation in your office, Tommy. Have the balls to take me to an interrogation room. Make sure to invite Leila Abadi Knudsen, my lawyer."

Finally, Tommy spoke. "Thank you for your cooperation in this matter. We won't be bothering you again with this."

Embla stared at Tommy angrily. "Is this because of your personal connection with . . ."

Tommy raised a hand. "He isn't going to tell you what you want to know. And we can't compel him. He hasn't done anything wrong. He met a guy for a drink. He shot a guy who was shooting at him."

"Mikkel Thorsen . . ."

"Is a lying sleazebag," Tommy finished for her. "I suggest you focus on Mikkel Thorsen, his wife, the two Russians you have in custody and close the fucking case . . . this one and Sanne Melgaard's."

"*Chef*?"

"Yes." Tommy smiled at her. "I believe him. You should too."

Embla nodded and then looked at me. "And will you talk to me if I need more information?"

"Yes. As long as my lawyer is present."

Embla left Tommy's office and I looked at him. "You could've warned me."

"And miss all the entertainment," he said. "You want to tell me exactly what's going on?"

"Yes." I sat down again, relieved to sit, relieved not to hide the pain. "But I need some painkillers first. Getting shot sucks."

I washed down the painkillers I had with me with scotch he kept in his office and then I told him all about Denmark's dirty Nazi secrets.

CHAPTER 40

That evening I invited Leila and Aisha for an early dinner at Hija de Sanchez Cantina in Nordhavn. I knew Leila had a weakness for Mexican seafood and I wanted to make her happy. Also, with fish on the menu, I didn't have to worry about halal with Aisha.

I got there early to meet with Sophie before Aisha and Leila joined us and ordered the restaurant's signature margarita, made with mezcal and chile de arbol syrup. The restaurant was cozy with shades of pastel pink, sandy yellow, and cobalt blue—and beautiful colorful Mexican rugs on the walls. I sat at a table for four by the glass windows.

"*Hej, Far.*" Sophie kissed me on my cheek and sat next to me. She held my right hand in her left, lacing our fingers together. "I hear Mikkel Thorsen is being questioned by the police."

"Who told you?" I asked.

"Tommy. I called him to ask how your meeting went. I wanted to get his version before I got yours."

"Ah."

"And . . . I have to say something to you that isn't easy, but I'm going to try. You left a letter for me at . . ."

"Oh crap." I sighed. "I got shot and . . . forgot."

"I love you too, Far." Sophie's eyes were full of tears.

"Hey, you can't cry . . . I'm trying to celebrate life and shit."

She let my hand go and put her head on my good shoulder. I wrapped my arm around her.

"When I said you had to see this through, I didn't mean you had to die to see it through." She buried her face in my shoulder.

"That's a very nice Etro shirt that you're sobbing all over," I told her.

"And covering in snot." She looked at me with wet eyes. "Did you find out who Arkitekt was?"

"I think so." I told her about the one page from the manuscript that existed, which had finally unraveled the whole thing.

By the time Aisha and Leila came, Sophie was in a better mood and the tears on her cheeks and my shirt had dried. Aisha wore a long white blouse over skinny jeans. She was still in mourning, as was Leila, who wore a white maxi sundress.

We ordered food. When Leila ordered a cocktail, I ordered a second one for myself. Sophie, who usually would order a drink, didn't; I guessed to keep Aisha, who didn't drink, company. After we finished our tacos and were nibbling on chocolate cake, I told Aisha about Mikkel Thorsen.

"Why did he kill her?" Aisha asked.

"I don't know." I lied easily. I didn't have any evidence against Arne Juhl, regardless of what I had told Mikkel. Also, I had been honest when I told Mikkel that I didn't give a shit about what Elias Juhl's grandfather had done. I cared about what Elias Juhl did or didn't do now.

"The police will reach out to you. And . . . Leila will make sure that . . . Look, I know nothing can bring your father or your brother back, but Leila will make sure you're compensated so that you can live a comfortable life."

She looked at me, baffled. "I don't care."

"Well, you should," I insisted. "You have a younger brother, and you can help him. You can use the money, depending upon how much it is, to help other immigrants get legal help. I don't know. What I do know is that your father would want you to live a full life."

"Nothing will take this hurt, this ugliness, away," Leila soothed. "But your father was innocent and now the world knows it."

"You said you'd help, and you did. You kept your promise to me." Aisha's eyes filled with tears. She came up to me, leaned down, and kissed my cheek. "Thank you."

My throat tightened. "You're welcome."

After Sophie and Aisha left, Leila took my hand in hers. "You're tired. You've had a long day. Let's get you to bed."

"Leila," I began, and she nodded.

"I know." She seemed resigned. "I'm going to put you in a taxi . . ."

"I bicycled."

"In your condition?"

"Yes."

I paid the bill and we walked out. She ordered a taxi on her phone, and I walked my bicycle to where she stood. She looked nervous. "I . . . I really liked . . . you know, *that* night."

"Me too."

"I'm going to Brussels," she blurted out. "I'm . . . *we* are moving to Brussels. They have been approaching me for the past year to work on some human rights cases and I finally said yes."

"Okay." My heart was breaking even before she told me what

I knew she would tell me. A part of me wanted to be mean and say, *Oh, so while I was in a hospital trying to survive, you were making plans for your future.* But I didn't. Not this time. Last time when we parted, I'd been an asshole. This time, I was going to be the man I had become.

"It's a fresh start." She smiled, but her eyes were sad. "For Edward and me."

"Yes." She'd gone back to him. Of course she had.

"You and I—"

"I know," I interrupted her. I didn't need an explanation. I understood.

Her taxi came.

I leaned down and kissed her cheek, my hands tightly gripping the bar handles of the bicycle. "Good luck, Leila. And be well." I meant it this time.

She got into the taxi and then rolled down her window.

"Thanks, Gabriel." She smiled.

CHAPTER 41

started the next morning with a spring in my step. I was ready to put the next part of my plan into action. So far, everything was going the way I had expected it would. I'd gotten shot and that was unfortunate, but I'd known the risks. I'd shot someone and I'd have to deal with that at some point and for a long while in therapy, but not right now.

I bicycled to work, and it wore me out, not just because of the exertion and my battered body, but because summer had gone on hiatus. It was twelve degrees, windy, and cloudy. It was not a good day.

I texted Victor Silberg and asked for a meeting. Since I was an invalid, he suggested that he'd see me in a couple of hours at Pastis.

"Does it still hurt?" Victor asked, looking at my bandaged arm.

I had put my injured arm in a sling made out of a cashmere scarf. I wore a T-shirt with jeans and slip-on Ferragamo moccasins, because I couldn't tie shoelaces without it hurting. I made up for my desperate fashion choices with a cashmere-and-silk Stetson hat, which kept me warm and stylish.

"Yes."

"I've never been shot," Victor said contemplatively.

"It's my first time," I told him. "I don't recommend it."

"What do you want to drink?" Victor asked, looking at his watch. "It's happy hour, not just somewhere but here as well."

I shook my head. "I'm pumped up with too many painkillers. If I drink on top of that I won't be able to drag myself out of bed." The mezcal from last evening had left me wiser about my beverage choices.

"And maybe that would be the right thing to do." Victor waved his hand slightly, but the waiter saw the regal movement and came to our table.

I got a Schweppes tonic water, while Victor got a beer.

"I need your help in arranging a meeting."

"With whom?"

"Elias Juhl."

Victor leaned back and looked at me admiringly. "The prime minister himself."

"Yes."

"Will you tell me what this is about?" he asked.

"Yes." I trusted Victor implicitly. I'd known him my entire adult life, as long as I'd known Eymen and Clara.

The waiter brought our drinks and we both ignored them.

"Juhl and Brother was a construction company, which has now become KBM," I began. "Jylland Murer was a secret subsidiary of Juhl and Brother that did business with the Germans during the occupation. A lot of business."

"Everyone did," Victor drawled. "My father was involved in hiding money for the Germans. Bankers those days, hell, even now us bankers are notorious about standing on the wrong side of history to make a profit."

"But that's public knowledge," I argued.

"True," Victor agreed. "My father was open about it. He also funded the Danish resistance, so he feels he evened it out. Tell me more about Jylland Murer."

"They used slave labor to build camps and prisons for Germany in Estonia and, really, all of Europe. They made bunkers on the west coast. They made a whole lot of money," I told him. "Arne Juhl was a young man then and he joined Holger Danske and became an informant for the Nazis."

"That is not in the history books." Victor raised his eyebrows.

"No."

"This would mean trouble for Elias Juhl even today," Victor said evenly.

"Yes, it would," I agreed. "On October 1, 1943, the Germans rounded up Jews in Denmark. But most of them had been hidden or moved to Sweden."

"Proud of that part of Danish history," Victor stated.

"On that day, twenty Jews were hiding on a farm in Helsingør," I narrated. "Arne Juhl told the Gestapo about them, and they shot the farmer, his wife, and two young children—seven and eleven years of age—as punishment, and twenty Jews ended up in Theresienstadt."

Victor picked up his beer and drank silently for a while, letting what I had said digest.

"Do you have proof?" he asked.

I shook my head. I told him about the book Sanne had been writing and the research she'd done.

"Do you think Oskar Sommer found out the identity of this informant called Arkitekt?" Victor wondered.

"I think so."

"Code name Arkitekt for a construction guy." Victor smiled. "I like it. It's ballsy. Speaking of ballsy, what were you doing rattling that snake Mikkel Thorsen's tail?"

"Mikkel Thorsen confirmed what I guessed. He'd never have sent anyone to kill me if that wasn't the case. I lied, told him that I had the manuscript and I had read it."

"How did you convince him you had the manuscript?"

"I had one page that Sanne sent to someone in Germany to verify," I revealed. "I used it as bait."

"If it's true that Arne Juhl caused the death of not just Jews but Danish citizens, Elias won't survive this election." Victor was thoughtful.

"What I don't know is how much the PM is involved," I admitted. "Or if it was Mikkel Thorsen on his own."

"Mikkel won't take a shit without Elias's permission . . . but on the other hand, he'd do what needed to be done to protect Elias." Victor tapped a finger absently on the table, keeping beat with "La Vie en rose" by Édith Piaf, which was playing in the background.

I told him the rest. About Mikkel Thorsen, his wife, the Russians, and whatever else I could think of.

He listened patiently and finally asked, "What's your endgame, Gabriel?"

"I want Yousef Ahmed to be cleared of the murder of Sanne Melgaard."

"And you'll probably get that once Tommy gets through with Mikkel, his wife, and the Russians," Victor pointed out.

"Maybe."

"Then why meet Elias Juhl?"

"I want to know what he knew."

"You don't want this whole Arne Juhl story to come out?"

"Don't care. Sins of the father. I don't give a fuck."

"Sins of the grandfather, and Elias Juhl would give many

fucks," Victor declared. "You want to meet in private with Elias Juhl, without anyone knowing about it?"

"Yes."

Victor nodded. "We have our summer party this Saturday."

"I know."

Victor grinned. "You already knew how you wanted this meeting to be set up, didn't you?"

I grinned back. "Yes."

"Gabriel Præst, you're smarter than you look."

Victor raised his glass, as I did mine, and in unison, we said, "*Skål.*"

CHAPTER 42

I wore linen pants, a white shirt, and a colorful silk scarf turned into a sling to hold up my left arm for the Silberg summer shindig.

I waited alone outside in the garden off of Victor's luxurious study. Their house in Klampenborg was old and grand. It was fully modernized and yet retained a palace ambience. The study was spacious, with more than a thousand books, arranged in perfect order by size and name of author in dark mahogany bookshelves. The study opened onto a garden through large open French doors. The green manicured garden rolled into a sandy beach, where the waters of the sound between Denmark and Sweden gently rose and fell in small waves.

It was a very good day for the summer party, and even at seven in the evening, the weather was balmy, a soft and cool breeze wafting through.

I watched the boats sail across the sound as I sat in a comfortable wicker chair. On the table next to me were two empty Champagne glasses and a bottle of a good bubbly that I had commandeered from the Silberg wine cellar resting in an ice bucket.

I heard footsteps behind me and rose.

Elias Juhl, the silver-haired fox, smiled at me.

We shook hands. I didn't introduce myself. He knew who I was.

He sat on the other side of the table in a matching wicker chair, both of us facing the water.

"May I?" He pointed at my sling and tilted his head toward the Champagne.

"Thank you," I said politely.

He poured us Champagne and we toasted.

"Victor throws one hell of a party," Elias commented.

"He does," I agreed.

Elias stared at the water, where a large cargo ferry was sailing what felt like incredibly slowly from this distance. I could smell frangipani flowers, which were blooming somewhere in the garden, thanks to a dedicated gardener who made sure that the tropical flower survived the Danish weather.

"What do you want?" Elias finally asked, looking directly into my eyes.

The man was intimidating, I had to admit, commanding respect, but I was all out of fear or respect.

"I want Yousef Ahmed's name to be cleared."

Elias nodded.

"I want Mikkel Thorsen to go to prison for his role in the killing," I added.

Elias nodded.

"And I want you to resign as prime minister," I finished. "You don't deserve to be in office. Not because of what your grand-daddy did, but because of what you did."

Elias nodded yet again. There was not a flicker of . . . anything on his face. I would never play poker with this man.

"How long does one have to pay for the sins of the father . . . the grandfather?" he wondered.

"My problem is not your grandfather."

"Let me clear up a few things. I didn't know about Sanne's murder. Mikkel did that on his own. He did a lot of things on his own, including attacking you and your family," he told me. "Do you believe me?"

"Does it matter?"

"Yes, it matters." Elias seemed genuine. "I didn't direct him to hurt anyone. I didn't even know what Sanne was writing about. The family knew that Arne played both sides . . . but we didn't know that he was an official Nazi informant. I found out from Mikkel. I told him that it couldn't hurt me. He didn't agree."

"He's your lapdog and you're telling me he did this on his own?"

"Yes." Elias shrugged. "I have no reason to lie to you. I could simply prevaricate. I'm a politician. I'm good at it."

I had to smile.

"You may not have been part of the crime, but you were part of the coverup."

"Yes . . . *way* after the fact." Elias sighed. "And I know what they say in political thrillers: it's not the crime, it's the coverup. I accept that."

"Are you involved with the Russians?" I asked.

He shook his head. He drank some Champagne. He looked relaxed, like we weren't talking about his future, the future of the country.

"Tomorrow, in a press conference, I'm going to tell the country two things. One, that my spin doctor, Mikkel Thorsen, hired a hitman to kill Sanne Melgaard and frame Yousef Ahmed, because she was blackmailing him. She knew about him laundering money for the Russian Mafia via his wife's position as a KBM board member. As you know, my family and I don't have any vested interest in KBM." Elias spoke like he was giving a speech.

Well, that is neat and tidy, I thought.

"Mikkel is confessing to the police as we speak," Elias confirmed.

"The press will dig into it."

"Ah, yes. The investigation will take KBM down but . . . it's not of consequence." Elias drank some more of his Champagne. "But I think the media will be too busy dealing with my next announcement."

I waited.

"I'm resigning from office, leaving it in the capable hands of my successor, Mathilde Windberg," he announced.

"What do you want in return?" I asked.

"No mention of Sanne's book or anything that came out of her research. You destroy everything." His tone was still pleasant, friendly, as if we were talking about the weather.

"How will you know that I've destroyed everything?" I asked.

"Victor said you will," Elias said confidently.

"Okay," I promised.

Elias took a deep breath and sighed. "I've had a good run."

"You certainly have."

Elias drained his Champagne glass and then stood up briskly. "Keep in touch, Gabriel. I think we can do business together."

"I'd rather get shot again." I didn't stand up.

As he was leaving, he turned around. "You didn't ask me what I will do next."

"I don't need to." I turned to face him and raised my glass. "You get to be the hero of the immigrants by sacrificing Mikkel Thorsen, so you can, what?" I thought about the various places an ex–Danish prime minister could end up. "Get a job in the EU?

NATO?" I paused when I saw his eyes change from cool to something else that felt a lot like respect. "Ah, you're going to NATO. Try not to start any wars, Elias."

He smiled. "I'll do my best, Gabriel."

I sat in the garden alone until I'd finished the bottle of Champagne. I walked toward the sounds of the party and waited at the entrance of the noise and glamour.

Clara was dancing with Eymen in the large living room, which had been converted into a dance floor, spilling open onto another garden. Sophie was doing an energetic jive with Noah, a cousin of Clara's. Bør was deep in conversation with a member of parliament. Tommy and Nadia were standing with some couples I didn't know, drinks in hand. Erik and Stine were sitting next to each other, her head on his shoulder—they were in harmony, coordinated, and happy.

Nico was dancing with Victor, her blond hair flowing around her shoulders, her eyes bright. Victor looked at me and lifted his chin in query. I nodded, *Yes, it was done.*

I stepped into the room to celebrate the summer with friends and family.

EPILOGUE

got the package nearly six months after the whole Mikkel Thorsen–Elias Juhl mess had hit the fan. It was from Frau Dr. Monica Franke at the Friedrich Meinecke Institute of History.

The package contained copies of several documents and a letter from Monica. "I found these in my office, mixed in with my papers. I don't know if these are of any use or importance, but I wanted to honor Oskar and get these to you."

I skimmed most of the documents, but stopped to read through one and felt a sense of closure.

Kodenavn: Arkitekt **(Code name: Architect)**
Staatspolizeileitstelle Kopenhagen (Gestapo Copenhagen)
GEHEIM (SECRET)
Tagesrapport Nr.73 (Daily Report Number 73)
Vom 3.,1 und 27.4.1945

1) Danish informant, code name Arkitekt, refuses to reveal further information about the resistance and

British orders. Arkitekt's family has royal support; interrogation is not recommended.

Waiting for instruction to reveal identity of Arkitekt as Arne Juhl to get further cooperation. May need transfer to Germany if identity revealed to protect informant.

Certified

(Illegible Signature)
Dr. Karl Heinz Hoffmann
Regierungsrat und SS-Sturmbannführer

There was a scrawled note on the document, and now that I had read through enough material penned by Sanne, I knew it was her handwriting: "*Needs to be authenticated. Waiting to hear from Friedrich-Meinecke-Institute (FMI). Add this to the source file once Dr. Sommer sends authenticated copy of original.*"

I put the package away in one of the cabinets in my office, locked it, and decided to forget about it . . . for now.

ACKNOWLEDGMENTS

Death in Denmark has been in the making for many years and many people helped me tell this story: my husband, Søren Rasmussen, who continues to talk to me about fictional characters from my book as if they were real people; my sons, Tobias Malladi Rasmussen and Isaiah Malladi Rasmussen, who read and reread the drafts and gave me constructive feedback; and my sister, Aparna Malladi, who listens to my stories and tells me hers.

I thank Fatima and Erik Aller for giving me a home in Copenhagen and being my family; Dr. Chekuri Suvarchala Vardhan and Dr. Madhav Yendru for giving me a home in India and being my family; and to Alice Verghese for being there for me no matter which part of the world she's in.

I am lucky to have a great circle of friends who hold my hand, lift my spirits, and are always on my team. Allison Blackwell, Anka Mensforth, Bernie Duffy, Edna Betgovargez, Jannette Avila, Oliver Brunchmann, Priyanka Rana, Soumitra Burman, Stephanie Machado, and Valerie Soulier, thank you for your wisdom, support, and love.

Without my agent Rayhané Sanders there would be no Amulya

Malladi books. She was giving birth (literally) and still checking up on my book when the wonderful Lyssa Keusch, editor extraordinaire, saved my life and took my book and me on.

This book contains some references to the Danish police department. I thank Karina Numelin Bjørnholdt, a journalist at *Politi Forbundets*, for patiently answering my questions. All mistakes made are absolutely mine.

And finally, I thank Copenhagen for giving me such excellent material to work with. I have written this book in a variety of locations across the city: Emmerys in Østerbro, Café Victor, Le Jardin, Pastis, Joe & The Juice in Hellerup, Mojo, Café Bopa, Restaurant Le Saint Jacques, and Marchal at Hotel D'Angleterre. I can't wait to go back and find new places I can write the next Gabriel Præst story.